I0556507

Between
LOVE
and
LOYALTY

SHANNYN
SCHROEDER

BETWEEN LOVE AND LOYALTY

PUBLISHED BY: Shannyn Schroeder

Copyright © 2016 by Shannyn Schroeder
ISBN 978-0-9978895-1-2

All rights reserved. Except for use in any review, the reproduction or utilization of this work in whole or in part in any form by any electronic, mechanical or other means, now known or hereinafter invented, including xerography, photocopying and recording, or in any information storage or retrieval system, is forbidden without the written permission of the publisher.

This is a work of fiction. Names, characters, places and incidents are either the product of the author's imagination or are used fictitiously, and any resemblance to actual persons, living or dead, business establishments, events or locales is entirely coincidental.

Printed in the USA.

Cover Design and Interior Format

© THE KILLION GROUP INC.

Chapter 1

FIONA CAVANAGH BURIED THE SHARP blade deep into a slab of clay, and tried desperately to *not* think of her mother.

"Ooo… someone's in a bad mood."

Fiona lifted her head and gazed at her friend Sarah Paulsen, who was also her boss. "Who says I'm in a bad mood? I only get to do longer projects with the kids when they're here on the weekend. There's not enough time to work in clay after school."

Sarah snickered and walked into the room. "You only want to work in clay when you're pissed off."

She said it as if it was a no-brainer. And since Sarah had known Fiona for years, it probably was.

Rather than acknowledging the fact that Sarah was correct in her assessment, Fiona continued to hack the block of clay into smaller pieces for the kids.

"Your mom?"

Fiona grunted assent.

"What did she do this time?"

Putting the knife down, Fiona stared at her. "She spent the morning pointing out that if I had stayed with Patrick, my father's career would be in better shape. As if it's my fault my ex is running against my dad."

"Your dad has been alderman for two decades. It's a lock."

Fiona blew at the curls that escaped her ponytail. "It should be, but ever since the latest polls, Patrick has been trying to turn this into a smear campaign, accusing my dad of sitting on his laurels. He talks about how change will be good for the city. How it's time to infuse some new blood in order to make the city better." She toyed with the knife. "My dad has been working his ass off for years to make Chicago better. He's fought for all kinds of improvements and Patrick makes it sound like Dad's been twiddling his thumbs and collecting a check."

"How is that your fault?"

"I broke up with Patrick. If I had played nicer and clung to him a little longer—like until after the election—he wouldn't be gunning for my dad's job now. Mom only ever saw how we looked on paper. She never wanted to listen to how I felt. Plus, I broke up with him over a year ago, but she acts like it was last week." Although Fiona had believed she'd loved Patrick, everything with him had been superficial. No wonder her mother liked him so much.

Fiona refastened her hair and grabbed her blade. She cut a few more chunks of clay, hoping it would be enough for the kids who would give up their Saturday to work on art with her.

"I'm sorry, Fi. I had no idea things were rough. I don't follow city politics, except for the mayoral election. And I definitely don't follow the aldermen who aren't in charge of my ward." Sarah squinted. "Actually, I'm not even sure who my alderman is. I should probably know that, right?"

Fiona always paid attention to elections having lived in politics most of her life. Her dad ran the first time when she was still in elementary school. It didn't take long before he learned the ropes of Chicago politics and became the man people either loved or hated. But she knew his true colors. This was the first election she'd be able to vote for him and her vote would actually count. In the past, his win had been guaranteed.

"I've worked so hard on his campaign this year, but it's never enough for her. I've knocked on doors and made countless phone calls, but Mom's biggest concern is my wardrobe and how I look in the media. Don't I *know* better? Image is *everything*."

Sarah burst out laughing. "I know you hate when I say this, but you sound just like her when you do that."

Even Sarah's smile couldn't lighten Fiona's mood. Fiona organized the chunks of clay on separate trays.

"Why do you let her get to you?"

"I don't know. Sometimes, I feel like she's right. She's been way deeper into this than I have, so she might know what she's talking about. I don't want be to be the cause of any problems."

She'd watched her brother Aiden do nothing but cause trouble growing up. How he'd managed to become a productive adult still puzzled her.

"Can I do anything to help?"

"Find me someone to fall in love with? Someone to take my mind off politics and appearances."

"I don't think falling in love will fix this." Sarah busied herself with straightening art supplies on the shelf.

"It couldn't hurt. I like being in love." She began setting the trays on the tables for the kids.

"That's your problem. You like the idea of love more than anything. You keep hoping you're going to find your prince and live happily ever after."

"Well, I don't need the forever kind of love right now. Short-term love is okay."

Sarah snickered. "You mean you want a one-night stand."

"Not necessarily. I want to go out and meet someone. I'm tired of being Fiona Cavanagh. I want to just be Fiona. At least for a little bit." As much as she loved her family, the name carried weight that people sought. Everyone loved knowing a Cavanagh.

"Then maybe you should stop choosing guys who want you for your family name." When all the paint bottles were facing front in a straight line, Sarah turned back to face her.

That last bit was all about Patrick. Patrick had worked for Fiona's father, but used her to get closer to the family and move up the political ladder. "You're right. You pick the guy for me."

"Are you crazy? How is that any better than your mother telling you who to date?"

"It couldn't hurt. I'm sure you'll find someone I would normally overlook. What does it matter if it's short-term?"

"Okay. We'll go out tonight." She turned toward the door.

Fiona's ability to fall in love quickly made Sarah a little nuts, but Fiona couldn't help it. The rush of falling for someone, the attraction and lust when he couldn't keep his hands off her, the lack of need for sleep. She did some of her best work while riding the high of new love. She could go days on a few hours of sleep.

As she leaned over the clay, her necklace dangled forward. She'd made the necklace within two weeks of meeting Patrick. It remained one of her favorite pieces.

Maybe it was time for something new.

New love, new jewelry.

"Hey, Ms. Cavanagh," Emily, one of her students, called from the doorway.

The kids were arriving for their art lesson. She'd have time to think about love and jewelry later. Time to get dirty.

∞

Connor Duffy swallowed a gulp of Guinness. Men around him jostled and yelled at the soccer game on the screens above them. He was too upset to even know who was playing. Dermott's was his usual place to view the games and he'd normally be as invested in the match as every other guy, but today he just wanted to drink.

Dermott Mulroney himself leaned on the bar in front of him. "What bug crawled up your ass?"

"I don't want to talk about it." He drank again. He wasn't ready to tell Dermott the news.

"You're ruining the atmosphere of my fine establishment. If you want to be pissy, go sit in the corner."

Connor knew Dermott was only trying to break him out of his funk, but he wasn't in the mood. He grabbed his beer and slid from his seat. He walked to the end of the bar and took the last stool, effectively putting himself in a corner. Dermott was the only person who he'd allow to talk to him like that. He was Connor's only real friend, even though he was old enough to be Connor's father.

Unfortunately, Dermott wouldn't take a hint and followed him to the end of the bar. "What's going on? It's not like you to pout."

"Not pouting. Pissed off. Another rejection."

"You had to know it wasn't going to be easy. Even those fancy New Yorkers can find out who Brady Cavanagh is."

"This was a local publisher. The editor called to talk to me.

She's real interested in my book." He drained his glass.

"Hell, that's not a rejection. Let's celebrate."

Connor nudged his glass forward for a refill. "She said interested, but not buying. If I had come to her a year ago, she said, she'd be all over it, but since the election is less than a couple of months away, there's no way to get it out before. It wouldn't have enough impact after."

"Shit. I'm sorry, boy."

"She said if I could change it and add more salacious details, newer scandals, she'd be more likely to buy. Apparently, my story isn't enough of a tell-all. Too bad I don't have an inside track. Everything I've got is old news." He sipped from his freshly poured beer. He'd been kicking himself all afternoon after getting the call. If he hadn't wasted so much time before settling down and writing the book, it wouldn't be such old news.

Connor knew there had to be dirt on Cavanagh, but he couldn't dig any up. The man had extremely tight-lipped people working for him. They all revered the man like a god.

In his gut he knew he'd never really be able to destroy Cavanagh. The man was untouchable. But Connor wanted the truth to come out. Cause a few chinks in the Cavanagh armor. Connor deserved at least that much.

"You're not giving up, are you?"

Connor didn't answer. Was he? It didn't feel like giving up as much as letting go.

"You deserve to have your story heard. They cost you everything—years in prison, your future, your family."

The last part dug into Dermott, but Connor knew better than to comment. The Cavanaghs hadn't taken away his family; Mom and Danny simply chose to move on without him, and he couldn't blame them. Dermott, however, blamed the

Cavanaghs for driving Connor's mother away. Dermott didn't talk about it, but Connor knew Dermott cared for his mother.

"You can't quit now. You've come a long way."

True, he had come a long way. When he'd started the book, it had been at the urging of his counselor, one Dermott had dragged him to because of his out-of-control anger. Dermott feared Connor would land in prison again. The guy had him write his story. Once he started, Connor didn't know how to stop. Letting it out had been freeing. It had taken years to write it in between jobs and working on his house. He wasn't a writer. He struggled with every word, but Dermott had convinced him the book was good and should be published.

Even if he couldn't bring Brady Cavanagh down, he wanted the Cavanaghs to at least suffer some. Wanted all of Chicago to know who they really were.

Dermott left him to drown his sorrows, but he didn't want the dull feeling alcohol would bring. He was tired of feeling like crap. Everything the Cavanagh name touched had that effect.

Suddenly, the crowd shifted too close for comfort. The mob of men quieted their cheers. Like the Red Sea, the group parted and then merged. *What the hell?*

Then, over the shoulders of the men nearest him, he caught a glimpse of wavy orange-red hair. Figures. Always a woman. The crowd shifted again as she made her way to the bar. Just his luck, Red and her friend, who he hadn't been able to see because she was so short, edged their way toward his end of the bar.

Red spoke up over the noise of the game to her friend. "Could you have picked a more crowded place?"

Her friend answered with a smile. "There's no pleasing you. You complained the last bar was too empty. Now you're mad this one is too full. I don't know why it's so crowded. I had no idea. There's no football game on until tomorrow."

A man standing behind her tapped her shoulder. "Got your days mixed up. The game's almost over."

The short brunette glanced up at the screen. "That's soccer."

Another yell rose from the crowd. Her eyes widened. "Well, at least you can have your pick."

Red shook her head and ordered two light beers. When she turned to face her friend, her gaze met his. Her wide, bright blue eyes sparkled. She looked half-lit. He smiled in spite of himself. A nagging feeling told him they'd met before, but he couldn't place her. He'd shared company with quite a few redheads.

The two women huddled together and spoke quietly. He looked up at the TV in time to see the last play of the game.

Red stood and moved around her friend to head his way. "You look like a man in the know. What's the deal with the crowd?"

"European football—soccer to you. This is the best place in the neighborhood to watch the games. Dermott springs for the premium satellite package so we can see them all."

"Huh." She sat on the stool beside him as if she hadn't come with a friend. "I didn't realize soccer was such a huge thing in Chicago."

Waves and curls spread past her shoulders and freckles sprinkled across her nose. Her smile took over her face and his brain shorted out.

She wrapped her lips around her bottle of beer and erotic thoughts he had no business thinking of flooded his mind. Redheads had always been a weakness.

She thrust her hand forward. "Fiona."

His heart stuttered with the recognition. Although they had never met in person, he knew her. Fiona fucking Cavanagh. What the hell was she doing in his bar?

"And you would be?"

He banked the rising anger. She obviously didn't recognize him because she continued to flirt.

"Connor."

"Nice to meet you, Connor. So, tell me about yourself."

His brain sped through the alcohol he'd already consumed. He needed to focus. The universe finally tilted something in his favor by dropping Fiona Cavanagh in his lap. "Not much to tell."

"Are you married? Girlfriend?"

He held her gaze and shook his head. He picked up his beer to soothe his throat, which grew drier by the minute.

"Boyfriend?"

He sputtered a bit before swallowing. "Hell no."

"I didn't think so, but…" She drank from her beer again probably because she didn't know how to finish. "What do you do for a living?"

"I'm a carpenter, furniture maker."

"Hmm…a man who's good with his hands."

Connor gripped his glass tightly to focus. He didn't want to be turned on by this woman, but she was making it difficult. Instead of thinking about using his hands to tangle in her curls, he tried to remember every detail he'd ever found on Aiden Cavanagh's little sister.

He'd known Aiden had a little sister, but that fateful year, she'd been out of the country doing something only rich kids got to experience. Ever since, she'd only appeared in the news as part of her father's campaign, the ever-dutiful daughter.

He'd take whatever he could get from her tonight. With a

few drinks, she might loosen her lips, much like her brother Aiden always had. He might get some salacious details yet.

Fiona was a little tipsy, but she knew a sexy man when she saw him. And Connor was definitely sexy. He was of the strong, silent, and brooding type. His short, dark hair required no work. It made him look like the kind of guy who had better things to do than style his hair.

He looked as if he didn't want to return her smile, but he did. At least what could pass as one. One corner of his mouth lifted into a crooked half-smile, but at least he responded.

At first, she thought Sarah had no idea who she was picking, but something about Connor pulled her.

His hand was calloused, but his handshake gentle. He was different from most guys she'd dated and different was exactly what she wanted. She watched his throat work as he drained his glass of beer.

"Let me buy you another," she said. The way his eyes narrowed, she thought he was going to turn her down.

He waved the bartender over. "Dermott, meet Fiona. She'd like to buy me a drink."

The old man raised his silver eyebrows. "You sure you want to waste your money on this ugly mug?"

"That's not how I would describe him." She slid a glance at Connor. Just then someone bumped her shoulder and she knew she'd left Sarah alone for too long.

"Are you going to introduce me?"

Fiona shifted back in her seat. "Connor, Sarah." She pressed back so they could shake hands. Then she burst out laughing, and when they didn't join, she added, "In my head, I said it the other way—Sarah Connor—with an Arnold Schwarzenegger accent."

Connor shook his head at her, but Sarah smiled.

The bartender slid a beer in front of Connor and Fiona dug in her pocket for money.

"Don't worry about it," the old man said. "That's the first smile I've seen cross his lips tonight. Well worth the price of a beer."

When the bartender walked away, Connor asked, "So what brings you two beautiful women out tonight?"

Sarah smiled. "Maybe we're here to watch the soccer game like everyone else."

"If you want to sell that story, you might want to make sure you at least know who's playing."

Sarah gave a careless shrug and squinted at the screen. "The guys in blue played the guys in green. Looks like blue won. Simple."

Fiona turned back and looked at Connor. He reached out and pushed her hair off her shoulder, allowing his fingers to linger a moment before resting his hand on the back of her chair. Slow heat spread through her body. "Sarah dragged me out to save me from myself. She was afraid I'd drown in self-pity. It's been a crappy week. She hoped my problems might be solved if I picked up a new man."

Connor's eyes dilated as he listened. "Are you always so forward?"

"Sometimes." At least when it had nothing to do with her family. She pushed the thought out of her head. She would *not* think of them tonight. "What's the point of playing games when we both know why we're here."

He leaned closer and she waited for a hint of aftershave to tickle her nose. Only the scent of soap and a hint of sawdust met her.

"I *am* here for the game."

"Well, then I'm sorry I interrupted. I'll take my drink elsewhere." She turned away and caught a glimpse of a smirk on Sarah's face before he spun her back.

"I've been interrupted for worse. And Dermott was right; I've had a crappy week too. Let's try this again." He extended his hand. "Hi, Fiona, I'm Connor and I'd like very much to forget the crappy week we've both had."

She took his hand. In truth, she probably would've given up on this mission had he been serious about getting rid of her. Instead, she stared into the dark blue of his serious eyes. "Hi."

Sarah tapped her shoulder again. "It looks like my work here is done. Do you need me to stay?"

Fiona winked. "I think I can find my way home. Are you okay to drive?"

Sarah nodded and then looked at Connor. "Would you mind showing me your driver's license?"

He stiffened a bit at Sarah's request. "Why?"

"If something happens to my friend, I'll be able to hunt you down and kill you."

How Sarah managed to say it with a straight face and look a little frightening, Fiona couldn't explain. Sarah was the most mild-mannered person she knew. But Connor pulled out his wallet and showed Sarah his license.

"Connor Duffy, be nice to my friend." She hopped off her stool.

When Sarah handed his wallet back, he looked at Fiona and answered, "I plan to be."

"I'll walk you out," Fiona offered. Turning to Connor, she said, "You'll be here when I get back?"

He nodded.

Fiona slid her arm through Sarah's and pushed through the

crowd to get to the door. The cool air felt good compared to the stuffy heat of the bar.

"Having second thoughts?" Sarah asked.

"About what?"

"Sexy Connor."

"No. I want to make sure you got to your car safely. And to thank you for tonight. I would never have picked Connor out of the crowd, but he looks like he might make the evening fun. As an added benefit, he doesn't appear to know me, so..."

"Remember, don't use your last name. If he looks for you online, he'll find out about your family. Keep it simple and fun. Don't fall in love tonight." She gave Fiona a quick squeeze.

"Even I don't fall in love in a single night."

She waited until Sarah got into her car before turning back to the bar. Connor met her inside the door.

"I thought we could sit somewhere a little quieter." He led the way to a booth on the other side of the bar, away from the TV. The room had quieted considerably since the game ended.

She sat in the booth and scooted to the inside. Surprisingly, he sat beside her instead of across from her.

"This okay?"

More than. She nodded. His broad shoulders nearly touched her. He waved a waitress over and ordered fresh drinks.

"So what do you do for a living?" he asked.

"I make jewelry to pay the bills, but I work part-time at a youth outreach center teaching art because I enjoy it. Tell me about being a carpenter." She sipped her beer and tried not to think about how close he sat, but his hard thigh brushed against her. She began to envision him naked.

"I build custom furniture and sometimes take on the odd

job." He took a drink from his beer and then turned the glass slowly in circles.

"What made your week so crappy?"

He stiffened a little and she knew she shouldn't have asked. "You don't have to tell me if you don't want to."

"A job I hoped to get fell through. You?"

"Family stuff I'd rather not think about."

What the hell were they supposed to talk about?

Connor licked his lips and faced her. "I suck at small talk. I like you, Fiona. I'd like to get to know you better. Are you interested in coming to my place?"

"Are you always this forward?" she asked with a smile.

"Sometimes. Especially if I think I'm in danger of losing the chance to be with a beautiful woman." He leaned closer and paused, his lips hovering in front of hers, as if asking permission.

She closed the distance and their lips touched. Warm and smooth, unlike his hand at her neck, which scraped a little at the sensitive skin. His tongue swooped into her mouth as he changed the angle of the kiss. A zing of pleasure shot through her and she knew she'd go home with Connor tonight.

She put a hand on his shoulder and pulled back. "Do you live close?"

"Right down the block."

"Let's go."

His eyes widened a bit, but he stepped out of the booth and tugged on a navy pea coat. When she moved toward the door, his hand fell to the small of her back guiding her through the crowd. He whispered in her ear, "Are you okay with walking? I didn't bring my car."

"That's fine."

"Don't you have a jacket?"

"You said it's close."

Outside the cool night air brushed over her. She hadn't brought a coat because it would have been one more thing for her to carry.

They hadn't gotten far before the breeze went from refreshing to cold and she shivered. She hadn't dressed for walking around.

"Shit. I'm sorry. Have my jacket."

Before she could refuse, he'd already slipped out of the coat and slid it on her shoulders. The coat held the heat from his body and his clean scent. Her shivering immediately stopped. "Aren't you going to get cold?"

"I'll be fine."

She pushed her arms into the sleeves and he put his arm around her shoulders. Since he'd admitted to being no good at conversation, she had to keep it going. "What do you do for fun? Besides pick women up at the bar."

His arm tensed momentarily. "I don't often pick women up at bars. I'm usually only there to watch the games and few women are around then."

"Are you trying to tell me you lead a lonely and celibate life?"

A quiet chuckle slipped past his lips. "No. I date. But I've been busy with jobs lately and relationships didn't pan out. But to answer your question, I read. It's a habit I picked up a long time ago and held onto."

"What do you like to read?"

"A little of everything. I usually read a couple of books at a time. I like thrillers, something with a twist. For nonfiction, I prefer stuff written by journalists as opposed to the celebrity crap." He pointed to a house. "That's me."

He lived really close. No wonder he didn't bother driving.

He jingled his keys in his hand before unlocking the door.

"Before we go in, I should warn you it's still under construction. I bought it as fixer-upper, so it's pretty bare."

"Does your bedroom consist of a sleeping bag on the floor and a milk crate for a chair?" God, she hoped not. She wasn't feeling that adventurous.

"Not quite." He swung the door open and flicked on a light. Barking echoed throughout the first floor. "That's just Max. He's harmless."

Oh, man. She was a total sucker for a guy with a dog. A big beast came running into what should've been the living room. Connor greeted his dog and Fiona assessed the situation. There was nothing. No furniture, no TV, not even a rug. Everything was bare.

Connor mumbled something and said he'd be right back. She took a few more steps into the house. The room was huge, big enough to be both a living room and a dining room, but she began to question if he really even lived here.

He returned, his footsteps echoing in the empty space. "Sorry, Max had to go out. I warned you it was empty. I've already finished the upstairs, though. That's where I spend my time."

He took his coat from her and hung it on a hook near the door. "Come on, I'll give you the grand tour."

Beyond the living room/dining room combo was the kitchen where Max scratched at the back door. When Connor let him back in he greeted Fiona by trying to jump on her.

"Down, Max. Sorry, he gets excited," Connor said while tugging at Max's collar.

"Too bad every man I meet doesn't get excited like that."

Max settled next to Connor's legs and Connor slid his gaze back up to meet hers. "I imagine men get plenty excited around you."

He stepped over his dog and backed Fiona against the wall. His lips were cold from the walk, but his skin was warm as his hand grazed her cheek on its way to cradle her neck. He might not be much of a talker, but Connor was a damn good kisser. His fingers tangled in her hair and brought her head back. He licked her neck and bit the sensitive flesh causing sparks to zoom through every nerve. Her blood raced and she pressed her body into his.

"Tour can wait," he said against her heated skin. He pulled away, leaving her much colder than she expected. Grabbing her hand, he pulled her from the room and toward the stairs.

Max's nails clicked on the hardwood floor as he followed. "Max," Connor called out over his shoulder, "stay."

Based on the roughness in his voice, he was as turned on as she was. He took the stairs two at a time; luckily, her legs were long enough to keep up with him. He maneuvered her through the dark and she couldn't see anything. At least he wasn't a messy guy, or they'd be tripping over stuff.

Connor released her hand, leaving her standing in the dark, and switched on a small bedside lamp. The glow illuminated the room enough to show that he spent time here. It looked like he combined two rooms to make this one big suite. The light wasn't bright enough to fill the room, but the king size bed stood only a couple of feet in front of her and that was all she needed to see.

She kicked off her shoes and pulled her shirt over her head. Connor just stared.

"Something wrong?"

His face looked a little strained, and for a minute she thought maybe he didn't like an assertive woman, in which case, she should leave now.

"Uh-uh," was his only response. He sat on the edge of the

bed and pulled her to him, his rough hands on her waist. He planted a kiss just above her bra between her breasts while his hands, warm and calloused, rubbed across her skin above her jeans. She reached for the button on her pants, but he pulled her hands away.

He trailed kisses down her torso and his fingers skimmed beneath her waistband. Her knees weakened at his touch, so she used his shoulders for balance. His broad, hard-muscled shoulders proved to be excellent anchors as he slid her jeans and panties down her legs. When the pants were gone, she reached around and unclasped her bra, discarding it along with everything else. She stood naked in front of Connor while he was still fully clothed.

He inhaled deeply and stood. By the time she blinked, his shirt had joined hers and he'd turned her toward the bed. She barely had a chance to ogle his chest before he pushed her down on the bed and covered her body with his. Connor continued his assault of her senses by kissing and stroking her.

The rough denim of his jeans matched the rasp of his hands on her body. "You're so soft," he whispered.

He wasn't soft—not at all, and she loved every delicious hard plane and muscle that pressed into her. His fingers stroked her and she moaned. He clamped his teeth gently on her nipple. If she didn't know better, she'd think the man had eight arms because of the diversity of sensual pleasure erupting all over her body as he explored. Her blood raced and she writhed beneath his hands.

"Close, aren't you, Fiona?"

She couldn't speak, couldn't even open her eyes, so she nodded and bucked her hips up. He held her close, trying to keep her still. The pressure built and her muscles clenched.

Then suddenly, he was gone.

She wanted to whimper. She eased her eyelids up and saw an evil grin on Connor's face.

"I'm coming back." He pushed his jeans down his hips and donned a condom. Leaning back over her, he whispered in her ear, his voice low and husky, "I want to be inside you when you come."

She shuddered knowing release was so close. She spread her thighs wide to accommodate his body. He slid inside her, filling and stretching her. Her muscles relaxed a fraction, but then Connor started to move. Tension skyrocketed in her body, coiling in her center, waiting to explode.

Connor propped himself on his forearms beside her head. Their breath mingled as their bodies collided. He felt so good. She wasn't ready to let go; she wanted to ride the wave a little longer. Connor's pace picked up and he shifted, pulling back.

Cool air breezed in the space between them. Connor hooked an arm under her knee, opening her further. Then he touched her with his thumb and she was gone. Every muscle tightened and stars burst behind her closed lids. She might've screamed out his name.

As her shudders and spasms slowed, Connor stopped and held her. His body was rigid, so she knew he hadn't finished, but he didn't move. She tried to shift, to thrust, but he held her down. His heavy breaths heaved from his chest and she knew he was trying to prolong this every bit as much as she'd tried.

He'd toyed with her, so it was only fair that she return the favor.

Chapter 2

"LET'S CHANGE POSITIONS," FIONA WHIS-PERED.

Connor held her tight, knowing if she bucked against him, he'd come. Pulling out left him cold and wanting, but at this moment, he'd give Fiona anything she asked. And she wanted a new position. He swallowed hard and moved to lie on his back, figuring she'd want to ride him and have some control.

"You're not done working yet." She turned over on her hands and knees and shoved her ass up at him.

He stared at her, not sure if he could move. She was pink and glistening from her come and he wanted to be back inside her. A burst of energy shot him out of bed and he knelt behind her. He grabbed her hips and brought her onto him. He almost came, especially when she tried to wiggle away. He gripped tight, possibly leaving bruises.

Connor inched out and slammed back into her causing her to yelp. He froze. "You okay?"

"God, yes. Don't stop." She grabbed his hand from her hip and forced it back to her clit.

Even from this position where he should be in total control, Fiona owned him. He stroked her until she came again.

This time, he couldn't hold back. Her walls tightened around him and milked him. He pounded into her one last time hard enough to cause them both to fall forward.

He eased off her, hoping his arms could support his weight; he had no strength left. Luckily he didn't have to hold it for long. Fiona rolled out from beneath him.

She was still panting, but her smile lit up the room. "Holy crap, that was great. I think it worked." She paused. "Yep. Bad week totally forgotten."

They laid together in silence, recovering. After a few minutes, Fiona sat up, her hair wild around her head. "Can you point me to the bathroom?"

He sat and pointed in the general direction of the hall. She'd figure it out. Before lying back on the bed, he disposed of the condom.

A shadow crossed him and he bolted up. Fiona stared wide-eyed and startled.

"Sorry. I must've dozed off." Then he realized she'd gotten dressed. He hadn't even heard her return from the bathroom, and she planned to leave. He hadn't gotten anything other than a great fuck. "You can stay."

"Thanks for the offer, but it's probably not a good idea." She shoved her feet into her shoes. "Do you have a sweatshirt or something I can borrow? I'm going to freeze outside."

He pushed off the bed and grabbed one from his dresser. Then he remembered her friend asked if she'd be able to get home. "How are you getting home?"

"I'm going to call a cab."

"Forget that. I'll give you a ride. Give me a couple of minutes." He'd already started toward the bathroom.

"Are you sure? I live kind of far."

"You don't live all the way up in Wisconsin, do you?"

"No."

"Then I'll take you home." It was the least he'd do for any woman who could make him come so hard he thought his eyes would explode. The car ride would offer him the chance to talk and pry some information from her pretty lips. He cleaned up and redressed while Fiona sat watching from the bed. His sweatshirt swallowed her; he couldn't even tell she had breasts under it.

"Ready?" he asked.

"Whenever you are."

He led the way out the back of the house to his truck. Max danced around and Fiona squatted to pet him good-bye. Once in the truck, she gave him directions to her house. She hadn't been joking; she lived far. It made him wonder what she'd been doing in his neighborhood.

They rode in silence and he knew he'd screw this up. The awkward after-fucking conversation always sucked. He had no idea how to maneuver her into talking about her family. Before he knew it, he pulled up in front of a big condo building.

"This is me."

"Can I have your number?" he blurted.

She smiled a soft, sleepy smile. "Let's not do this."

"Do what?"

"I know it's the polite thing to ask for my number, but don't ask if you don't have any intention of using it."

"Here." He reached into the slot on the dashboard and grabbed a business card. "You call me if you're interested."

He handed her the card and threaded his fingers into her hair pulling her across the seat toward him. He kissed her breathless and then whispered, "Be interested."

She nodded slowly and climbed out of the truck. He waited until she entered her building before driving away. Fucking a Cavanagh probably wasn't his wisest move, but he saw no other way to get close. While she'd been looking for a fuck, he hoped he'd be able to get more.

Fiona had been an unexpected but very welcome addition to his night.

Fiona let herself into the condo with a smile on her face. She tossed her keys on the kitchen counter, grabbed a bottle of water, and headed for a shower. She felt limber and relaxed, but energized.

While rinsing the shampoo from her hair, an idea for a new necklace struck her. She'd been in a slump and needed to create some new pieces. She dried quickly, pulled on shorts and a T-shirt, and went to her office. Her mother thought the spare bedroom was a luxury, but it turned out to be a great workspace. She had room for all of her tools and the odd stuff she bought simply because it looked cool.

Her mother had little patience for Fiona's love of things. In some ways, Fiona was a bit of a pack rat, but she'd been able to use that quality to her advantage. She made jewelry from all the trinkets she came across and bought *just because*. Mom had mostly ignored Fiona's jewelry designs until her mother's friends took notice. After all, who wouldn't want a one-of-a-kind piece?

Sheila's friends helped launch Fiona's business, and although she could open a storefront of her own, she preferred to stay small. She had an online store and did some pieces on consignment at a few Chicago shops. Her money was steady, but because she was still relatively unknown, Sheila wasn't happy.

Fiona didn't want to use the Cavanagh name to get places. She just wanted to be herself. As she pulled out her tools, she thought about Connor and the way he'd whispered her name while they had sex. He had no idea who she was and he wanted her. He required nothing other than the night. She wondered how long that could last.

She began sketching her ideas for work and toyed with the concept of leading a double life. Could she be with Connor and keep her family a secret? Would he get suspicious?

Fiona pushed everyone from her mind and set to work. She worked through the night and hadn't realized it until her phone rang. When she focused on the window, sunlight crept around the edges of the blinds. The phone stopped and started again.

Mom. She was the only one who called until Fiona picked up. Rubbing her eyes, Fiona grabbed her phoned and answered. "Hi, Mom."

"Hi, honey. I'm calling to make sure you haven't forgotten about the fundraiser tonight."

"Huh?"

"I knew it. I've told you about this repeatedly. We need the entire family to attend. You probably haven't purchased a dress, either. Goodness. Be ready in an hour. I'll be there to take you shopping."

"Mom, I have clothes in my closet. I'm sure I have something appropriate." She mentally scanned her closet and knew it was nothing more than a prayer. She usually donated the crap her mother made her wear.

"Fiona, we've been over this. You cannot walk around like some artsy hobo. The constituents have expectations."

"The constituents should be more concerned about Dad's policies than where I bought my dress." Fiona went to the kitchen and poured a glass of orange juice.

"An hour, Fiona." Then she hung up.

It looked to be one hell of a day. She changed into a pair of ripped jeans to make her mom crazy and paired them with a comfy gray sweater. She finger-combed her curls and lay on the couch to wait.

Sheila Cavanagh was never early nor late. If she said an hour, she would arrive in exactly sixty minutes. By Fiona's estimation, she had fifteen minutes for a power nap.

When her doorbell rang, she didn't bother to answer. Fiona stumbled off the couch, grabbed her purse—the giant one which held everything she could ever need—and went down to meet her mother.

When the elevator door opened, Fiona saw her mother tapping her feet. "Hi, Mom."

"Why didn't you buzz me in?"

Because I didn't want to hear the criticism of my place. Again. "I was ready and I want to get this over with as soon as possible."

Sheila stared at her for a moment. "You haven't slept." One eyebrow shot up. "Why not?"

Fiona rolled her eyes. She and her mother had never had the kind of relationship where they shared personal details. "I worked last night."

She pushed through the exterior door and walked out onto the street. Sheila followed at a clipped pace. Fiona stood a good five inches taller than her mother and used her long legs to her advantage.

Sheila walked around to the driver's side door. At least she drove herself today. Fiona hated when her mother sent a town car with a driver. Once in the car, Sheila removed her sunglasses and stared at Fiona. "Are you seeing someone new?"

Connor swept into her head and Fiona wondered what her mother would think of him. *Hi, Mom. Meet Connor. I picked him up at a bar and all I know about him is that he makes furniture and he's great at making me come.* Fiona snorted to keep her laugh in.

Lack of sleep was starting to get to her. She shook her head to dissuade any further questions.

They drove to Michigan Avenue to hit all of her mother's favorite stores. Sheila meant to keep it simple by sticking to the department stores: Saks, Neimann Marcus, Bloomingdale's. Stores Fiona never stepped foot in. If Target was sufficient for the first lady, why the hell wasn't it okay for the daughter of a lowly alderman?

But Fiona knew it was useless to try to talk her mother out of it and so she paraded through the dressing rooms in whatever Sheila tossed at her. Three hours later, Fiona was the proud owner of five new dresses. Obviously, Sheila didn't want to have to make any more trips to ensure Fiona dressed appropriately.

Over the course of their shopping expedition, Fiona didn't speak; she knew better and let her mother steer the conversation. She half-listened to the details for the evening and other upcoming events.

"Don't forget we have your cousin Kelly's wedding next month. She said she's keeping it small, but you know how that side of the family is. For the wedding, you can probably wear one of the dresses we bought today."

Fiona nodded. She'd forgotten about the wedding. She hated weddings. Correction, she hated being a single guest at a wedding. People would grill her about when it would be her turn. They'd quickly glance at her ring finger in search of a diamond, wondering why she wasn't announcing her engagement. They'd question why she wouldn't rush the crowd of single women to jump and catch the bouquet.

Maybe she could conveniently get the stomach flu the night before.

They pulled in front of Fiona's building. She hefted her bags and hip-bumped the door.

Her mother rolled down the window and called, "Take a nap. And do your hair."

After an incredibly long and restful nap, Fiona did as she was told. She struggled with the flat iron to straighten her hair into the sleek look her mother preferred. Half an hour through the process, she became frustrated. She grabbed Connor's card and dialed, not quite sure what she planned to say.

"Hello?" His deep, rough voice came across the line above noise in the background. He was working.

"Hi, Connor. It's Fiona."

"Hey. Hold on a minute." A moment later the background quieted. "I'm glad you called."

"Sorry to interrupt your work."

"One of the perks of working for myself is that I can take a break when a beautiful woman calls."

She smiled, even though it was just a line.

"Something on your mind?"

She'd forgotten she'd been the one to call. "Um, yeah. I have this family thing I have to go to, but I was wondering if maybe you might be free late tonight."

"How late?"

"Ten, maybe eleven?" It would give her enough time to make an appearance, have a crappy dinner, and shake hands with people who would vote for her dad. Nervous flutters in her stomach reminded her how much she wanted Connor to say yes.

"You want to meet somewhere, or come over here?"

"I can come to your house." *Yes. Something to look forward to during this dreadful night.* "Should I call when I'm on my way?"

"No, I'll be here."

"Okay, see you then."

"I'm looking forward to it."

Fiona disconnected and went back to wrangling her hair into place. With thoughts of Connor undressing her, she chose an emerald-green bra and panty set to wear under the conservative gray dress her mother had chosen.

Fiona fidgeted at the banquet table. Her cheeks hurt from holding the same smile for hours. Her father stood to finally take the podium and her smile dropped. Watching him take command of a room always inspired her. She tended to get a little choked up when he went into full-on patriotic mode.

The thing was, he believed everything he said. Despite the phoniness of the politics and the glad-handing, he made her believe. Over the years, he'd made a difference in the city and she wanted to think that even if he weren't her father, she'd still vote for him.

He started every speech in much the same way: Chicago is a great city, rivaled by no other. She leaned forward and held her chin on her fist to listen to her dad. God, she loved to hear him speak. Emotion swelled and she began to think about what kind of jewelry she would make for this election. Ever since childhood, she made something special for the election, a bit of a good luck charm for her father to have while campaigning.

She remembered his first election. The flurry of activity around their family was overwhelming, but the first time she heard her dad speak, she'd recognized it as something special. Her chest filled with so much emotion, she had no way to explain it. Instinctively, she knew he was where he belonged—doing this. Most kids never understood that about their parents. They didn't get to see them at work, doing something they were passionate about.

Brady Cavanagh was as passionate about the city of Chicago as he was about his family. When Fiona made him a flower out of tissue paper for election night, she figured he'd keep it safely tucked in his pocket for good luck, but when he took the stage, her flower stuck in his lapel, having replaced the rose her mother had put there.

Not only had Fiona felt special that night, but she also felt part of something bigger. For all of his faults, her father cared about many things. That caring reverberated every time he spoke to a crowd.

The timbre of his voice reminded her of another deep voice, which had a much different effect on her.

She closed her eyes and a picture of Connor popped in her head. The freedom of the night before took over. Her eyes flicked open and she realized if she bolted from her seat, it would cause a scene, so she leaned back and let memories of last night transport her to relaxation.

Connor's ragged breath echoed in her ear and she felt his rough hands stroke and rub and grab her in all the right ways. She shifted her hips as the thoughts turned her on. None of her father's words penetrated the fantasy. Her skin warmed and her breath hitched.

She shook her head to clear her mind, needing to focus on her dad for the evening.

"This city needs experience and dependability. I stand before you today to ask for your support in keeping Chicago strong."

When her father wrapped up his speech, the crowd clapped and reporters snapped photos. Her mother called Fiona up on the stage, using nothing more than her eyebrows. As Fiona stood to join her family, she briefly wondered if all moms had that ability.

Without grinding her teeth too much, Fiona managed to make it through another hour of listening to people stop her dad and ask questions about his policies. She couldn't understand why they wanted her in attendance. She added nothing to the conversation. Her mother simply expected her to smile and be pretty.

Her father spoke about utilizing tax breaks to lure more business to the city. Fiona needed a break. She eyed the door and wondered how far she'd get before anyone noticed her missing. She'd driven herself, which made escape even more tempting.

She touched her father's arm and leaned forward. "Excuse me. I need to go freshen up," she said politely. Her plastered-on smile earned her a wink from the older man her father spoke with and a peck on her cheek from Dad.

When she got to the hall near the bathroom, she waited to see if her mother would follow. Five minutes passed and Fiona snuck back to the edge of the banquet hall. Everyone carried on without her. Even her mother seemed to be in full party mode.

It was now or never. She made a break for it.

Connor worked late trying to get caught up on an order for a dining room set. The table had been constructed for a while, but he was behind on getting the eight chairs done. He'd wanted to have the chairs finished so he could move onto staining them, but he was working slower than usual. Thoughts of a sexy redhead distracted him enough that he'd made some rookie mistakes.

He brushed sawdust from his shirt before heading upstairs.

The clock read nine, so he had time to eat a quick sandwich and take a shower. The anticipation of seeing Fiona again surged through him. He'd tried to do some more digging to understand how she fit into the family dynamics, but he came up empty. Other than usual campaign appearances, Fiona didn't appear to have much to do with the rest of the Cavanaghs.

Getting details from her without causing suspicion would be a challenge. In the meantime, he'd enjoy the other benefits of being with Fiona Cavanagh. In the back of his mind, a little voice told him he should feel guilty for sleeping with the girl, but his dick quashed that noise.

He stood barefoot at the kitchen sink chomping on a ham sandwich with Max sitting at his feet, waiting patiently for a bite. Connor tossed the dog the last bit of bread and drank from a bottle of beer. The doorbell rang. He checked the time and went to see who was there.

On his front porch stood a very dressed up, sleek, and rich-looking Fiona. She definitely looked like a Cavanagh tonight. When he swung the door open, her face brightened with a huge smile.

"You're early," he said by way of greeting.

"I can go drive around the block for a while if you want."

"Hell, no." He reached out and pulled her into his living room. "What happened to your hair?"

Her wild curls were gone. She touched it self-consciously and he realized it sounded more like a criticism than a question. And in a way, it was. He preferred her crazy curls. "It looks good, just different."

She sighed. "I had to go to a fancy dinner and my mother likes my hair tame. Tomorrow it'll be back to a frizzy mess."

"I like the frizzy mess." He ran his hand down her sleek hair. The same silk he'd tangled his fingers through the night before, but so different.

She leaned in and kissed him. It was a quiet, searching kiss.

He tried to pull away, but she followed. Against her lips he said, "Hold that thought. I worked late and I'm covered in sawdust. I was on my way to the shower."

Her lips curled into a smile. "Mind if I join you? The minute water hits my hair, the curls spring back."

Her offer had him hard and he nodded.

On the way up the stairs, she asked, "Do you have some clothes I can borrow? A shirt and some jogging pants or something? I have your sweatshirt but forgot it in my car."

"You're one of those women, huh?"

"*Those* women?"

He smiled and went to the bedroom to find her something to wear. "The ones who like to borrow a guy's clothes."

"Actually, yes, I am one of those. A man's shirt makes a woman feel sexy. It's big and smells like him. But I hadn't planned on stealing your clothes tonight."

He grabbed a T-shirt for her. If he had his way, she wouldn't need anything else. "What was your plan?"

She stepped out of the heels she wore and turned so he could unzip the dress. "My plan was to taunt you with my sexy underwear, have sex with you, and then leave the way I came."

He dropped the shirt he held. His breath hissed along with the zipper as he caught a glimpse of green satin. He kissed her back on the path left bare by the gaping material. She smelled as soft as she felt.

She turned and dropped the dress. The stiff material stood a little on its own and she stepped out of it. His mouth watered looking at the green satin cupping her pale breasts. He would've been better off waiting to undress her until they were in the bathroom; they might not make it that far.

Fiona took another step toward him and kissed his cheek and then his neck while tugging his shirt away from his jeans. He grabbed her shoulders. "Wait. I'm all sweaty and dusty."

She raised an eyebrow. "I like the way you smell." She tucked her nose to his neck just below his ear and sniffed, her soft lips grazing the sensitive skin. It was the one spot on his body a woman could use to bring him to his knees and he never shared that tidbit of information.

Leave it to her to find it without trying. Again, she pulled his shirt, allowing her nails to scrape against his stomach and then chest. He yanked the T-shirt from her hands and whipped it over his head. Her fingers were already busy at the button of his jeans. His dick strained against the seam and instead of freeing it, Fiona stroked him through the denim.

"I don't think a shower is what's really on your mind, Connor."

"It was until you showed up. Now, the only thing filling my head is you." He stared into her big blue eyes and saw the heat and desire. She was easier to read than a picture book. "Come with me."

She giggled. "I'd love to *come* with you. A couple of times maybe."

He held her hand and pulled her toward the bathroom. He started the water, knowing it would take a minute to heat up. He took that time to slowly remove her remaining clothes. She stood naked, uninhibited under his gaze. Her skin pinked up with arousal as he slid his jeans down.

Fiona reached for his hard-on, but he maneuvered her to the bathtub. "Shower's ready."

He held her hand as she stepped into the tub. Although the bathroom fixtures were new since his remodel, he'd wished he'd thought ahead and put in a double showerhead. He stepped back and let her have the spray while he lathered up.

She ducked her head under the water and he waited for her hair to come to life, but it still snaked down her back in a smooth river. As if reading his mind, she said, "The curls pop when it starts to dry."

While she busied herself with shampooing her hair, he took the opportunity to rub his soapy hands down her front, paying special attention to her breasts.

"You know, I'm not really dirty. I took a shower before going out tonight. I just offered to wash my hair because you looked so disappointed about the curls."

"I was disappointed. I like the curls. Running soapy hands all over your naked body is a bonus."

She rinsed the shampoo from her head and then faced the spray to get the soap off. She gave him a quick kiss and stepped out of the shower. "I'll be waiting in the bedroom."

Connor watched her naked ass sway as she left the room with his towel on her head. He proceeded to take the fastest shower he'd had in years. Maybe even faster than the first time he'd had to share a shower with a roomful of men.

He flicked off the water and pulled a towel from the cabinet behind the door. Without Fiona in the room, his dick had softened a little, at least enough to be able to wrap the towel around his waist. He looked in the mirror and realized he'd forgotten to shave again.

In the bedroom, he'd hoped to find a naked Fiona lying sprawled across his mattress. Instead, she stood in front of his bookcase, petting Max's head, while wearing the T-shirt he'd dropped on the floor. She was right; a woman wearing a man's shirt was sexy. Especially when the woman in his shirt was Fiona.

Noticing him in the doorway, she said, "You really do like to read. You're into politics, huh?"

She sounded like this was an unpleasant prospect. It opened the door to conversation to see how she'd react. "No more than anything else. You have to admit Chicago has an interesting political history."

She shrugged, but said nothing, not even a mention of her powerful father. Connor could almost see her fortifying a wall around the subject. He crossed the room, dropping his towel along the way. Her hair was still wet, but the curls were springing back, just as she said they would.

He threaded his fingers into the wet curls and brought her face to his and kissed her. He thrust his tongue in her mouth and pressed her body against him. When he ended the kiss and pulled away, her eyes were clouded with desire.

He understood about not wanting to discuss some things. Neither of them wanted to talk. They had time. He'd figure out how to draw her out and open up. He reached under the shirt and found nothing but smooth skin. With his hands on her bare ass, she panted and moaned. He guided them back to the bed.

Fiona was a loud lover and he liked that she held nothing back. She knew what she wanted in bed and wasn't afraid to ask for it. As she lay naked and writhing beneath him, he couldn't imagine her lying there with the slick hair and fancy dress. He liked the wild Fiona.

When their shuddering finished, he rolled off her and they gasped side by side.

"I'm glad you came by tonight." It sounded lame, but it was true.

"So am I." She sat and her curls stuck up everywhere. "Don't stare. I know my hair's crazy." She smoothed a hand down the locks as if it would have an impact.

He grabbed a handful of curls and pulled her down to him. "I like the crazy."

She lowered her head and kissed him again. "That's good because the crazy always comes back."

Somehow he thought she spoke about more than just her curls.

Before he recovered from her kiss, she scooted off the bed and gathered her clothes. He propped himself on his elbow. "You don't have to go. I'm not so territorial that I can't share my bed for the night."

"I appreciate the offer, but I don't sleep much at night. It's my best time to work."

The sound of vibrations had them both looking for phones. Connor doubted it was his; the only calls he received were work-related during the day. Fiona fished her phone from her tiny purse and frowned.

"Bad news?"

She shrugged and the relaxed look on her face disappeared. She shimmied into her panties without a word. The phone went off again. Her pace increased, like she was in a sudden hurry to leave.

Fiona zipped the dress, slid into her shoes, and shoved her phone back in her purse.

He had no idea what to say to make her stay. This might be his only chance to learn about her family. "Fiona."

She looked up at him, a tense expression replacing the relaxed one she'd had moments ago. Whoever called caused the change in her and he didn't like it. "When can I see you again?"

She bit her lip before answering. "I'm not sure."

"How about dinner tomorrow?"

Shifting further into the shadows of his room, she said, "I

don't think so. I've got some stuff to do."

Was she seriously brushing him off? He replayed their brief evening together and decided she'd enjoyed herself every bit as much as he had. Why wouldn't she want to continue?

"Then you pick the day."

She plopped on the corner of the bed furthest from him. "Look, I like you, Connor, but—"

Whoa. She was *not* going there. No fucking way was a Cavanagh going to reject him. "Stop. I get it. Why did you come here tonight?"

Her voice whispered in the dark. "You invited me and I wanted to see you."

"Then why blow me off?" He had a hard time keeping his cool. If she'd been any other woman, he would've simply thanked her for the fuck, but he needed more from Fiona and his anger slipped through.

"It's complicated."

Complicated? "Are you married?" He'd done plenty of research and nothing showed her having a husband. In his eagerness to find out about her position in the family, it was possible he'd missed something.

She sighed heavily. "No, I'm not married. It's my family."

Yes. He sat up to get closer. "What about them?"

She shook her head, her messy hair slipping forward and covering her face. "Nothing. I can't talk about it. I just...I have to go." Standing, she turned to him. "Thank you for tonight."

"So that's it?"

"It's all it can be."

She wanted to keep him as a secret. The tightness in his chest loosened. This would work to his advantage. As long as her family didn't know about him, he could continue the charade until he learned what he needed.

He followed her to the door. "Okay," he said as she gripped the doorknob.

Without turning, she asked, "Okay, what?"

Coming up behind her, he settled a hand on her shoulder, brushing her curls aside to feel the soft skin under his fingers. "If this is all we can have, I'll take it."

She spun quickly and the moonlight from the window glinted in her eyes. A slight curve of her lips told him it had been the right approach.

He lowered his mouth and brushed against her. "Call me," he whispered against her lips.

Then she slipped out the door and down the stairs without another word. No promise to call, nothing. He had no idea if he'd put something in motion, but he hoped so.

Chapter 3

FOR THE NEXT FEW DAYS, Fiona had stared at Connor's texts. How about dinner? Dinner's not complicated.

How little he knew of her life. She shot him down every time because she didn't want him to find out who her parents were. The thing she liked most about him was that he knew the real her without any preconceived notions.

She wandered through the banquet hall debating whether she should go see Connor, when she saw her father without Mom.

She headed in his direction and stood beside him. He was deep in conversation with a younger man, one Fiona didn't recognize. Not that she knew all of her father's campaign donors.

"Michael, this is my lovely daughter, Fiona. Fiona, this is Michael Cartwright."

The man shook Fiona's hand and smiled. "And what do you do for a living, Fiona? I haven't heard your name bounced around in politics."

"I'm an artist."

His eyebrows shot up. "Interesting."

"And what about you Mr. Cartwright?"

"Michael, please. As I was telling your father, my construction company is looking to expand. We hope to get the bid for the expansion on the riverfront. Maybe you could put in a good word for me."

Her father chuckled a politician's laugh.

"Sorry, Mr.—Michael, but I stay as far away from policy and politics as I can." She flashed a friendly smile, the one her mother liked so much.

The men relaunched their conversation about zoning and possibilities for improvements, but Fiona tuned them out. Although it was supposed to be a friendly conversation over drinks, Fiona knew it to be what it was: a power gauge. Each man was feeling the other out to see who would be top dog. Fiona almost rolled her eyes. Mr. Cartwright should've realized her dad would always be on top.

She quietly excused herself and walked outside for some fresh air and the chance to maybe call Connor.

The air was colder than she expected and her skin pimpled and as she sucked in a deep lungful.

"Still trying to escape?"

The voice startled her and Fiona looked to her left. The man the voice belonged to startled her even more. "Patrick, what are you doing here? This isn't an open event."

"I know. I was in the neighborhood."

She crossed her arms and ran her hands over her chilly flesh.

"Actually, I came to see you. I thought maybe we could have coffee or dinner sometime." He'd edged closer, close enough that Fiona knew he hadn't been standing out there long. She felt the heat of his body.

"First off, if you wanted to contact me, you know my number. Second, why the heck would you want to meet?" Patrick was up to something, but she couldn't figure out what.

He reached out and played with the ends of her hair. "I always did like your hair like this. I wanted to talk and see if you might be interested in getting back together. Give us another shot."

A bark of laughter shot from her. "What? Why would I want to do that?"

He stiffened for a moment. "I'm going places, Fiona. I'll never settle for alderman the way your dad has. I have my sights set on bigger things. We could go far in this city. The results of this election won't even matter. Choose your side wisely."

She placed a hand on his chest to make sure he didn't come closer. "Just as I told you when we were a couple, I have no desire to be part of Chicago politics. I'm not my mother. As far as stepping on my father to reach your goals? Good luck with that."

As she turned to go back into the banquet hall, a movement nearby caught her attention. She turned fully and looked near the shrubbery alongside the building. Sure enough, a guy climbed out from behind the bushes. And he had a camera.

Fuck!

Her jaw clamped tight. She knew better than to approach the idiot. At least now she knew what Patrick was up to. Why he wanted to get her photo, she had no idea, but it wouldn't be for anything good. Inside the hall, she looked for her mother. When she found her, Fiona pulled her from the crowd, which of course irritated Sheila.

"Fiona, couldn't this wait? I have people to talk to." Her mother spoke with a steady smile on her lips.

"I wanted to let you know that I went out for some fresh air and ran into Patrick."

Mom's façade dropped. "What? When?"

"A few minutes ago."

"What is he doing here?"

"I wondered the same thing. He said he wanted to talk to me about getting back together, but when I turned him down, I noticed a guy in the bushes taking my picture."

Her mother's face turned to stone and Fiona's stomach fell.

"Do you know who?"

Fiona shook her head.

"Was the photo incriminating or embarrassing in any way?"

"Of course not. What do you think I would be doing outside with Patrick?"

"With you, I'm never quite sure." Sheila threw her shoulders back and renewed her smile. "I'll let your father's media people know. In the meantime, please avoid these kinds of things. They never do turn out well for you." She patted Fiona's arm.

Fiona's jaw dropped as her mother walked away. How could her mother have possibly turned this back on her? She'd done nothing but her duty as a daughter all night. She didn't invite Patrick to show up and she'd done nothing but try to get rid of him.

She couldn't win. Fiona made her way back through the throngs of people eager to speak with her father and she kept walking until she reached her car.

She drove to the one place she'd wanted to be all night: Connor's house.

Fiona stared at Connor's house. She had no idea why she was there. She should've called, especially after dodging his invitations for a date.

He'd left an open invitation. *But to just show up at his house?* Her eyes popped wide with a reason. She still had his sweatshirt.

She could return it and gauge his reaction to her presence.

She grabbed the sweatshirt and left the car. In front of his door, she took a deep breath and knocked. Max barked, but no other sounds came from inside. Another bark, then she heard Max run through the house. Maybe Connor was out. She looked down the block at Dermott's bar.

The door swung open and she was surprised to see Connor fully dressed, work boots and all.

"Fiona?"

"Hi." She held out the sweatshirt. "I wanted to return this."

He didn't reach for the shirt. His eyebrows rose expectantly.

Okay, so not responsive to seeing her. She shrugged and then turned, but he grabbed the sweatshirt she still held.

"You look like you had a bad night." His voice was quiet and his face softened. "Come in."

"Thank you," she answered and walked into the house. Again, she glanced around the empty space unsure of exactly what she'd expected by coming here. Max sat at her feet, so she played with his ears.

"Max, get off her fancy shoes."

"He's fine."

Connor walked toward the back of the house. Over his shoulder, he called, "I have a pot of coffee on in the kitchen."

She followed, and he poured her a cup.

"Milk or sugar?"

"Both please."

She sat at his kitchen table and he dropped a container of sugar and a half-gallon of milk in front of her. She stirred them in silently. He stared at her the entire time, but said nothing.

Her hands cupped the hot coffee and she sipped.

"You might sleep better at night if you weren't hopped up

on caffeine and sugar."

Fiona looked at him. He had the half-smile going on and she relaxed.

"Why are you really here, Fiona?"

She sipped the hot liquid to buy her time. Why was she here? It wasn't just the sex, although it had been pretty freaking hot between them. How could she tell him she needed a break from her family? She wanted to hide out for a little while in a place where her mother couldn't find her.

He drank his coffee silently and she would've given anything to see inside his head. She probably shouldn't have come here. She couldn't explain it, but she liked being with Connor. "I wanted to see you again."

"Wanted to see me or screw me?"

"Both?" she answered with a smile.

Still nothing. She definitely called it when she saw him as silent and brooding. Setting her cup back on the table, she said, "I guess this was a mistake. When you said you were okay with what I could give, I thought you meant it."

"You haven't called. I thought we were done."

"Me too. I don't like games. But something happened earlier tonight and all I could think about was you."

"What happened?"

She shook her head. Words bubbled at the back of her throat, seeking escape, but she swallowed them.

He sighed and pushed off the counter he'd been leaning on. "As much as I'd enjoy taking you to bed, it's not an option for me right now. I'm headed back downstairs to work. I'm behind on this project. You can join me if you want, but it's dusty down there."

Connor kept trying to spend time with her out of bed, so uncharacteristic for most guys. She didn't think she'd ever met a man who wouldn't take her up on her sex-only offer.

He looked at her over his shoulder. "You won't let me take you on a date, you can at least talk to me while I work."

She hesitated and when a line of frustration creased his forehead, she stood. "I don't mind talking to you, but I won't talk about my family."

He stepped closer, so close that heat bounced off his body and onto hers. "Why not? Are you in the mob? A spy?"

She chuckled. "No to both. All you need to know is that sometimes I need a break from them. Talking about them doesn't give me a break."

"Hard to get to know someone when she blocks out a hefty piece of her life." His words were quiet, but she heard the irritation in them.

Standing on tiptoe, she planted a kiss on his lips, inviting him for more. Her tongue probed and he gripped her hips before pulling away.

"I have work to do." He turned back toward the door behind him.

She rolled her eyes, but followed him. He really wasn't going to have sex with her.

He looked at Max and said, "Sit." To her, he said, "I don't let Max downstairs. He's too destructive."

He led the way into the basement. The space was a completely unfinished—all concrete floor and walls. It smelled of Connor. The sawdust and hard work scent of his skin. On one side of the basement sat a massive table. The wood was bare and four chairs surrounded it.

Connor ignored her and began moving wood and tools on a workbench. She went to the table and ran her hand along the smooth edge. The design was simple, but beautiful.

A noise behind her startled her and she turned to watch

Connor slide a piece of wood into a machine. He turned it on. She recognized it as a lathe and he was making a chair leg. She stared at the muscles on his back as they bunched. Then she shifted to the side to better watch him work.

The roped muscles on his forearms bulged and making it one of the sexiest things she'd ever laid eyes on. Sawdust littered the area and stuck to the hairs on his arm. She closed her eyes as warmth flooded her body at the memory of those forearms braced at the side of her head while he drove into her.

This man might've ruined her for others for a long time. After sleeping with him only twice, she was fantasizing about getting him naked again, and she wasn't sure if he even liked her right now.

The whine of the machine and the grinding of wood created a rhythm that lulled her into peace. She sat on one of the chairs, relaxed, and watched Connor move. He wasn't relaxed. His muscles were hard, but not tense. She couldn't see his face, but she imagined the focused and determined look. He was the kind of guy who didn't like to make mistakes.

After a few minutes, the noise stopped and his stance shifted. The jeans made his ass look really good. He bent over and blew dust out of the way. She could almost feel his breath against her skin when he'd kissed and sucked at her collarbone.

Holy shit. She was getting turned on watching a man work on wood. She snorted back a laugh. She must be tired if she found the ridiculous pun funny.

He turned and stared at her. "Problem?"

"Not at all." Her gaze darted away. She didn't want him to know she'd gotten hot and bothered watching. She shook her head and stood. Her mouth was incredibly dry, so she swallowed hard. Her words came out quiet and breathy. "You look busy. I'm going to go now."

One of his eyebrows cocked up and his mouth twitched. Damn it. He saw right through her.

She jogged up the stairs as quickly as her heels would allow and said a quick good-bye to Max, who greeted her at the basement door. From behind her, she heard a quiet laugh.

This is exactly what Sarah had warned her about. She never should've shown up here. He was supposed to be a one-time thing. She'd already turned it into three times and her mind raced down the path to find time number four, where they would definitely be naked again. She walked to her car and hoped the cold night air would cool off her body.

Two days and two fucked up and incomplete chairs later, Connor still had Fiona on the brain. He'd had no luck digging up dirt on Fiona and proof of nothing new on her father.

He couldn't stop thinking about getting her naked again, which was exactly what she wanted.

Maybe he'd find nothing on her because she truly didn't know anything about her father's dealings. He stared into his fourth beer for the night.

Was he thinking clearly, or was it the alcohol talking?

He thought of Fiona bucking naked under him, screaming his name and decided his dick was doing all the thinking.

Maybe one more beer and she would leave his brain. Or his dick would give up. Either would work. He could pick up another woman if he wanted to get laid. He glanced around the bar. Not a redhead in sight.

He pushed off the barstool and headed for the door. He stumbled back to his house and took Max for a walk.

The dog yanked and pulled at the leash. "Slow down, boy. No running tonight."

As if he understood, Max slowed to a trot, keeping the leash taut. The cold air helped clear Connor's head. He was buzzed, not drunk, but not okay enough to drive. On his way back home, he pulled out his phone and dialed Fiona's number.

If she answered, he'd invite her over. If he got her voicemail, he'd drop it.

One ring, two, three, he pulled the phone away to disconnect when he heard a quiet, "Hello?"

"Hey, sweetheart. It's your favorite booty call. Want to come over?"

"Connor?"

"How many other guys do you call for late-night sex?"

"Are you drunk?"

"Close, but not quite." He walked up the front steps and let Max free of the leash.

"Why are you calling me? I thought you were pissed off."

"I was. Maybe am still a little. But I've been thinking about you. We had fun. And I'm horny." He looked at what should be his living room. What he wouldn't give for a couch to fall on right now. He went to the kitchen to make sure Max had food and water.

"My situation hasn't changed."

"Neither has mine."

"What does that mean?"

He laughed. "Hell if I know. Fiona, you're the kind of woman who can appreciate a straight answer, so I'll give it to you. I miss your body and I'd really like to fuck you right now."

His proposition was met with silence. Maybe he'd offended her. Then he thought about how she'd come onto him.

"No more questions about my family?"

"I don't care who your family is or why you want to keep them a secret." In that brief moment, he almost believed himself.

"And no commentary about it," she snapped out.

"I can have sex with you without judgment." He hoped. "You'll have to come here because I can't drive."

Silence.

He continued, "You know you want to." He lowered his voice. "I saw how turned on you were in my workshop. If you want, we can have sex on the table in the basement. I can't think straight because I keep imagining you naked on my workbench."

Her breathing was uneven, so he knew his words were working. On him too, and he shifted his cock in his jeans.

"I'll tell you what, Fiona. I'm going to take a shower and have a cup of coffee to sober up a little. I'll leave the door unlocked. If you're not here by the time I finish, I'll go off to bed by myself." Then he disconnected. If she were half as hot and bothered as he was, she'd be speeding all the way to his house.

He took his shower and tried not to think of Fiona's slick body in front of him or the way her wet curls snaked around his hands. He dried off and opted for a bottle of water instead of coffee. If she didn't show, he didn't need another sleepless night.

Two gulps of water down his throat and he heard a quiet knock on the front door. Max scurried through the house. For such a big dog, he liked to act like a puppy. "Hello," Fiona called out.

Connor didn't reply but walked from the kitchen toward the door. Her cheeks were pink probably from the cold air, but he liked to think their conversation had something to do with it.

Her pale skin flushed when she was turned on.

She had her hair twisted up into some kind of crazy ponytail and she wore ratty sweat pants.

"Hey."

She closed the door behind her and brushed her hand across Max's head as she walked by. "Thanks for inviting me. If it's any consolation, I've been thinking about you too."

She hung her jacket on the post by the stairs and kept walking toward him. Her thin T-shirt revealed she didn't have a bra on. Her nipples poked through and before she could touch him, he lowered his mouth and sucked a stiff peak through the shirt.

She inhaled sharply and the air trembled on her exhale. She rubbed her hands over his head and through his hair as he moved from one breast to the other. Her hips gave a little thrust, but she was too far away to collide with him.

Connor slid his hands beneath her shirt. He loved the softness of her skin. He lifted the shirt to have full access to her bared breasts. He kissed his way down her torso and knelt in front of her. He peeled her pants down, following with his mouth. Her legs quivered as his lips grazed her mound.

Her nails dug into his shoulders. He worked his way back up her body and kissed her. He broke away and they stood staring at each other, panting.

He *really* wished he had a couch right now.

She stepped out of her pants. "Upstairs?"

"Yeah."

She turned and took the stairs two at a time. He didn't try to keep up, but he loved the view.

An hour later, Connor lie awake in bed, trying to figure out the words to say to convince Fiona to stay, at least for a while.

He enjoyed the feel of her warm body curled next to him. No. This wasn't supposed to be about enjoying her, which he was. He needed to get information on her father. He stroked his fingers down her back and she sighed. Her light breath skimmed across his chest. They were both relaxed and comfortable.

As if on cue, she sat up and pushed her hair away from her face. He loved to watch her body in the soft glow of the bedside lamp. Shadows played across her pale skin, making him want to explore all over.

She turned and leaned her body across his chest. She gave him a hungry kiss and said, "I'm starving. Do you have anything to eat, or are you one of those guys who only has beer and condiments in his fridge?"

He rose up and kissed her neck. He knew exactly what he'd like to eat. "Depends on what you're looking for."

She shivered and pulled away. "I've already had a helping of that. And although I completely enjoyed it, I'd love some breakfast." She crawled backwards off the bed. "And then we can have seconds up here."

She pulled his T-shirt over her head. "Maybe even thirds. It's not good to go to sleep on a full stomach."

He liked it when she toyed with him, and he enjoyed the idea of her staying even more. "I can make breakfast."

He climbed out of bed and put on underwear. Food sounded good. Connor knew just what he'd cook for Fiona. He lucked out when she'd asked for breakfast. No woman could resist his chocolate chip pancakes.

In the kitchen, Fiona sat on a chair and propped a foot next to her ass, the T-shirt barely covering anything. He groaned as he pulled ingredients from the cabinet. "If you actually want to eat food, I suggest you put your foot down, or I'll take you right here on the table."

"Sorry," she said without a bit of remorse. She stood and walked around the small kitchen.

When he turned to get a bowl and measuring cups he almost ran into her—twice. He set the items on the counter and spun back to her. "Here," he said, grabbing her waist. He set her on the counter beside the ingredients. "You can watch and tell me about yourself while I cook."

She swung her legs out behind him and he was keenly aware of the nakedness they led to, but he focused on mixing pancake batter.

"What do you want to know?"

This was what he'd been looking for. Time with Fiona to sneak under her defenses. "Whatever you want to tell me. I don't want to ask about something off-limits, so you choose. Although it might be nice to at least know your last name. We've been naked together a few times, but I only know you as Fiona." He whisked eggs and milk together and waited for a response.

"I wish I could just be Fiona everywhere I went," she mumbled, then quickly covered as if he shouldn't have heard the admission. "Wells. Fiona Wells."

He tried not to let the lie get under his skin as he mixed the remaining ingredients and turned the flame on under the griddle. He should've expected the lie. "Tell me, Wells, Fiona Wells, do you like chocolate?"

"Doesn't everyone?"

He smiled and leaned over to kiss her. "You're supposed to be telling about yourself."

"My life's not exciting. I've lived in Chicago my whole life except for a year in high school when I studied abroad in Paris. Went to college and majored in art, much to my mother's dismay. *Art is such a useless degree.* It wasn't until her friends started buying my jewelry that she accepted I was never going to be a lawyer or an accountant. I make my jewelry when I'm inspired, usually late at night, and a few days a week I teach at the youth outreach. That's the extent of my life. See, not exciting."

He scooped the first pancakes onto the griddle and looked at her from the corner of his eye. "Paris sounds pretty exciting." That had been the year he and Aiden had gotten into so much trouble. It also explained why she didn't know who Connor was.

"It was. I had a great time, but I was too young to appreciate it. I want to go back someday."

He flipped the pancakes and grabbed a couple of plates from the cabinet above Fiona's head. The action caused him to lean over her and she took the opportunity to kiss his chest. He caged his arms around her on the counter. "I wasn't kidding when I said you better watch yourself if you want food."

She smiled and pointed. "My pancakes are burning. You don't want to have to start over."

He pulled the first pancakes off the pan and poured more. "What do you do for fun?"

"I don't know. I don't go out much. I'm kind of a homebody. I like to watch cheesy horror movies. I've never had many hobbies because I have my art. I love it and I'm lucky enough to get paid to do it."

Connor plopped pancakes onto the other plate. She had no political aspirations. Homebody was an understatement. Where most of the Cavanaghs clamored for the spotlight, Fiona clung to the shadows.

"How about you?" she asked as she hopped off the counter.

"My time is filled with work for money and work on this

house. Any down time I have, I read. I already told you that. And I go to Dermott's to watch the games."

She settled in at the table and he put a plate in front of her. "How did you get into watching European soccer?"

"My dad. He was an Irish immigrant and he brought his love of the game with him to Chicago. He used to take me to the bar to watch the games with him."

"Are you close?"

He felt her gaze on his back as he reached into the refrigerator for the syrup. He hadn't wanted to get into a personal and heavy conversation. At least not on his end. But maybe it would get her to open up. "We used to be. He died when I was fourteen."

"Wow. That must've been hard."

He nodded and hoped the conversation would end.

"What about your mom? Any siblings?"

He shook his head. "My mom went back to Ireland with my brother a few years after my dad died."

Fiona's eyes widened. "She left you here? You were just a kid."

He couldn't tell Fiona he'd given his mother his money and urged her to go. He couldn't go with *because he'd been in jail.* "I did okay. This life was all I'd known."

He handed her a fork. "Dig in before they get cold."

She slopped syrup all over and cut into the pancakes. He waited while she tasted and gave him what he wanted. She closed her eyes and moaned in appreciation.

"You know, if the whole carpenter thing doesn't work out, you can always be a short order cook. You definitely have the guys at IHOP and Denny's beat."

He dove into his own plate. "Fuel up. I'm hungry for more than pancakes."

Fiona scarfed down the pancakes. Although she'd needed escape from the politics and her mother the other night, things had gotten worse over the last two days. Some political blogger had posted the photo of her and Patrick and included a scathing commentary, which called into question her loyalty.

The picture did look like an intimate moment and it had taken place right outside her father's event. Her mother was livid.

Losing herself in mindless sex was exactly what she'd needed. And now she was enjoying delicious pancakes.

Determined to keep politics from her mind for a while longer, Fiona finished her pancakes and added one more. After eating it, she eyed another but decided against it. She pushed her empty plate away. "Thank you. Those were delicious."

"Sure you don't want anything else?"

"I'm stuffed." She stood and took her plate to the sink. He didn't have a dishwasher that she could see, so she started the water to wash the dishes.

He came up behind her with his plate and set it in the water. "You don't need to do the dishes."

"They aren't going to do themselves, and you cooked."

"Maybe we should wash together." He moved her hair to the side and his arms circled her waist. He kissed her neck and nibbled her earlobe.

Jolts of pleasure zinged through her. She tilted her head to give him better access as she picked up a sponge and began wiping a plate. He made it so easy to forget her family.

Connor's hands moved to her hips, pulling the T-shirt up. She began to breathe heavily and scrubbed a harder and faster on the dish in her hand.

"Like that?"

She knew her voice would be rough, so she nodded. His fingers skimmed across her inner thigh and she spread her legs for him. When he stroked her, her knees weakened. The plate slipped from her grasp and clanged into the sink.

Fiona turned in his arms and grabbed his head, leaving a soapy trail in his hair. She dragged his mouth to hers.

Then she let him take her against the kitchen counter until they were both blind and exhausted.

When he lowered her legs back to the floor, he steadied her hips and waited. It was late and she should go. He probably needed to work in the morning. And she had enough going on to fuel her for at least a few hours of work. She finally finished the dishes with Connor's gaze burning into her. You'd think the man hadn't gotten laid in years the way he looked at her like he still hadn't had enough.

But she knew better than to believe he didn't have women after him. He had his own house, a job, and he could cook. Maybe just pancakes, but it was real food. And he was freaking hot. He might not be the happiest or funniest guy in the room, but his sex appeal made up for his reticence.

She dried her hands on a towel and turned to face him, hoping her face wouldn't betray her lust for him. "Thanks for breakfast in the middle of the night and the multiple orgasms. Definitely made my evening better."

He leaned against the doorway with his arms crossed. Not angry, just casual. His body filled the doorway and she skirted past him.

"I'm going to grab my clothes and head home." She grabbed her pants from the bottom of the stairs where Connor had stripped them off and then she headed up.

Connor still said nothing but followed her upstairs. In the bedroom, Max lifted his head from his spot on his bed in the corner. He tilted his head as if he wasn't sure it would be worth getting up.

Fiona picked through her clothes on the floor and straightened them. She pulled her panties and pants on. Connor sat beside her on the bed.

"My offer stands. You can stay."

The proposition taunted her. She wanted to stay. To sleep in the comfort and safety of his arms for the night. But she also knew the desire to do so was her main problem. She'd believe she was half in love by morning, and she promised herself and Sarah she wouldn't let that happen.

He nuzzled her neck again. "It'll be fun."

She had no doubt, but she pushed off the bed and handed him his shirt back. "That's why I shouldn't stay." She pulled her shirt on, already missing the warmth and scent of his clothes.

How the hell did this happen every time? "Maybe I'll see you this weekend?"

Connor stood. "I have plans this weekend."

The acknowledgement of his social life away from her stung in a way it shouldn't have. She'd admitted to herself that he probably had a line of female admirers. Her crazy fantasies started running before she even knew they existed. "See you around then."

She headed for the door. His sigh crept toward exasperation, and he followed her to the front door. She pulled her keys from her coat pocket and buttoned up.

"I don't have plans with another woman."

"I didn't ask. It's none of my business." She tried to sound believable because she didn't have a right to ask and it shouldn't matter.

He wrapped one of her curls around his finger. "I know you

didn't ask. I'm making it your business."

She didn't know what to make of that. Connor had called himself a booty call. A booty call didn't provide unnecessary details.

Breakfast. That's what changed things. A booty call wasn't supposed to share meals, was it?

His quiet laugh pulled her from her rampant thoughts. "I see your brain going a mile a minute." He kissed her and every thought fled her mind. When he pulled away, he asked, "Do you have plans this weekend?"

She blinked and tried to form a coherent thought. "I'm working at the outreach center Saturday, like I do every week."

"I'm going camping. It's probably the last warm weekend we'll have. If you want to come with me and Max, we can wait until you're done."

"Oh, um…I don't know." Her heart kicked up a notch. A booty call didn't make weekend plans together. She didn't know what to make of the offer.

Connor brushed a kiss over her cheek. "Think about it. I'll call you tomorrow."

"Okay." One thing she could say for Connor was that he was definitely laid back. His no-pressure tactics worked too well on her as evidenced by her quick arrival after his drunken phone call. It was like he was inside her head and knew when to push and when to step back.

A prick of panic poked at her and she left his house before she could convince herself to stay.

Chapter 4

CONNOR HAD FINALLY FINISHED THE last of the chairs for the dining set. Using Fiona's body to satisfy himself had cleared his head. He'd get the first coat of stain on the bare wood and then pack for camping.

Although he loved his house, even with the work it needed, the urge to leave the city to get to wide-open space never left him. Maybe it was the time he'd spent in prison that caused it. The confinement, being surrounded by people with no escape. It had been years since he'd been released, but the lure of fresh air and the outdoors hadn't diminished.

Even during the summer months, when the parks were filled with families and groups of campers, he could be alone. He loved his solitude, so he had no idea what had possessed him to invite Fiona. She didn't seem too interested, but it would give him a chance to get further under her defenses, away from the city and far from the reach of the Cavanaghs.

Plus, having a warm body to hold onto during the long, cold night might make the intrusion worth it. Connor grabbed a couple of sheets of sandpaper to smooth over the chairs and table before staining. The fine grit paper made the wood feel more polished even without being finished. He dusted the furniture and got his cans of stain.

Just as he popped the lid off the can, his phone rang. Fiona. "Hello."

"Hi, Connor. I know you said you'd call, but I was wondering if the offer to go camping still stands."

He'd thought she wouldn't want to go. But she was making the first move again and she wanted to spend time with him. "Sure. What time do you finish on Saturday?"

"I'm usually done about one, but I can get out a little early. How about we meet at my place at twelve. Will that work?"

He'd planned on heading out Friday afternoon and waiting until Saturday afternoon was probably the latest he'd ever gone. "Okay."

She grew silent, but didn't hang up.

"Was there something else?"

"Um, yeah. I'm not a real outdoorsy person, so I have no idea what to bring."

He sat on one of the newly finished chairs. "Pack a backpack with warm clothes. Think layers. Hiking boots or comfortable shoes. I'll bring everything else."

"Are you sure?"

"Do you have any camping gear?"

"No. But I could bring food."

"I have what we'll need." It was a small lie. He'd make this camping experience one she wouldn't forget. She'd learn the fun of being an outdoorsy person.

"See you Saturday then?"

"Yeah. Unless you want to come over tonight?"

"I have plans for tonight with my friend Sarah. Can you shoot me a text of where we'll be staying in case Sarah needs to reach me?"

"We'll be at the campground at Starved Rock."

"Okay. Thanks. See you Saturday."

Connor hung up and stared at the can of stain on the table. What had he agreed to? Irritation dug at him. This would probably his last weekend of camping until spring and now, not only was he cutting it short, he was going to be with a woman who didn't know how to camp.

He pushed the irritation aside. He'd invited her and if it ended up being a disaster, he'd go camping alone a different weekend. It'd just be colder than he liked. He needed to focus. Fiona volunteered to spend time with him, which meant things were falling into place. Maybe this weekend would put him in a position for his plan to work faster. No editor would wait forever on his book. He needed information, and the sooner he got what he needed, the sooner he could forget Fiona.

As he stroked the rich dark stain over the naked wood, he couldn't help but think of Fiona's pale skin. He made a mental note to pack the small heater so he could enjoy getting her naked in the tent.

So much for focus.

He supposed missing out on a hike would be worth it if he spent the time inside Fiona.

Saturday afternoon, Connor drove his packed truck to Fiona's place. They'd only met a little over a week ago and they were going camping together. He still couldn't get over how strange it felt. He'd never invited a woman to go with him. Then again, he'd had sex with Fiona more times than he had almost anyone else since being a teen. Especially in one week's time. A nasty bit of nagging guilt tugged at him.

He'd gone into this expecting to use her, but although he'd

been giving her what she wanted, something felt off. He'd convinced himself they were using each other. It was time for him to get what he'd been looking for.

He called her phone when he was a block away.

"Hello?" She sounded a bit breathless, which didn't bode well for him getting to the campground.

"I'll be at your place in a few minutes. Are you ready?"

"Yeah. I'll be out front waiting." She disconnected.

Hmm. He liked a woman who managed to be on time. Then he pulled up in front of her building and swallowed a curse. She stood wearing old, faded jeans, knee-high leather boots with a small heel, and a skimpy jacket, which didn't appear to be lined.

She waved at him and he put the truck in park. She climbed in, rubbed Max's head, then flashed a brilliant smile at Connor.

"Tell me you have a warmer coat."

"This is the warmest one I've got. But I packed a couple of sweatshirts."

"You're going to freeze your ass off."

Her lips quirked up even farther on one side. "That's okay. I can stand to lose a little back there."

"I'm serious. And your ass is just fine." He watched the blush creep across her cheeks. "What do you wear all winter?"

"I go from my house to the car to whatever indoor place I'm headed. I told you I'm not an outdoors person."

"Forget it. We'll stop on the way and buy you a coat."

She inched closer to him on the bench seat. "Or you could keep warm."

"I plan to do that anyway. Trust me, you want a coat."

She shrugged and shifted back to the passenger seat and buckled up. He drove out of the city in silence and stopped at a sporting goods store. He cracked the windows open for Max and took Fiona shopping.

He grabbed a parka and tossed it to her. "Try this."

She slid her arms into it and then glanced at the tag dangling from the sleeve. She inhaled sharply. "I didn't bring much money. I have about sixty bucks and my driver's license. I didn't even grab a credit card because I was afraid I might lose it."

"I got you covered." He zipped the coat up and saw that it fit perfectly. "Now let's check out boots. You won't make it through half a hike in those. And they look unlined, so your feet will freeze." He turned toward the back of the store and she scurried to keep up.

"I asked you what I should pack. These are boots."

He stopped in his tracks and she crashed into his back. He turned around. "Not for hiking. They're barely suitable for walking."

Christ. What had he gotten himself into? There went any enjoyment of his weekend if he had to teach her everything.

"You know, this was a bad idea. You go on without me." She shrugged out of the coat. "I'll call a cab to take me home."

He hadn't meant to let her know how he felt, so he scrambled to fix it. "It's fine. I asked you to come and I'm not rescinding the invitation. It'll be fun. What size are your feet?"

After getting Fiona the gear she needed, including finding a hat to fit over her hair, they headed back to the truck.

"I'll pay you back when we get home tomorrow. I don't expect you to cover my expenses."

He looked at her in her puffy parka and smiled as he turned the key. "Consider it a gift. You're all set for camping. Maybe you'll like it so much you'll want to go again."

She leaned across the seat and kissed him. Her lips connected with his, warm and inviting. When she pulled back, she whispered against his mouth, "Thanks for the present. I have one for you too."

"Yeah? Where?" His voice was a little strangled and his jeans tightened uncomfortably.

"You'll have to unwrap me to find out." She brushed her lips against his again and then flopped back against the passenger door.

He lowered his window more to allow the cool air in. If she kept him this hot, he wouldn't need the heater he'd packed for her comfort.

Fiona sat on a rock near what Connor said was a campsite. Max lay at her feet and she petted him while watching Connor assemble a tent. It didn't look all that big. In fact, she didn't see how she would fit. His broad shoulders filled the doorway flap thingy and she suspected if he laid in it, his feet would stick out. She never should've accepted his invitation. She didn't belong here.

Worse, he regretted asking her. He wouldn't admit it, but she saw the look in his eyes when she'd admitted to never having camped. She sighed and stood up. "Is there anything I can do?"

He looked over his shoulder at her. "You can gather some firewood. Dry stuff. Nothing that looks like it just fell."

Finally, something to make her feel useful. "I'll take Max. We'll be back soon."

She wrapped Max's leash around her wrist so he wouldn't wander off, not that it looked like he wanted to. She picked up some branches and a couple of logs she thought would make a good campfire. It was wood. She couldn't screw it up, right?

As she walked into the woods, she breathed deeply. The

fresh, crisp air filled her lungs. The day still felt warm and after a few minutes of picking through the trees, she wanted to take her coat off. She didn't see why she needed such a heavy jacket. She would've been comfortable in the one she'd been wearing.

Max sniffed around and barked at a squirrel. She hoped he wouldn't need to relieve himself because she hadn't brought a bag to clean up. When her arms were full, she tugged Max back in the direction of the camp. She had a moment of panic she might've taken a wrong turn, but Max guided her. He knew exactly where to find Connor.

The tent was fully assembled and Connor sat on the rock she previously occupied. She dumped the wood on the ground at his feet. "Is this enough?"

"For now." He shifted on the rock. "I'm going to go on a hike with Max."

A statement not an invitation. She didn't know how to respond.

"Do you want to come?" He looked as unsure as she felt.

"Not if you want to be alone. I can hang out here." And do what, she didn't know.

"Come on. I'll keep the hike short."

His invitation warmed her in ways it shouldn't. She didn't know what she was doing with him. He had somehow twisted her into a relationship of some kind. Guilt plowed into her chest. Holding back so much of herself wasn't fair to Connor even though he let her.

He whistled and Max stood and trotted over. Connor loosely grabbed the leash and started walking.

Romantic walk in the woods this wasn't. He didn't speak, so neither did she. At first, silence engulfed her uncomfortably, but then she began to hear the sounds of nature: birds chirping, squirrels chattering, chipmunks scurrying beneath dry leaves.

She watched Connor walk. He paid no attention to her, so she turned her focus to her surroundings. She'd never been to the park before, but she could immediately see the appeal. Many trees had already started to lose their foliage, but enough remained that the kaleidoscope of colors made her itch for a paintbrush. She rarely painted for pleasure anymore. She used her creative energy for her jewelry. But every now and again, something she saw begged to be painted.

She pulled her phone from her pocket and snapped a couple of pictures. She'd use them as inspiration. If not for an actual painting, for a fall line of jewelry. As they walked deeper down the trail, the wind shifted and the trees swallowed the warm sunlight.

Fiona shivered and burrowed her hands into the pockets of her lined coat. So Connor had been right. Maybe she did need a warmer coat for being out here. She hadn't paid attention to how long or how far they'd walked. She trusted Connor would get them back to the camp before it got dark. Her nose started to numb and just as she was about to say something, they turned a bend and she stared at the campsite.

Connor still hadn't spoken to her. She didn't know if she'd make it the weekend without him talking. She understood he was a quiet guy, but this edged toward the ridiculous.

He picked up a few pieces of wood and began creating a tower in the fire pit.

"Can you point the way to the bathroom?"

He dropped the stick in his hand. "I'll walk you."

A sharp whistle and Max walked beside him.

She hurried to catch up. "I can handle going to the bathroom."

He didn't respond. She paid close attention to the path they took. There was no one in sight. Maybe there was a reason he didn't want her to walk alone. "Is the park not safe?"

He looked at her over his shoulder. "You're safe."

The two words simply stated fact, but he didn't answer her question. Obviously she was safe with him. A person would have to be crazy to mess with him. She knew if she prodded, she probably wouldn't get anything further so she dropped it. A moment later, she arrived at the bathroom.

When she emerged, Connor and Max were waiting and they walked back in silence.

Connor immediately went back to building a fire. She took the spot on the rock and watched him work, fascinated by the deft movements of his hands. He pulled a box of matches from his pocket and lit the wood.

"Isn't that cheating? Aren't you supposed to strike a rock or rub sticks together or something?"

He prodded a branch and added a couple more twigs. "Rest assured if I was stranded without matches, I'd get a fire going. I don't see the reason for making extra work for myself." When the fire blazed, he stood and surveyed the area.

Her gaze followed his. "Not a lot of people around."

"Most people are done camping for the season. You'll find a few diehards out there. I like a site that offers me some privacy. It allows me to break the rules and let Max off his leash."

"He has to stay on a leash all weekend?" The flames licked and warmed her face.

"Those are the rules. But this late in the season, no one hassles me."

Max sat comfortably at her side. Petting his head, she questioned again why she came. She could've found somewhere else to hide out after that stupid political blogger published the photo of her and Patrick. She kept seeing the headline: **FIONA CAVANAGH AND PATRICK NEALE – WILL HER ROMANCE RUIN DAD'S CAMPAIGN?**

She'd been spitting mad, but Mom's cooler head prevailed and Fiona knew she needed to escape. Maybe by the end of the weekend, it will have all blown over and she could go back to her quiet, almost anonymity.

Connor knew he was being a dick, but he didn't know why. He suddenly felt crowded, like there wasn't enough room for him to breath, which was ridiculous since they were surrounded by nothing but trees and air. He settled on a log across from Fiona.

She stood and fisted her hands on her hips. "Why did you invite me if you didn't want me here?"

"What?"

"You obviously don't want me here. You've barely said two words to me and those I had to pry out."

"I want you here."

"Please."

Although she meant it to sound pissed off, he recognized the exasperated word for what it was. Hurt. He hadn't wanted that. He stood and walked around the fire to meet her. "I'm being a jerk. I'm sorry. I don't even know why."

"Because you don't want me here. It's obvious. What I don't get is why you invited me."

He held her hand and pulled her toward the log. He sat and tugged her to settle between his legs in front of the fire. With his thighs wrapped around her hips and the scent of her soft curls in his face, he finally relaxed. *This* was why he'd invited her.

No! The scream resounded in his head. He'd invited her to get information about her family.

"Camping is something I've always done alone. Except for Max. I didn't think about sharing this time with anyone."

She stiffened in his embrace, so he rubbed his palms down the front of her thighs, willing her to relax.

"When I asked you to come with me, I didn't think you'd say yes, but I wasn't hoping for a no either. I asked because I wanted to spend time with you outside of the bedroom and since you've refused every date I offered, I figured this would be a compromise."

Fiona melted against him and his shoulders released some of the tension. "I come out here for peace. It's my time to decompress. I have to adjust to having someone here, that's all."

Her head rested against his shoulder. "You can pretend I'm not here. Draw a line across the middle of the tent. You stay on your side and I'll stay on mine."

He pushed her hair to the side to expose her neck. "Not gonna happen."

He kissed her pulse and slid his hands past her coat and under her sweatshirt. Her stomach muscles quivered under his touch.

Then she put her hands on top of his to stop him. "I wasn't going to say yes."

She spoke quietly as if confessing.

"Then why did you?"

"Because I needed to escape my family again. If I stayed anywhere near my house, I'd get dragged into whatever my mother wanted. It's exhausting being someone other than who you are." She closed her eyes, and he cradled her against his chest.

His fingers resumed their exploration and she didn't stop them. His hands were cold against her warm skin. He didn't wander under her bra or into her pants. He just wanted to feel her skin.

"Hungry?"

Her eyes popped open. "Starved. What's for dinner?"

"Hot dogs and s'mores."

"What are you, twelve?"

"You said you've never been camping. Everyone's first camping experience should be hot dogs over an open flame and s'mores." He slid away from her body to go to the tent where he'd parked the cooler. "You're not vegetarian or something, are you?"

She laughed. "No. But what would you have done if I was?"

He shrugged. "Driven into town to buy you something to eat." He grabbed the skewers and hot dogs from the cooler. "There's beer in the cooler if you want one."

"Sounds great. One for you too?"

"Sure."

She popped the top on two bottles as he ripped open the package of hot dogs. He'd thought about bringing his campfire stove, but decided against it. No need to do anything fancy for one night of camping. Maybe they could come back in the spring and spend a long weekend.

Whoa. She wasn't supposed be around in the spring.

He skewered a hot dog and handed the stick to Fiona. "Why can't you be yourself around your mother?"

Her hand holding the beer twitched. He broke the rules by asking the question, but he deserved to know, didn't he?

"Because she has certain expectations that I always fall short of no matter how much I try."

"Then why try?"

"You promised no questions about my family."

He lifted a shoulder like it didn't matter. It was the most she'd said about her family and it still wasn't much of anything.

He charred his hot dog until near black and then pulled it from the flames.

"That's gross. It's burnt."

"It's the way I like it." He put it on a bun and added ketchup and mustard.

Fiona kept her hot dog at the edge of the fire, barely making any marks on it. Then she squirted ketchup directly onto the dog.

"I brought buns."

"I like it like this."

Then she proceeded to eat a hot dog so obscenely, he couldn't believe his eyes. All he wanted was her naked again. She licked the ketchup as it dripped down the length. When her lips circled it, he groaned, even though he knew a bite would come next.

She chomped hard and laughed with a mouthful.

"You're an evil woman." He tossed the rest of his food to Max and advanced on Fiona. Her eyes widened, but she held her position. He stripped her coat from her body and lowered his head to kiss her.

He pressed his hard dick into her hips, the denim between them too constraining. He reached for the button on her jeans.

Her hips jerked out of reach. "I know you don't think I'm getting naked out here."

He looked over his shoulder and then over hers. "There's no one around."

"Maybe not. But it's freaking cold."

"Hold on." He went into the tent and brought back the extra blanket he packed. He wrapped the blanket around her and then popped the button on her jeans. "Trust me."

He sat on the log, positioning Fiona with her back to the fire, keeping her warm, so she could straddle him. In one shove he knocked her jeans and panties to her ankles. He stared at the hiking boots he made her get. He cursed under his breath and untied one.

She held his shoulders and he yanked the single boot off and she stepped from the restraining clothing. He kissed her hip and trailed his tongue across her torso as he fumbled with the button on his own jeans.

His cock sprang free and he realized he'd forgotten the condom. Tilting his body up, brushing his cold, bulky clothes against Fiona's smooth nakedness, he caused another shiver. He handed the condom to her for safekeeping, but she ripped it open immediately.

Before she removed it from the package, Connor went back to touching her. He massaged her thighs and his fingers crept slowly toward the apex. She tilted her hips forward, begging for his touch. He stroked her gently and she began to ride his hand.

The woman had no patience. He wrapped his left arm around her hips to hold her steady. He looked up from his position and smiled. She returned a glare.

"Trust me." He used his mouth and hand until she swallowed moans and her fingers scraped and grasped at his coat. She was wet with wanting him, but he wanted her almost at her peak before he drove in.

When her legs began to tremble, he snatched the condom from her hand and slid it on. The moment allowed her to recover, so he lapped at her one more time. Her body stiffened and he pulled away.

She was breathless, but managed to say, "Now who's being

evil?"

He brought her down on top of him and thrust as deep as he could. As soon as he filled her, Fiona took over the pace and rode him fast and hard. She bounced on him, pulling almost all the way off him before slamming back down, teasing him the way he'd teased her.

Until he couldn't take it any longer and grabbed her shoulders. He drove into her and exploded. She ground her pelvis into him and followed.

The blanket had slipped from her shoulders and rested around their waists, covering their connection. She laid her head on his shoulder and panted to catch her breath.

"I thought you said s'mores were for dessert."

He laughed. A real, deep, free laugh. His first in a long time. And it felt great.

After gorging on too much chocolate and marshmallow, Connor leaned back against the log and grabbed his book to read. Fiona settled next to him, the blanket still snug around her, even though she'd reclaimed her pants. She licked melted marshmallow from the edges of her graham cracker and he tried not to stare.

Max whined next to her before standing and barking. Connor sighed and stood. "He probably needs to pee again."

Fiona stood. "I'll take him. I have to pee too."

He closed his book and set it beside the tent. "We'll go together."

"I'll be fine with Max. I have a black belt in karate, so I can hold my own. Plus, you're not supposed to leave a campfire unattended, are you?"

She didn't wait for an answer. She picked up Max's leash in one hand and handed Connor her gloppy mess of a dessert to free her other hand to hold the blanket around her. "We'll be fast. Time us." She leaned up and kissed his cheek. Her lips were still sticky.

Connor watched Fiona and Max head up the path until they were out of sight. He tossed her food into the fire and then paced, waiting for them to come back. He knew the park was relatively safe. And Max would alert them to any danger. But Fiona had no idea what she was doing. Black belt or not, he couldn't imagine Fiona kicking anyone's ass. Striking someone in a karate class wasn't the same as being assaulted unexpectedly.

When ten minutes passed, he began the trek to find them. That's when he heard her scream. He bolted from the site, calling her name.

The smell hit him before he saw Fiona and Max. Skunk. He should've warned her Max would get into a fight if given a chance. A moment later, Fiona came toward him, blanket pulled around her face so he could only see her eyes. They were watering something fierce.

"Did you get sprayed?"

"No. Just your silly dog. Doesn't he know he'll always lose against a skunk?"

"Not always. He's killed a couple in my neighborhood. Still comes home smelling though." He took Max's leash. The dog looked up at him with pitiful eyes. Connor addressed him, "Yes, dummy, you did it again. Another bath for you."

"I reek of skunk. I don't think he got me, but I was close enough to Max. This is disgusting. How am I going to get rid of this?"

Connor sighed. There was no way she'd be comfortable surrounded by the stench overnight. Neither would he. "We'll pack up and head back. I've got the stuff at my house to remove the smell."

He put his arm around her and Fiona burrowed closer to him. "I bet you're really sorry you invited me, aren't you?"

"Nope. Now, I get to take you home and give you a special shower. You wet and naked is never a disappointment."

Connor packed the campsite in record time and used the blanket to cover Max in the truck. Fiona rode with the window open sucking in fresh air.

Once they were back at his house, she stripped and the simple removal of her clothes helped got rid of much of the stench. "You can throw these clothes away."

He handed her a mixture of peroxide, baking soda, and dish soap.

"I don't know if it's safe to use on your hair. I use it on Max without an issue, but I don't want you mad at me if you go blonde." He began to mix another batch to wash his dog.

"I've never been blonde. Maybe I should give it a try."

Connor couldn't imagine her as anything but a redhead. He leaned in and kissed her hard. "Don't even think about it. I like your hair."

He left her to take a shower, even though he wanted to join her. Max needed him more right now. After washing Max, Connor went to the truck and brought in Fiona's bag. He set it outside the bathroom door and went to his bedroom to get fresh clothes. Max followed him around like a pitiful puppy, as if he knew he'd ruined Connor's plans by getting skunked. Again.

Max nudged him with his nose and Connor rubbed Max's head. "It's okay, boy. You haven't scared her off yet. If skunk didn't do it, I'd say we're pretty safe."

"Safe from what?" Fiona asked from the hallway outside the bedroom door.

"Nothing." He joined her in the hall and inhaled. "You smell good."

She gave him a little shove. "I smell like you. Your soap, your shampoo."

He nuzzled her neck. "Uh-uh. Underneath, it's all you."

"Well you smell like wet dog."

"I'm on my way to the shower now."

Chapter 5

FIONA WATCHED HIM GO INTO the bathroom. She didn't know what to do with herself. It was late and it had been a long day. Although she should be tired, she wasn't. But she didn't have anything to work on.

She walked downstairs and grabbed a beer from the fridge and checked out the living room. Connor had cans of paint sitting on the floor and tarps rolled up in the corner. Maybe he was finally going to do something with the room. She set her bottle down. The lid on the first can read "living room," so she pried it open. A pool of lush forest-green paint.

Using a stick, she stirred the paint before dipping her fingers in. She swiped her fingers across the wall. Not a bad color choice. She replaced the lid and picked up her beer.

"Fiona?" Connor's voice carried from upstairs.

"I'm down here."

His footsteps thudded down the stairs.

"What are you doing?"

"Checking out your color choice." She pointed to the smudge on the wall. "It looks good."

He stood staring at her like she was crazy. He dressed in a

fresh pair of jeans and a snug T-shirt. Must be time to go. If he planned on her staying, he wouldn't have gotten dressed, right?

"I'm about done with my beer. Then we can go."

"Go where?"

She took a drink of beer and stared at his bare feet. "I figured you wanted to take me home."

"I thought you didn't want to be home this weekend."

She shrugged. Her mother had had a day to cool off and the blogger had time to move on. Hopefully. "It's probably fine."

He sighed and walked closer. She continued to stare at his feet until his hand cupped her jaw, bringing her face to meet his. "I didn't say you had to go."

His breath fluttered against her cheek and she whispered, "I didn't want to assume…"

"Consider this your formal invitation." He kissed her and took the bottle of beer from her hand. Then he stepped back.

"Hey, that's my beer."

He took a swig. "Was." He did his little half-smile thing where only the corner of his mouth lifted on one side.

She wondered if he ever really smiled. Like a happy smile. "I'll grab us a couple more bottles. Why don't you lay out the tarps?"

"For what?"

"I'm not tired. I like to work late. Let's get your walls painted."

"You sure?"

"Yep." Part of her wanted to see the living room as a real space. One that reflected Connor. What she'd seen of his life showed a lonely existence and an empty living room didn't help.

Grabbing another beer from the fridge, she shook her head.

She was doing it again. Creating a happily-ever-after with a man who was *not* her Prince Charming. For once, she wished she could be more like her brother Aiden and keep her emotional distance.

∞

For two days with Connor, Fiona had been able to forget about politics, her family, and most of all, Patrick Neale. The damn political blogger—Fiona finally found out his name: Marco Weston—continued to use the photo of her and Patrick outside the banquet hall to make it look like she was more interested in Patrick than her father's campaign.

Over the weekend, Weston managed to dig up some old photos of her and Patrick to run with Patrick's response, for which she could kill him. Patrick allowed Weston to interview him and he admitted to talking with her about a possible reconciliation.

She was done listening to her mother. No way would she let that sit. Patrick made it sound like getting back together was imminent. She'd contacted Weston herself to set the record straight. Unfortunately, the interview hadn't gone quite as she'd planned.

Now she stared at her phone, knowing her mother was at the other end. "Hello, Mom."

"How could you, Fiona? I told you I would handle it."

"But you weren't, Mom. He interviewed Patrick who made it sound like we were headed toward coupledom again." The thought heated her blood and she wanted to hit someone.

"Why would you allow that to bother you?"

Her mother made no sense. Every little thing, like the color of Fiona's dress would bother her, but God forbid Fiona got upset over someone spreading rumors about her.

Her mother continued, "No one gives credence to the drivel that man writes. It would've blown over if you had ignored him. Now I have to interfere."

"Something you excel at," Fiona mumbled.

"Excuse me?"

"Nothing. I was trying to help. Can't you see? Not only did he make it look like Patrick and I are dating, but he made it seem like I was invested in Patrick's campaign. That my loyalties were torn. I couldn't sit by and allow people to believe him."

"And if only you stated your position that way. Instead, you allowed your temper to speak for you. Luckily there were no sound bites."

"I'm sorry." As usual. "Is there anything I can do?"

"Your father has an interview this afternoon. Dress appropriately for television."

"Am I going to have to speak?"

"Only if a question is directed at you. Otherwise, you're there to show your support."

She scribbled the information on a scrap of paper and looked at the clock. She had a few hours, which was plenty of time to pick out an outfit and take a nap. She set two separate alarms to make sure she didn't oversleep. As she closed her eyes, she thought of sitting by a campfire in Connor's arms.

Connor's phone vibrated in his pocket. He cut the power to the saw. Checking the screen, he did a double take. Dermott rarely called. "What's up?"

"You at home?"

"Yeah. Why?"

"Turn on the TV. Channel twenty. Your boy Cavanagh and

his daughter are on."

Connor dusted off his hands and turned on the TV he kept near his workbench. The picture waved on the screen since the TV was old and reception far from great, but Fiona came into focus good enough. The reporter pretended to be deeply invested in Brady's answers, so Connor turned the volume up.

"Your opponent has accused you of living off your past success. We've covered all of the great things you've accomplished over your career in serving the city, but tell us about your plans for the future, Mr. Cavanagh."

Brady Cavanagh adjusted a perfectly straight tie before speaking. "I plan to continue to serve my constituents. I've been working closely with many businesses looking to expand. I want to bring those jobs, that revenue, to my neighborhood. To my people. My opponent can throw any accusation out he wishes to, but the fact remains, my track record proves my ability to serve the people. All he has is a list of wishes with no real means of accomplishing the tasks."

The reporter settled back in his chair. Connor's eyes were glued to Fiona, who sat stiffly beside her father, smile frozen in place. Anyone who knew her would recognize the false pleasantry.

Brady continued to drone on. "I've always put my constituency first. Nothing more needs to be said."

The reporter leaned forward again, this time zeroing in on Fiona. "In bringing up Patrick Neale, I don't think it would be fair to ignore his statements last week. Ms. Cavanagh, would you care to address that?"

Fiona's eyes fluttered. "There isn't anything to address. I met Patrick when he worked with my father. We dated for a while and things didn't work out. We haven't dated in over a year. Last week, he approached me about a possible reconciliation, which I promptly turned down."

What? How had Connor missed that bit of information? He'd checked for new stories daily. After a quick thought about the timing, he realized it was when Fiona had been looking to escape by going camping with him. While his brain processed this information, he watched as Fiona reached out and covered her father's hand with hers.

"Regardless of what some blogger chooses to say, my father knows he has my full and complete support." Now the last vestiges of phoniness melted away as she looked at her father and offered a warm, genuine smile. "I've always believed in my dad, and nothing Patrick Neale says is going to change that. Brady Cavanagh works for the city because he loves the city. I'll stand by him because I know he makes things better."

Connor stood, tension bunching his muscles. He stabbed the power button on the TV and stomped upstairs. He needed to find out what had been said about Fiona. Max met him at the top of the stairs and followed as Connor made his way up the second flight.

Fiona's words turned over in his head. She believed in her father. He saw the look on her face and knew she meant it. She'd spent so much time trying to escape her family that he'd been sure she wasn't like the rest of them. That she was different.

At his computer, he did his usual searches, but this time, added in Patrick Neale's name. Sure enough, a blog post popped on the first page. Connor clicked and his stomach clenched. Picture upon picture of Fiona and Patrick Neale. Some were obviously old, but the top photo had been taken last week, the night she'd showed up at his house and they hadn't fucked. She'd been upset and turned to him. He hadn't offered her any comfort, yet when he called her drunk the next night, she came over.

Even then, she'd let nothing slip. Her family must've applied pressure because of this. Maybe her family even told her to go away. Brady had a habit of sweeping problems under the rug.

And then they trotted her out on TV days later.

God, how he hated her family.

Fiona's smiling face, beaming up at her father intensified his anger. He didn't know what to believe.

One thing he knew for sure: never trust a Cavanagh.

Later that night, Connor sat at Dermott's bar getting drunk. Fiona had called and he ignored it.

He told Dermott about Fiona, and Dermott let out a long, low whistle. "Shit, just like the rest of them. Liars, the whole lot."

Rehashing it didn't make him feel any better.

"Does she know you know who she is?"

Connor shook his head. "Not that I'm aware."

"The publisher wanted newer stuff on them for the book. Use her and get the information. Think of the advantage you'd have." Dermott wiped down the bar while he talked, but Connor saw the fire in the old man's eyes.

"I've been trying, but she says nothing about her family at all. Except to say her mother puts pressure on her to be something she's not. When I ask questions, she ignores them or gets mad. Talk of family is off-limits."

Connor finished his beer and thought about Fiona. He should just walk away from her, but Dermott made a valid point. If the publisher wanted newer, fresher details, he had to get them from Fiona. Everything else he'd found would be as old as his story.

Sliding off the stool, he waved at Dermott. This was one

of those nights he was grateful he lived in walking distance of his favorite bar. That had been by design. He wanted to be near Dermott, the closest thing he had to family. Dermott had taken a chance on him after he'd gotten released from jail. Although he'd probably only done it out of loyalty to Connor's mother, he'd watched out for Connor. Only Dermott knew the truth about him.

Two houses down from his, he could hear Max barking and howling, and Connor stopped in his tracks. Fiona sat on his porch, huddled into her thin coat. Where was the woman's brain? Why wouldn't she have waited in her car? Or better yet, waited for him to return her call?

She looked up and caught his gaze as he neared. Something shot through him, something he couldn't quite name and didn't want to figure out. He wanted to cling to his anger and resentment, which might lead him nowhere, but in his current state he didn't think he could fool Fiona about his feelings.

Fiona stood and met him at the bottom of his stairs. "Hi."

The single tentative word caused a storm of confusion in his chest. The breeze swept her hair across her face and she batted it away.

"I'm sorry I showed up uninvited, but—"

"It's not a good time, Fiona." The words snapped from this mouth. He sounded like a dick, but he couldn't muster the energy to give a fuck.

Max howled again and Connor attempted to move around Fiona.

"Did I do something to make you mad?" She reached out and touched his arm.

Although he couldn't feel anything more than the pressure of her hand, he knew what her fingers felt like digging into his flesh, and his blood stirred in ways that weren't safe for either of them. "No."

"Then what's wrong?"

"I don't want to talk." This time he succeeded in brushing past her.

"Then let's not talk," she called from her place behind him.

Connor paused, but forced his feet forward. Unfortunately, she took his lack of refusal as an invitation. He wanted to tell her to leave, but couldn't. He pushed the door open and let Max jump on him. He ruffled the dog's fur and hugged him. The simple act eased some of the emotion roiling in him. "Come on, boy."

Max ran ahead to the back door, smart enough to know there would be no walk tonight. When Connor returned to the living room, Fiona stood against the closed front door. Her coat hung on the stair rail. Her nipples protruded through her thin shirt and he realized she wasn't wearing a bra again. She didn't speak, as he'd expected her to. She simply stared at him.

He walked closer with the intention of telling her to leave. He wasn't ready to deal with her on any level yet. And when he was, he'd be sure to be sober. "You should go."

Connor reached for the doorknob, but she slammed her back against the door to stop him from opening it. "I don't want to. I thought we weren't going to talk."

She hitched her chin up, her eyes defiant. She was looking for a fight as much as he was. She grabbed the waistband of his jeans and yanked.

Her fingernails barely brushed his skin and his dick started to get hard. "I can't give you what you're looking for. Not tonight."

Fiona pushed off the door and cupped him with her free hand. His dick twitched with her groping. "I'm pretty sure you can." Her hand left his waist and wrapped around the back of his head and pulled his face to hers.

He didn't resist the movement, mostly because he enjoyed her hand on his crotch, but when she pressed her mouth against his, he didn't open. He didn't want to taste her. Didn't want to feel the relief she offered.

But she insisted. She wasn't being gentle, nor was she asking him to be. She shoved her pants down and stomped on them until she was free from clothing. Then she set to undoing his pants. He said nothing, just let her do what she wanted.

When his cock sprang free from his jeans, and her cool hand wrapped around him, he reached for her, but she shoved his hand away. She lowered and took him into her mouth. At first, the shock of her warm mouth and cool fingers startled his sensitive flesh. Connor braced one hand against the door and grabbed her hair tightly with his other hand. He closed his eyes and enjoyed the sensations of Fiona licking and slurping against him.

Then he made the mistake of opening his eyes and looking down. At that moment, she chose to look up into his face, her lips wrapped around his cock, and he couldn't stand her wide-eyed enjoyment. He shoved away from the door, dislodging her from her position and grabbed her by the shoulders, raising her to her feet.

Connor bent and pulled a condom from his pants pocket. Fiona reached for both the condom and his dick, but he held her back. He rolled the condom on.

"Connor, I don't mind—"

Before she could finish whatever she planned to say, he spun her around and pressed her against the door. He moved her hair aside with one hand and bit down on the soft skin of her neck while his other hand roamed down her front.

She was already wet. When his fingers entered her, she rocked against him.

He bent his knees and shoved his cock into her. Her sudden sharp intake of breath was the only indication of surprise. She didn't push him away and she said nothing. He kept one hand twisted in her hair, arching her back toward him. She braced her left forearm against the door as he pounded into her. He wanted to use her the way he'd felt used. But not Fiona, she wasn't going to let that happen. She guided his hand back to her and used both their hands to stimulate her clit. He tried to jerk away, but she held tight.

Within minutes, they were both moaning and grinding against orgasm. He pumped into her angrily and felt her tremble. His mind saw black, he heard nothing other than Fiona's soft, "Oh God, yes." His muscles went rigid as he emptied into her.

She finally released his hand, which was now wet and sticky with her come. He pulled out of her and kept one hand on her back, not wanting her to turn around. He didn't want to look into her eyes and see any emotion. He removed the condom and yanked his pants up so he could walk to the bathroom.

He cleaned up and avoided his face in the mirror. When he returned to the living room, Fiona had already redressed, the only sign of their fucking was the smell of sex in the room and the bite mark he'd left on her neck.

She stared at him, but her eyes held none of the anger or resentment or hatred he'd expected. She simply raised one eyebrow. "Want to talk about it?"

A loaded question. Fuck no, he didn't want to talk, least of all to her. So he answered the one way he could to get her to back off. "Do you?"

"Nope." She looked over to where her coat hung. "Do you

want me to leave?"

Fiona's heart pounded and it shocked her to realize she feared the answer. Connor scrubbed a hand roughly over his face. He'd been drinking, but he wasn't drunk. When she decided to show up at his door, she wanted escape. She wanted to be the Fiona she'd been this weekend, not the Fiona who'd had yet another fight with her mother over her lack of family commitment.

No matter what she did, her mother wouldn't be happy. Fiona thought the interview went well, but of course Mom found flaw with Fiona's comments.

When Fiona arrived and saw the shadows in Connor's eyes, she knew he needed an escape as much as she did. She couldn't explain what had just happened between them. She wasn't quite sure, but it had been different. It wasn't the rough sex. It was raw. Connor clung to something so deep, he didn't want to let it go.

His lack of answer was enough and she reached for her coat.

"No."

He spoke the word quietly and she wasn't sure she'd heard him right, so she stopped. She turned to face him. He looked a little beaten down, the same way she felt. "No, what?" She wanted to hear him say it, needed to hear it.

"I don't want you to go."

Her heart slowed and she finally inhaled fully, but now she wasn't sure she wanted to stay. Whatever had happened left them in a tentative place, awkward in a way they hadn't been over the past week. She wasn't ready to lose the freedom she had with him. So if he wouldn't talk about his problems, she would help him ignore them. For her, life as usual.

"I skipped dinner. Any chance of getting some chocolate chip pancakes?"

And with the simple question, the darkness in his eyes lightened and he nodded. Connor led the way into the kitchen and he let Max back into the house.

The dog rushed to her for attention and she gave it willingly. When Max was satisfied, he wandered off. Fiona pulled her hair into a ponytail and hopped onto the counter to watch Connor cook. He beat the batter and set the bowl beside her thigh while the pan heated. He reached up and brushed a finger gently over the spot where he'd bitten her. The soft stroke sent a shiver through her.

He cleared his throat and said gruffly, "Sorry about that."

"I'm not." She slid from the counter and wrapped her arms around him. At first he stood stiffly, but she didn't care. She rested her cheek against his chest. Finally, he wrapped his arms over her shoulders and around her back and held her. She sighed.

They were okay.

She gently extracted herself. "Get cooking. I'm hungry."

He smiled, and although it didn't make it all the way to his eyes, it was a start. He swatted her ass. "Then get out of my way."

They shared a meal and spoke quietly about Connor's work. He didn't ask about her family issues, and she knew he understood she only came to him to get away. She wondered how long she could keep it up without him wanting more.

While they washed dishes together, Connor asked, "Doesn't your family wonder where you disappear to when you come here?"

Fiona shrugged. In all honesty, she hadn't given it much thought at all. "It's not like I live with my parents. As long as

I fulfill my familial obligations, they don't notice me and what I'm doing."

The little snippets of truth she let slide around him offered her so much relief. She wished she could let it all loose.

"I have a hard time believing anyone could *not* notice you." His arms circled her, his hands leaving wet prints on her shirt. He nuzzled her neck and licked the bruised teeth mark. "Are you spending the night?"

"No." She couldn't. As much as she loved the escape he offered, she couldn't pretend her life didn't exist.

His warm sigh brushed her skin. "So I'm still the late-night booty call."

She didn't know how to explain why he couldn't be more. Then she had a thought. "You could come to the Halloween party at the outreach center. It'll be fun."

"A Halloween party?"

Excitement filled her. No one paid attention to her work there. "Yeah. We all dress up in costumes and play games with the kids. We could go out afterwards."

"What about your family?"

"They never come to the party. I stopped inviting them a long time ago." But this was a tricky election year. As a heavy contributor, her dad might want to make an appearance. If Dad brought it up, she'd ask Aiden to come as the family representative. Problem solved.

"Maybe."

"You need a costume. Those are the rules."

"I'll come as a carpenter."

"That's not a costume—it's what you are every day. Although I really like the sight of you in a tool belt." Her words created the image in her head. Maybe she could stay a little while longer.

"Send me the information and if I'm not working, I might stop by. Are you going to wear a sexy outfit?"

"It's a party for kids, so no, but I'm willing to change for you after."

He tugged her closer and she felt his erection poke her. His hands edged under her shirt, and she knew she wouldn't be leaving anytime soon.

Later that night, while she slid a beautiful antique button onto a wire, Fiona examined what happened with Connor. Something had shifted between them, but she didn't know what. He'd been angry and she'd felt like it had been directed toward her, but he didn't explain. While anything in his life could've caused the raw emotion, Fiona felt responsible. He'd taken her up against the door like he wanted to punish her. Unfortunately for him, it only turned her on more. If he'd expected her to run away screaming, he'd been wrong.

She didn't know what she was doing with Connor or where she'd expected it to go, but she couldn't stop. She'd only known him a short time, and she felt best while with him. Even when he was angry and bent out of shape. She suddenly wished their relationship had started under different circumstances. What would happen when he found out her real identity? Would he ever be able to see her as a girlfriend instead of a booty call?

Fiona twisted wire in place and her gut matched the knot. Life would be so much easier if Connor would talk to her, let her know what he was thinking, but she couldn't ask for what she wouldn't give.

How long could she hold out like this? Being secretive wasn't her style. Every time Connor looked at her for information, it ate away at her. Her openness annoyed her mother.

Mom would be so proud now, wouldn't she? Fiona dropped her tools and decided sleep might be more productive. Things weren't that bad. She had a date with Connor for Halloween. They could be together like a regular couple for at least a little bit, kind of like when they went camping. And there were fewer than three weeks left until election night.

Then she would come clean to Connor on all counts.

Connor stood under the hot spray of the shower questioning his sanity. He should've made Fiona leave before she'd gotten naked. No matter what he did, he couldn't deter her. He didn't understand her game and he'd give anything for even a hint. She was a Cavanagh, which meant he couldn't trust her. The problem was, he had a hard time remembering that when they were together. Especially when he looked into her big blue eyes.

He needed a plan to be able to get what he needed from her without falling into whatever trap she intended to lay. Frustration still gripped him when he stepped out of the shower. He pulled on some underwear, made a pot of coffee, and sat at his computer to do the research he needed. He sipped on the strong coffee while scrolling through another round of Google hits for Fiona.

Her work with the outreach center still popped up first, before the connection to her infamous father during an election. The photos taken of her and the kids at the center showed the Fiona he knew: a bright, lively woman who loved art. These were followed by her online jewelry store. A few clicks later, he found the Fiona he'd grown to despise: the sleek, polished Cavanagh. Then he found a picture of Fiona with Aiden.

The years had been kind to his former friend. Aiden looked cleaner than ever. Maybe he'd finally grown up. Before Connor knew what he was doing, the search had shifted and Aiden's life appeared on the screen. Two articles in and Connor realized Aiden had become everything Brady Cavanagh had ever wanted in a son. Connor had done his job.

Unfortunately, he hadn't known the long-term effects of the agreement. Right after prison, he'd approached Cavanagh, seeking to make it right, but Cavanagh had just wanted to throw more money at him. As if money could repay the years he'd lost. He scrolled back to Fiona. He couldn't wrap his head around her being part of that family. But he had the proof staring him in the face.

The little voice in his head he'd learned to listen to pointed out she routinely came to him to escape her family.

Focusing on Fiona wouldn't get him what he needed. He cleared his search again and started with Brady Cavanagh. Whatever Brady did and covered up was the information Connor needed. Once he had Fiona's trust, he could get her to confide her father's wrongdoings and then he'd...

What? Would spilling all the horrid details of all of Brady's politicking change Connor's life? Connor shoved away from the desk. He knew he'd never be able to ruin Cavanagh. If the news reports over the years had never knocked him out of the running, Connor's personal account wouldn't either. Connor recognized he was losing sight of his original plan. He wanted his name cleared. He wanted people to know he wasn't guilty of hurting that girl. Mostly he wanted the Cavanaghs to admit to destroying his life for their benefit.

While it was true that he'd made the decision by himself, Brady had made it seem like no big deal. Confess, get a pile of cash to help his mother and brother, and no more. Brady supposedly had not expected Connor to actually have to serve time. It *had* been an accident after all.

Connor paced the room and knew he was lost. He got dressed and went to the basement. Wood always made sense. Tools in his hands put him at peace. With any luck, the noise would drown out the echoes of Fiona's gasps and moans in his head.

He had no idea how he was supposed to keep this up.

Chapter 6

CONNOR FELT THE VIBRATION OF his phone against his hip and turned the sander off. A text from Fiona. She'd been coming to his place most nights, looking for whatever escape he provided but he found himself enjoying her company as much as he did the sex. None of which helped his cause. She rarely let anything slip about her family. When campaign crap appeared on the TV, she flipped the channel.

Her text offered information for the Halloween party he hadn't yet agreed to attend. He dialed her number. When she answered, he said, "I didn't say I'd come to the party."

"I know. I was being optimistic. You complained about being a booty call. This is your chance to go somewhere as my date. But you have to be in costume."

"I'll go as a carpenter."

She tsked at him like an old lady. "I already told you that doesn't count. Use your imagination."

"What are you wearing?"

"Right now I'm wearing an old T-shirt and nothing else. How about you?"

The thought of her wearing next to nothing made his jeans uncomfortable and he groaned. "I meant for the party."

She giggled. "You'll have to show up if you want to see."

"Who's going to be at this thing?"

"My friend, Sarah, who is also in charge of the center. I introduced you to her the first night we met. The kids from the program and maybe some of their parents."

She became abruptly quiet and unease crawled across Connor's shoulders. He said nothing. Just waited for her to continue.

"There's a chance my brother might show," she finally added quietly.

When he didn't respond, she continued, "I wasn't going to tell you because I didn't want you to freak out, especially since I put talk of my family off-limits. But then I figured if he did come, you would feel blindsided and get pissed off."

How could he get out of showing up without making Fiona want to ditch him altogether? Aiden would recognize him. "I thought you wanted to keep me away from your family."

"It's not like that. Aiden is different. He doesn't care who I'm with. It's not like he's going to run out and tell the world who you are."

She had no fucking idea how small the chances of that happening were. Aiden would want to keep him a secret more than Fiona did.

"You'll still come, right? It'll be fun."

He couldn't say no to her. He couldn't refuse anything she asked which was a problem. A huge one. And he had no idea how it had happened. "Yeah, I'll be there."

"Great."

He could hear her smile and liked knowing he was the cause. They disconnected and Connor went back to sanding wood.

All he had to do now was come up with a costume to hide his identity from Aiden. Between a well-designed costume and careful avoidance, the Halloween party could come off without a hitch.

Then he'd have enough of Fiona's trust that maybe they could spend some time at her place. A little reconnaissance in enemy territory might work to his advantage.

He told himself that it didn't matter that he no longer saw her as the enemy, even though her family was.

Connor stood at the door, not quite sure of his next move. The gauze over his face scratched and itched, but he figured it would make a better disguise than a mask, which could be easily removed. He inhaled a slow deep breath and then entered the outreach center.

Kids ran by him without a second glance. He heard music and noise coming from a room off to the right, so he headed there. A small gym had been turned into a party room. Streamers dangled and twirled and fake fog swirled around his legs. He stood still and looked over the sea of people. A few adults milled around, chatting with each other as kids played games or snacked on food at the long buffet table.

From the corner of his eye, he caught sight of Fiona. The green skintight outfit she wore drew Connor's gaze down her back to her ass. He immediately imagined peeling the material from her body. She held onto the arm of a man. He didn't need to see the face to recognize Aiden.

He shook his head and turned in the other direction, immediately running into Sarah. She was dressed as Dorothy from *The Wizard of Oz*, but her face was anything but sweet innocence.

"Excuse me, but this is not an open party."

"Fiona invited me." He extended a hand. "Connor."

"Oh, she told me she invited you, but I didn't think you'd show." She eyed him up and down. "You get points for actually wearing a costume."

"Fiona left me with the impression that I didn't have a choice."

Her smile broadened. "You don't, but most guys like to cheat. I think it's instinct. Guys always look for a way to ignore the rules."

Connor chewed on that for a minute. Looking back on his life, he couldn't argue the point. This time, however, it hadn't even occurred to him. He just did what Fiona asked.

"Care for a tour? I'm sure Fiona is around here somewhere. She's dressed like Poison Ivy. She's hard to miss."

He glanced over his shoulder. "A tour sounds good."

Especially if it kept him away from Aiden.

Sarah hung a basket with a stuffed dog on her elbow and tilted her head to lead the way.

"Hey, Miss Sarah," a little princess called as she ran past followed by a second princess.

"Girls, no running." Her voice had Connor straightening his spine.

Both screeched to a halt and began to tiptoe away.

"You sound like a principal," he whispered.

A smile eased onto her face. "I pretty much am. My job isn't so different. I make a point of getting to know the kids and they see me as the boss. The one who could throw them out of the center and bar them from participating."

"You'd do that?" He knew a center in a neighborhood like this was all the kids had to look forward to.

"No, but I let them believe in the possibility. A little fear is a good thing." She walked on and began to explain the different types of classes held in each room. Occasionally, a parent or a kid interrupted them and Sarah always paused to chat.

Connor watched adults interact with the kids, playing games, talking, laughing. He could only imagine what a place like this could've done for him and his brother when they were little. Then he thought of Fiona's role here. He knew Sarah ran the place, which was a position he could easily see a Cavanagh in, but Fiona worked directly with the kids.

She stayed out of the spotlight. So unlike a Cavanagh. The Cavanaghs were not the kind of people who liked to get their hands dirty by actually mingling with the people they supposedly helped. In their minds, money could fix anything.

But Fiona didn't fit that mold and the knowledge rattled him.

Before he had time to examine it further, Sarah's phone rang. "I'm sorry. I have to take this. If you walk down this hallway, you'll get back to the gym. Fiona's probably there."

Connor nodded and followed her directions, but overshot and went outside for fresh air. He leaned against a column and wished he still smoked. A night like this called for a cigarette. Instead, he attempted to inhale some fresh air and got a lungful of exhaust instead. The lack of fresh air made him think of camping, which unfortunately made him remember camping with Fiona.

He pushed it aside and reminded himself that the Fiona who went camping was not the Fiona he was really dealing with. Here in Chicago, she was a Cavanagh. He had to keep the two straight. He heard the door clang behind him and when he turned, he came face to face with Aiden.

Connor didn't speak, only nodded a greeting. It was possible Aiden wouldn't pay enough attention to recognize him.

Aiden stared into his eyes, and Connor knew when recognition hit. So much for his costume being a disguise. The damn thing hadn't helped at all.

"Holy fuck. What the hell are you doing here?"

"Aiden."

A range of emotions crossed Aiden's face before Connor could develop an answer for Aiden's question. "You're the guy Fiona's with? What the fuck are you doing with my sister?"

A smirk lifted Connor's mouth. "You really want the answer?"

Aiden stepped forward with fists clenched.

Connor glanced down at Aiden's hands. "You might want to rethink. Remember what happened last time."

"I was drunk and high last time. I'm in full control of my faculties now. I knew you hated me, but why the hell would you go after Fiona?"

The accusation poked at him, but the conversation felt natural. Just like it always had with his friend. "I didn't *go after* her. She came onto me at a bar and introduced herself as Fiona Wells."

"But you knew who she was." Aiden's gaze shifted.

"Yeah, but surprisingly, I never lied about my name and it didn't ring any bells for her."

"She was away at school. She never knew." Aiden's shoulders sagged.

Connor could almost feel the weight pushing between them, compressing the past into a flurry of emotions. If only he could turn back the clock. The number of things he'd do differently. He couldn't help but wonder if he and Aiden would still be friends if things had taken a different course.

"You can't continue to see her."

"Why not? Afraid of the truth?"

Aiden's weary gaze met his. "Hell, yeah. I care about her. If you want to come after me then bring it, but Fiona isn't part of this."

Connor was taken back by Aiden's honesty. "She made herself part of it."

"I tried to make things right. You know I did."

Old anger swelled in Connor's chest. "There is no making this right unless you tell everyone the truth. Are you prepared to do that?"

Aiden shook his head. "I can't."

"That's what I thought."

"It wouldn't change anything anyway." He took a deep breath and stared out at the street. "I'll tell her to stay away from you."

"I'm sure you will, but she doesn't strike me as the type of woman to listen to her big brother." Besides, Connor knew Aiden wouldn't tell Fiona the whole truth out of fear that Fiona would get to hear Connor's side of the story. Connor could tell her and possibly ruin Aiden's relationship with her, but it wouldn't be enough. Brady Cavanagh wouldn't suffer.

Aiden took another step. They stood eye-to-eye. "I've reformed my life, but if you hurt her, I will come after you."

"You can try." Deep down, Connor knew he might hurt Fiona, but the chances of her destroying him were much greater.

Fiona swept through the party a second time and still couldn't find Connor. Sarah said he was here, but now Fiona worried Aiden found him and said something to scare him off. Not that Connor would scare easily. She stood in the hallway, thinking she should be able to spot him easily.

A mummy filled the doorway of the front entrance. Gauze dangled from his jaw and his broad body didn't look like it had been stuffed into a sarcophagus for centuries. When his gaze landed on her, she knew it was Connor.

She headed toward him. "Nice costume."

He stroked a hand down her side. "Not as nice as yours."

She suppressed the shiver his touch brought. "Come on. I feel like you've been avoiding me all night."

"Why would I avoid you?"

"Because you didn't want to meet my brother. You don't have to worry. He's gone. The party's almost over. Let's go dance to *Thriller*."

"You dance. I'll watch."

Fiona led the way back to the gym where the first strains of *Thriller* played. She grabbed the hands of kids surrounding her and began to dance. She felt Connor's gaze following her every move and it turned her on. She'd wanted to have more time with him tonight. She'd hoped to have a night with him out as a couple instead of hiding in his house.

Well, hiding didn't normally involve sex, and they'd been having plenty. She had the impression Connor wanted more, but maybe she'd been mistaken. Late-night sex seemed to appease him now.

She just didn't know if it would continue to be enough for her.

When the song ended and the lights came on, brightly flooding the room, Fiona met Connor at the snack table. "Almost ready to go?"

"Yes." His voice was tight.

When his gaze raked over her costumed body, she knew he was as turned on as she was. "I have to pass out goody bags to the kids on their way out. Then we can leave."

"I'll help."

She reached under the table and slid a box out. He bent over and picked it up for her. Having a burly guy around certainly came in handy.

"Follow me," she said and led the way to the front door.

Fiona watched as kids shoved gloved hands through sleeves on their coats. Others had to bend wings to make jackets fit. Some whined and cried that they didn't want to go home yet.

Sarah's voice rose above the crowd. "When you have your coats on and are ready to go, make sure you see Miss Fiona at the door for your treats. Have a wonderful evening and thank you all for coming."

Connor and Fiona handed bags to eager hands. "Who's going to clean up all the mess?" Connor asked.

"Sarah has some teen volunteers who will stay and clean up. We're really done as soon as this box is empty."

He handed a bag to Melanie, who was dressed as a princess. "Happy Halloween."

Melanie's eyes widened. "Mummies can't talk. They don't have tongues. They just groan."

Fiona watched as Connor's eyebrow disappeared above his line of gauze. The corner of his mouth lifted as well. "Uhn." He said at Melanie.

"Much better," Melanie added as she grabbed her bag and ran out the door.

Connor shook his head, but didn't stifle the laugh that bubbled out. His charming half-smile always sucked her in, but his laugh was like sin. Deep and rumbly, it was a sound she'd like to be surrounded and soothed by.

He caught her staring at him. "What?"

"First, it was sweet to accommodate a little girl's request. Second, you don't do that nearly enough."

"Accommodate girls? I'll accommodate you shortly."

Fiona rolled her eyes. "No, I meant you don't laugh nearly enough. I like the sound of it."

He shook his head at her and continued to hand out bags. She couldn't quite understand this man. The grunt he offered Melanie fit his exterior, like it was a normal mode of communication, but he was so much more than the caveman appearance. It was all in his body language. She'd seen him build furniture from a block of wood, watched him play with his dog like a kid on the playground, and felt him worship her body during sex. He didn't speak much, but he communicated well.

With the box empty, Connor ripped it and broke it down for recycling. "If you want to stay and help Sarah, we can."

See? Few words, but such a generous offer. "No, she'll be fine. I came early to set up. Besides, I'm really beat."

His arm snaked around her waist and he lowered his lips to her ear. "Need me to carry you home?"

His breath caressed her neck and that oh-so-sensitive spot below her ear.

"Tempting offer," she whispered.

"I have better ways to tempt you."

"Promise?"

"Oh, yeah." He nipped her earlobe sending a shiver down her spine.

She pressed a hand to his solid chest. "Let me say good-bye to Sarah. Meet you in your truck?"

"I'll wait outside the door."

"I can find your truck."

"I'm not letting you walk this neighborhood dressed like that."

She rolled her eyes again. "You're probably worried I might

get a better offer."

"Yeah, that's it."

She patted the mass below her hand. "You never know. Batman might be out there to take me."

"Let him try."

Warmth pooled in Fiona's belly as she pulled away from Connor. He headed to the door and she went to find Sarah. The election was less than a week away. She needed to tell Connor the truth. Things between them were in an odd place. Part of her feared the truth would drive him away.

Sarah stood in the middle of the gym telling the volunteers what to do. "Hey, I thought you left."

"I'm going now. I wanted to check to make sure you had everything covered."

"We're good." She tilted her head and smiled at Fiona. "So, Connor, huh?"

"Yeah."

"I thought he was a one-night thing. Someone to let you escape your family."

"He was. He still is, I guess. I haven't told him who I am yet."

Sarah's brow furrowed. "How did you manage to pull that off? He met Aiden, didn't he?"

"I don't think so. Besides, Aiden dressed as a zombie tonight, remember? He didn't match my dad's campaign photos. But I was just thinking about how I need to tell Connor the truth."

"Do you want this to go somewhere?"

Fiona shrugged. "I don't know. Maybe. I really like him. And the sex is phenomenal. I'm afraid the Cavanagh name will scare him off, though. What should I do?"

"There is no right answer. If you don't tell him, he'll find out eventually. Using a fake name for a one-night stand is one thing, but you can't base a relationship on a lie."

Fiona knew her friend was right. A ball of dread settled in her stomach. She hated the lies, but they gave her peace.

She left the gym and grabbed her coat. Her phone bleeped letting her know she had a message. She leaned against the wall and listened.

"Fiona, we need to talk. Call me."

It was never good when her brother left a message without revealing the purpose for his call. She stared at the screen. Call him now or later? Connor stood outside waiting to take her home and ravish her. She didn't want to postpone, but the thought of Aiden calling and interrupting them later was worse, so she dialed.

"I'm glad you called me back."

"What's up? We just saw each other."

"I met your boyfriend."

Connor hadn't mentioned it. Why didn't he tell her?

"You can't be serious about him, Fi. He's not the right kind of guy for you."

"Careful, you're starting to sound like Mom." The muscles in her neck tightened. Aiden rarely commented on her choice of companionship.

"You can't trust him."

"You move pretty fast. What'd you do, run home and boot up your investigative search engines? How could you possibly know I can't trust him?"

Silence greeted her question. Aiden's heavy breath whispered over the line. "Because you can't. He's not who you think he is."

"What do you mean? He lied about his name?" They really were alike if that was the case. Connor couldn't get mad at her if he was guilty of the same thing.

"No, he's not a good guy."

Aiden was talking in circles and her patience had run out. "He's never been anything but good to me. Even when he probably shouldn't have been."

"You're not going to listen to me, are you?"

"Unless you give me an actual reason to break up with him, no. I like him." She was falling for him fast, but if she admitted it to Aiden, he would probably get their parents involved.

"You need to trust me. I know what I'm talking about."

Fiona heard something under the words. A warning in the quality of Aiden's voice. But then she looked up and saw Connor helping a teenager haul a bag of trash out. He'd already unwrapped his face, but gauze still dangled from his body. She studied him for a minute. He wasn't a bad guy. No way could she be that far off in her feelings. Could she? She hung up and walked out the door.

Connor helped her with her coat and studied her face. "Something wrong?"

Aiden's accusations stuck in her throat. She shook her head and whispered, "Take me home."

Fiona was uncharacteristically quiet on the drive to her house, and Connor didn't know what to make of it. She'd been her usual flirtatious self before she went to find Sarah. Now shadows of something haunted her eyes. She wasn't the same woman who'd been dancing with children an hour ago. She wasn't even the same woman who'd allowed him to angrily fuck her against his front door.

She pulled the mask off her eyes and her whisper broke the silence in the cab of his truck. "My brother called right before we left."

Shit. He should've known. Aiden had found a way to fuck up his life, even now. "And?"

"Why didn't you tell me you met?"

Met. Not knew each other. Aiden hadn't told her everything. "I didn't want to ruin your night."

"So you obviously didn't hit it off."

He pulled up beside her building and cut the engine. His next words would determine the course of whatever they had going and his ability to get information. "He didn't like me. Said I wasn't good enough for you."

He offered the truth without being totally honest. No wonder he and Aiden had made such good friends all those years ago.

"He said you're not a good guy."

Wasn't that the truth. "By his standards I'm not. I know you're out of my league. He didn't tell me anything I didn't already know."

Her blue eyes widened. "But you stayed."

He reached out and twirled a red curl around his finger. "I don't seem to be able to say no to you. As long as you want me, I'm here."

"Come inside."

"You sure?" The question was loaded. Every one of their trysts had been at his house. Other than dropping her off at home, she'd never invited him in. Part of him wanted to see her space, how she lived, but the practical part of him knew he might find some information in there.

She nodded and climbed from his truck. He locked up and followed. She said nothing on the way up in the elevator, but she reached over and linked her fingers to his. His plan fell to shit every time she touched him. He couldn't think of her as one of the devious Cavanaghs. Especially when a simple conversation with her brother stole so much from her.

He wished he had the words to convey how he wished she'd been born into any other family because if she had, he would've fallen completely in love with her by now.

The thought should've rattled him more than it did. Knowing what could've been was something he'd lived with for years. Knowing what was impossible and regrettable barely made a blip on his radar.

Her apartment was dark and he shuffled his feet, waiting for her to turn on a light. Instead, she continued to walk through the rooms until they reached her bedroom. Light from the street filtered through curtains and he could make out a bed and a dresser, but not much else. She turned, wrapped her arms around his neck, and kissed him.

Her lips trembled under his and he pulled away. "What's wrong?"

"I don't want to talk." She stepped back and began to unwrap the bandages he had covering his body.

She slowly circled him, balling up the gauze as she went. Once his torso was clear, she knelt and continued to unwrap him. She looked small and helpless with none of the flirty playfulness she usually exhibited in the bedroom, or anyplace where they'd gotten naked. She finished and tossed the balled-up gauze onto the chair in the corner.

Turning her back to him, she lifted her hair from her shoulders to reveal the zipper for her costume. His fingers were cold from outside and compared to them, her skin felt feverish. Goose bumps rose on her flesh as she peeled the costume away. She wore nothing underneath and he hardened at the sight of her.

She tugged his T-shirt, fingers skimming his stomach, and followed with her lips and tongue. He yanked the shirt over his head to give her the access she wanted, and while she licked his nipple, she unbuttoned his jeans. He toed off his gym shoes and walked her toward the bed. She needed something from him, but he wasn't sure what, so he let her take the lead. He shucked his remaining clothes and covered her body with his. He kissed her slowly, waiting for her response so he could figure out what she needed. Her hands moved slowly over his skin, like her fingertips were reading braille.

Slow. She needed slow, careful attention. But why? His mind raced, but her hands distracted him. He let his body do its own discovery of hers, with the hope of finding something new. He grabbed her wrists and pulled them over her head. He held them with one hand while his other continued to explore. If she wanted slow, he'd give every inch of her deliberate attention. If nothing else, it would make her forget whatever worried her.

Fiona made no attempt to pull out of his grasp. Her gaze remained focused on his every movement. Even when he lowered his mouth to kiss across her hip and he released her wrists, she didn't move. She wiggled beneath him and he lowered his mouth to her pussy, which was already slick and wet. Damn, she tasted good. When he flicked his tongue over her clit, her hips jumped and her hands grasped at his head.

He pulled away and sucked at her inner thigh. She tried to push his head back, but when he bit the soft flesh, she inhaled sharply and simply ran her fingers over his scalp. He kissed his way down her long leg and pressed his thumb into the arch of her foot. Her moan was so loud, her neighbors would think he was still eating her. He moved to her right foot and then licked his way up that leg. Fiona's skin was flush and warm.

When he reached her pussy again, he began to lick, pulling a gasp from her. She was close, but he wouldn't let her get where she wanted. Not yet. Even though it meant he had to ignore his throbbing cock. All he wanted to do was bury himself in her.

Fiona scraped her nails on his shoulders, trying to pull him closer. He splayed his hands on her inner thighs, spreading her wide and dipped two fingers in. Her hips created a rhythm and he pressed down to stop her. This was his show. He sucked on her clit and her calves closed in on his shoulders. She bucked and held him where she wanted and so he continued to play until her release was imminent.

"Connor."

There was no better sound than his name on her lips.

"Don't stop."

He mumbled against her, "Wouldn't dream of it."

Her hips jumped and her thighs trembled. Her muscles clenched on his fingers and he wanted it to be his dick, so he pulled out. She whimpered.

"I'm not done with you yet." He put on a condom and rubbed himself against her.

"Now," she whispered.

He slid in, pulled out and then slid deeper.

Fiona pulled at his shoulders. "Closer. Come closer."

He lowered himself and wrapped his arms under her. She folded her legs and locked them behind his back.

"Closer," she begged.

Connor buried his face in her neck, inhaling her scent and rocked slowly. She held tight, and he knew what she needed.

Fiona was saying good-bye.

Chapter 7

FIONA LAY SPENT AND SWEATY and gloriously satisfied. Connor had suspected something was wrong, but he'd yet to ask. He had no reason to put up with her bullshit, but he did. Over and over. When they'd left the party, she planned to tell him the truth, but now, laying here with him, she couldn't. She wasn't ready to lose him. And she was pretty sure she would.

The heat from his body kept her warm. She lay on his bicep and he toyed with her hair. What if she just blurted it out? *I'm a Cavanagh.* What was the likelihood the name would mean anything to him? She squeezed her eyes shut and tried to imagine his response.

Nothing. He wouldn't say anything. Connor wasn't demonstrative in too many ways. With him it was the small things. Touching her hair. His half-smile. But she could imagine the hurt in his eyes.

"You want to talk yet?"

She turned her head and opened her eyes. The streetlights illuminated the room enough so she could make out his silhouette, but not much else. Perfect for making a confession.

"My cousin is getting married in a couple of weeks. I'd like you to go with me." Shit. That wasn't supposed to come out.

"A wedding?" He shifted away.

"I know it's short notice, but…"

"Isn't your family going to be there?"

"Yeah."

Connor remained silent, staring at the ceiling. Yet another bad idea she had.

"I'm sorry I asked. I hate going to those things alone. You know how family gets. They start in with the questions about why I'm still single and what I'm doing to change it. It's a bad idea. If you're there, they'll start making assumptions. Forget I said anything." She sat up and grabbed her robe.

She went to the bathroom and freshened up. She had no idea what she was doing anymore. The pathetic invitation made her sound weak and that thought bubbled in her stomach. In the Cavanagh family nothing was worse than weakness. What had she been thinking? Connor managed to turn her world upside down and they hadn't even been on a proper date. How would she explain him to her family?

A soft knock sounded on the bathroom door. Connor poked his head in. "You okay?"

She smiled and hoped it looked real. "I'm fine."

"Look, it's not that I wouldn't go with you, but…it's a family thing. And your brother made his feelings clear."

She tightened the belt on her robe. "It's okay. Forget I said anything. Really. It was a dumb idea."

"Fiona—"

"It's no big deal, Connor." She brushed past him, glanced at her bedroom, and went to her office instead. She heard water running and then the toilet flushed. If Connor sought her out, she had no idea what to do or say.

Saying nothing would be best, so she grabbed her tools. She pulled her hair up and tied it in a knot to keep it out of the way and then rummaged through the bowls and containers of stuff. One day, she'd get organized. She was an impulse buyer when it came to trinkets she could use to create jewelry. The problem lay in the fact hat she kept buying despite the growing piles.

To a certain degree, the piles added to her creativity because she never knew what would stimulate her imagination. She dug through a mountain of buttons and felt Connor's presence. He didn't say anything, but she felt him looming.

She gazed at the mess on the table and compared it to his clean, organized workshop. Thinking of his workshop led to thoughts of his muscled arms flexing while turning wood, sanding a smooth finish, and a flush crept across her body.

He cleared his throat as if she wasn't aware of his presence.

She glanced at him, not wanting him to see the blush on her skin because he would know what she'd been thinking. He always did.

"Do you want me to go?"

Did she? She hadn't spent the night with him since the disastrous camping trip. Having him here, in her home, made it a relationship, not the late-night booty call he'd been. He always extended the invitation for her to stay at his place, even knowing she wouldn't. Except for that camping weekend. If she told him to stay, it would change the parameters of everything they shared.

Hadn't she already done that by asking him to the party? And then to the wedding? She'd started changing the rules without thought.

He shifted and walked across the small space. "Can I watch you work for a while? I'd like to see what you do."

"Sure, but it's not exciting." She pointed to the extra stool she had in the room, which currently held a sweatshirt, a scarf, and a book. She didn't have too many visitors here.

He scooped up the items and looked for a place to put them, but set them on the floor. He picked up the stool and placed it beside hers at her worktable.

Fiona tried to focus. Connor wore nothing but his underwear and all that bare skin distracted her. He leaned forward and rested his chin on his fist, eyes intent on her hands. She worked the wire and twisted with pliers to secure the piece. She couldn't remember a time when she'd been studied while she worked. "You want to try?"

"Me? I don't think I can."

"You build furniture. I think you can handle a couple of pieces of wire." She set pieces in from of him. "I'll help."

He looked at her from the corner of his eyes, but picked up the pliers. He fumbled them as he tried to thread the wire. His fingers looked huge holding the tools she used every day.

"The wire is flexible. It's not like you can break it. You don't have to be careful. Wind it around and then snip it. Once it's wrapped, use a smaller piece and thread it through to connect to the chain."

Connor's breath huffed out in frustration after a couple of tries. "This isn't my thing. I'll just watch you work." He shoved everything back in front of her.

Rather than make him feel bad that she'd have to undo what little he completed, she opted to start something new. She pulled a length of chain and cut it. Then she dug through a tin of jewels, rocks, and charms. She laid out a sampling and held some up to the chain to see what would work together. Sometimes she had a plan when she created; other times, she played around until she found the right look.

Once she started, she got into her groove and forgot Connor watched.

"Wow."

His word startled her and she jolted a bit. "What?"

"You make it look so easy."

"It's not difficult. Here." She grabbed his hands to the piece she worked on.

"No. I'll fuck it up."

"I won't let you." And she sincerely hoped she spoke the truth because she was falling in love with the necklace. She guided his hands in place and showed him what to do. When he got stuck, she took over.

Connor picked up his stool and put it directly behind hers. When he resettled on the seat, his thighs cradled her hips and his chest pressed at her back.

Talk about not being able to focus. His arms caged her in and his breath whispered across her neck, tickling her ear.

"Let me try again," he said and reached for the pliers.

They worked together to finish the necklace, their hands intertwining and working as a team. His large, scarred hands contrasted against her pale skin. When the necklace was complete, Fiona said, "Let me get a clasp on, and we're done."

He fingered the chain. "It's beautiful."

A blush warmed her cheeks as she added the final touch. "Thanks."

Connor's hands left the table and stroked her thighs through the silk of her robe. His palms were warm and she could feel the rough calluses through the thin material. He kissed the side of her neck and nibbled her earlobe as his hands searched for the opening of her robe. His erection poked into her back and the tug of desire pooled deep in her belly. She dropped her tools to the table with a small clang. She shifted her hips back and rubbed his thighs.

Connor tugged the belt loose and then his hands became very busy. One stroked up her inner thigh, while the other sought out her nipples. He knew exactly what to do to turn her on again and again, as if she hadn't just had very satisfying sex. She was wet and wanting a release within minutes.

Fiona reached behind her and held onto Connor's neck, the soft brush of his short hair tingled against the pads of her fingers. She became boneless as his fingers plunged into her and his palm applied just the right pressure to her clit. She met his small thrusts with her hips while pressing her back into his chest. She couldn't get enough of him, couldn't get close enough, couldn't feel enough.

He pinched her nipple and picked up the pace of his hand. Every nerve was tighter than any wire she worked with. She was on edge and wanted more.

When he pulled his hand away, she stopped breathing.

He kissed her shoulder. "Turn around."

He shifted and she heard the condom wrapper. Where the hell had that come from? She looked over her shoulder at him before lifting her hips. She moved her robe aside, wanting him to take her.

But he grabbed her hips again. "Face me."

Connor spun her and brought her to his lap. He spread the robe wide so it slid from her shoulders, only her arms keeping it on. He rocked himself, rubbing his cock against her, sending delicious licks of pleasure through her body.

He pushed her back and then brought her down on top of him. He stretched and filled her. Connor wrapped his arms around her and they sat close for a moment, cocooned in each other, breath mingling, fingers playing, lips touching.

He caressed her face so gently, it was hard to comprehend

they were the same rough hands whose calluses rubbed past her robe. He let her hair down and ran his fingers through it, spreading it wildly over her shoulders. One hand twisted at the back of her scalp, enough to give him control without causing pain. Her chin lifted and he kissed and licked and bit across her neck, down to her breasts, and sucked a nipple into his mouth.

Fiona couldn't stand it any longer. She needed movement, friction, release she'd been denied. She bucked her hips and ground onto Connor until he groaned. He moved onto the other nipple, but managed to lift her hips with one hand and brought her back down hard. Shockwaves speared through her, but it still wasn't enough.

"More," she croaked out.

So he did it again and again. Everything in her felt hard and tight. He pumped twice more and then slid a hand between them. This time when he pulled out, his thumb rubbed her clit and she slammed into him shattering everything in her. She screamed. Maybe it had been his name, but she couldn't tell.

Fiona moved forward and gripped him around the neck wanting to crawl into him. Connor's hands grasped her ass and he pumped fiercely against her, knocking into her worktable. She held on as tightly as she could until she broke again. She could hear nothing but his ragged breath, see nothing but starbursts behind her squeezed-tight eyelids, feel nothing but Connor cradling her.

A tear streaked down her cheek as she shuddered. His muscles tightened beneath her and Connor's pace slowed. He rocked into her, mumbling into her hair. "I got you."

She had no idea how long they sat with Connor holding her. He began to smooth her hair away from his face and he kissed her ear, her jaw, and then found her lips. After a slow, soul-searing kiss, he looked into her eyes, but she still couldn't read him. And God, how she wanted to. She wanted to know if it was as different for him as it had been for her. If his world felt as destroyed as hers did.

If he loved her the way she knew she'd fallen for him.

He pushed away from the table, knocking over a few things in the process. Fiona went to unwrap her legs, but he held her tight.

"Just hang on." He carried her to her bed and set her down gently.

Exhaustion hit her then, every muscle turned to mush, every bone, gone. Her eyelids felt heavy, but she kept them open enough to say, "You can stay."

He carefully brushed hair away from her face. "Some other time. I need to go take care of Max."

"Okay." She was both relieved and disappointed. It was the first time she'd invited him to spend the night, so she should be mad he turned her down, but at the same time, without him there, she could sort through her own feelings and figure out what she was going to do.

Fiona's eyes closed before he'd even gotten dressed. Connor stood in her bedroom, wearing his jeans and holding his T-shirt, and watched her sleep. Her breath slipped into a contented sigh. The urge to crawl into bed with her and hold her against his body struck him with unbelievable force.

What the fuck was he doing?

This woman kept him off balance, and he couldn't think straight. He'd believed she was going to toss him out and say they were done. Part of his brain was resigned to the inevitable, but she then asked him to a family wedding. What the hell was he supposed to do with that? Although Aiden was aware they were seeing each other, but he couldn't imagine facing all of the Cavanaghs at once.

He shook his head and grabbed his shoes. Easing from her room, he pulled the door closed behind him. He found a light switch and flicked it on. It bathed the living room in a warm glow and Connor did what he couldn't when they'd arrived. He took in Fiona's space. A lot of color. *Everywhere*. It was a little chaotic, but it worked. On the shelf above her TV, he saw family pictures. Aiden and Fiona starred in most of them. She had only one of the whole family. Her parents stood stiffly, formal smiles on their faces, arms around Aiden. Fiona stood off to the side, as if not really a member of the family. Fiona had her mother's eyes, but he saw no other resemblance.

But the pictures of her and Aiden…they were real.

He poked around Fiona's living room but found nothing related to her family other than the pictures. The artwork on the wall was hers. Her squiggly signature swirled in the lower corner of each. Books on the shelves were fiction, trashy romance, and some nonfiction on jewelry and various art books.

He didn't know what he'd hope to find. A diary detailing all of her father's transgressions? That shit only happened in the movies. He finished getting dressed and turned off the lights. He no longer knew what he was doing with Fiona or what his purpose was.

Connor drove home tasting Fiona on his lips. It took all his control to not turn his truck around and go back to her place. He now understood her reluctance to spend the night with him. Things were becoming too real between them.

He needed distance to keep his head on straight. At home, he let Max out into the yard and took a shower, washing away all but the memories of the evening. After he fed Max, Connor got onto his computer and began digging through Cavanagh-related material again. He read article after article. Was there anything he could gain from Fiona that wasn't here? She didn't appear to be part of their lives other than brief photo ops where she looked miserable.

The Cavanagh Foundation was a huge donor of the outreach center where Fiona worked, but even there, they didn't participate or visit. Like most things with the Cavanaghs, they threw money at it and went on their merry way.

Not finding any answers on his computer, Connor pushed away and went to the basement. Back to the wood that always brought him peace. A way to work with his hands to build instead of destroy. Dermott had given him that outlet.

Dermott had given him plenty of opportunities and advice over the years. Connor hadn't been very good at heeding most of the advice, but this time he listened too well. Dermott told him to get close to Fiona.

Connor went off the deep end and was falling for her.

He grabbed some sandpaper and rubbed furiously on the ornate table leg. He never wanted to fall in love. Definitely not with a Cavanagh. Nothing good would come from it. They could never be happy.

His past would prevent it. She'd either hate him for it or her family would drive them apart. No way could Brady Cavanagh look at Connor with his daughter and be happy. The *scritching* sound of the paper against wood soothed him. The pads of his fingers became scratched and rougher than usual.

He imagined how it would feel against Fiona's skin.

"Fuck!" he yelled to no one. He crumpled the sandpaper and threw it across the workbench. Fiona needed to get out of his head. His productivity suffered. His heart wouldn't survive.

Max moaned from the top of the basement stairs. His best friend always worried when Connor was upset. Connor left the basement and turned off the lights. He couldn't work and he couldn't *not* work.

"Come on, Max. Let's go for a run." A midnight run might clear his head. Bare minimum it would fatigue his body so he could forget Fiona for a while. At least that was his hope. He pulled on a light sweatshirt and slipped back into his gym shoes.

Max waited impatiently at the door, his tail knocking against his leash dangling on a hook. Max had the right idea. Live life for the moment. Enjoy a run. Nothing more was needed.

If only Connor's life could be half as simple.

For the next week, Connor saw Fiona every night. As the election neared, her frustration increased. And still she refused to open up about her family. Brady Cavanagh had trained her well.

The closest she came to admitting anything to him was when she told him she would be too busy with family things for the next few days and wouldn't be able to see him. She didn't mention the "family things" had to do with the election on Tuesday.

And with the election on top of them, he had no chance for any new information for his book. Brady would win—or wouldn't—and life would continue on. But what of him and Fiona? Everything he thought he'd wanted from her he didn't get, but he got something else entirely.

He had nothing to do until after Tuesday, so he worked. Seeing Fiona's workbench had made him a little twitchy. He couldn't comprehend being able to produce in such chaos, although it appeared to work for her. With his free time, he'd decided to make her a cabinet for her jewelry supplies. The box was finished and the first couple of drawers were ready.

He used plain white pine because Fiona wouldn't want something stained and simple. She'd want color, so he left it naked and ready for paint. He hoped he'd made it big enough. She had a lot of crap piled up in tins and bowls and muffin pans. How could she find anything?

The one thing she did seem to have organized was her collection of tools. To aid her in that effort, he added hooks to the side of the tabletop cabinet. She could hang her snips and pliers from the hooks beside her materials.

Connor managed to mostly put the Cavanaghs out of his head, but since Fiona was a Cavanagh and she was always in his head, it was difficult. If he kept his focus on her, he could almost forget the election.

Almost. The local TV stations carried candidates' commercials and political signs littered lawns through every neighborhood. And with the advent of the election, his last hope of adding to his book faded.

Despite his best intention, he found himself tuning the small TV in the basement to election coverage on Tuesday night while he sanded the cabinet for Fiona. He drilled holes for hardware and shook his head at himself. He'd gone into the hardware store and picked out the girliest knobs he could find, and they fit Fiona. He hoped she liked them.

He'd missed her over the past couple of days. He wanted to go to her condo and spend a few hours with her, but he still couldn't make himself show up uninvited. Which was weird given that she'd done it to him since the beginning. Plus, a wealth of lies created a gulf between them.

By late afternoon, the polls were showing the race between Cavanagh and his opponent was close, surprising many. Connor wanted to reach out to Fiona. Was this good news for her? Did she want her father to win again?

She must've since she'd gone out of her way to keep up appearances for him. After weeks, Connor still didn't have a good understanding of her relationship with the rest of the Cavanaghs.

At dinnertime, he made a quick sandwich and went upstairs to read. Maybe watch the rest of the election coverage. It was like a sick addiction. He needed to know.

As the night wore on, it became apparent that Brady Cavanagh would keep his seat as alderman. By the ten o'clock news, Cavanagh's opponent had conceded. Connor was about to turn the TV off when Brady Cavanagh stood before the cameras with his acceptance speech. Connor heard nothing but the usual empty promises about making Chicago the best city possible. Blah-blah.

In the background, behind her father, Fiona stood, looking strained with a polite smile on her face. To most viewers she probably looked like a loving daughter, doting on her father, excited about his win. But Connor saw the real Fiona, the one who hated the pomp and flash of politics.

Connor waited until the news went back to the anchors and he dialed Fiona's number. He wasn't sure if she would answer, but he had to try.

"Hello?" The room behind her blared obnoxious noises, like a New Year's Eve party gone wrong.

"Fiona, it's Connor."

"Hold on." The background noise softened and she came back on. "What's up?" she asked hesitantly.

"What's up with you?"

She sighed heavily. "You saw me on TV, didn't you?"

"Yep."

"Look, I'll explain everything later. I wanted to tell you, but it never seemed like the right time."

He knew the feeling well.

"Do you hate me?"

"No." His response came quickly, but after he digested the question, he realized his answer was truthful. As much as he despised her father, he held no animosity toward Fiona. He didn't know exactly what he felt about her.

Painful silence met him, and he thought she'd hung up.

"I'm glad," she responded quietly, then followed with a groan. "God, they're calling me for more pictures. I promise we'll talk later. I'm sorry I lied about my name, but you see what a circus this is. Being with you let me be me."

He heard someone calling her name and it was getting louder. Her hiding spot would soon be discovered. "Everyone has secrets. It wouldn't be fair for me to hate you for holding onto yours."

"That's very mature of you. It's almost like being in a real relationship."

"My door is open if you need to escape."

"I wish I could, but this will go most of the night and then my mother has me roped into crap for the next couple of days. I thought the campaigning was bad. Now it's like we have to go around thanking all of his supporters. Then I have my cousin's wedding. I just wish I had a normal life. You have no idea how much I envy you."

"You can join my normal whenever you want." In saying the words, he knew how true they were. "About the wedding. Still need a date?"

"Are you serious?"

His brain scrambled. "Yeah."

"Thank you. I can't wait." He heard the smile on her face and knew it was real, unlike the one she wore for the cameras.

Whoever had been calling her name now pounded on a door. "Fiona, are you in there?"

"I have to go," she whispered. "I miss you."

She disconnected before he could respond, but he answered anyway, "Miss you too."

And he spoke the truth. Going to the wedding would make what they had real. Show her family he wasn't going anywhere. Now that her last name was out in the open between them, he had to figure out a way to let her know he and Aiden had once been friends. He just hoped she would be as forgiving over his secrets as he'd been of hers.

Chapter 8

ELECTION NIGHT FINALLY WRAPPED UP and Fiona watched her father make his rounds shaking hands as people said their good-byes. Her feet hurt and her cheeks ached from the standing and smiling and faking of everything.

But her dad was happy. Mom was ecstatic. Their lives would go on as they had for years. Over the past week, Fiona realized that her mom worried about losing who they were. Sure, part of it was about the status and the recognition, but she'd been a politician's wife for so long, she didn't know how to be anything else. Fiona wished her mother could recognize that she was more than a wife. She headed multiple charities and organized lavish fundraisers. Her mom had skills.

When the last aide closed the door, Fiona collapsed onto the couch, grateful she'd booked a room at the hotel where her father had based campaign headquarters for the night. She kicked off her painful heels and decided to leave before her mother got any ideas about what she should be doing. All she wanted right now was a bed.

Too bad Connor couldn't share it with her.

Hmm…maybe if she called and asked him to join her. Fiona jumped off the couch and scooped up her heels, newly invigorated by the thought of being tangled in luxury sheets with Connor all night. And they could spend the entire night together without upsetting the delicate balance of whatever they had going on because the hotel was neutral ground.

Fiona grabbed her purse and said a quick goodnight to her mom and Aiden. She glanced around for her father, but didn't see him. She turned back to her mom. "Can you tell Dad I said goodnight? I'm beat."

Her mother reached out and touched her arm. "Can't you wait a little while longer? I'm sure he'd want to talk to you."

"I'll see him tomorrow." She didn't want to get roped into spending any more time there than necessary, especially now that she wanted to call Connor. She slipped out the door and down the hall to her room.

Fiona had barely wiggled out of her dress when a knock sounded at her door. She wrapped a warm, fluffy robe around herself and answered.

Her dad stood, holding two ice cream floats, looking tired with his tie loose around his neck and the first buttons undone on his collar. She always liked the relaxed version of her dad much more than the buttoned-up lawyer. "Dad."

"You left before these were delivered. I wanted to have some time with my little girl."

It had been a long time since she'd spent time alone with her dad, that is, time unscheduled by her mother. "Are those root beer floats?"

"Nothing but the best for you. Can I come in?"

"Sure." She opened the door wider and allowed him to enter. She locked up behind him, knowing she was giving up her opportunity to call Connor. She followed her dad to the table and took a seat. He had something on his mind and rather than poke at him, she waited.

She swirled the straw around the melting vanilla ice cream and scooped some into her mouth. Then she leaned over and slurped the creamy root beer foam from the top of the concoction. The sweet flavor slid down her throat, evoking many pleasant childhood memories. Sharing root beer floats equated to alone time with Dad, usually late at night, so Mom wouldn't know about the sugar splurge. Fiona smiled at the memories.

"That looks good."

"What?" Fiona asked, breaking away from the past.

"The smile on your face. I haven't seen much of you lately, but when we've spoken, you haven't sounded happy." Her father mostly played with his float, much like he did years ago.

She wondered why he always got one for himself if he never intended to drink it.

"You know how I get with Mom, especially when she's election-crazed. She's *always* a little too obsessed with appearances, as if some tabloid or newspaper would actually want to follow me around, but when it's election time, she acts like I could be the downfall of all things Cavanagh."

"She doesn't really believe that."

"Could've fooled me."

"She just wants what's best for you."

"She got to decide what was best for me as a child. I'm an adult now and I get to choose."

"Tell me about this new man in your life."

The casual statement made by anyone else wouldn't have made her blink, but her dad's eyes were far from casual. So much for the evening not being bad. "Aiden needs to keep his mouth shut."

Dad pushed his glass away. "Aiden is being a good brother.

It's his job to watch out for you."

Fiona snorted. Aiden had never been good at the big brother role.

"He told me about this man, and he's a poor choice, Fiona. You know I usually stay out of your personal life."

Another snort.

"*I* do. Your mother is a different story."

He had her there. Technically, he did stay out of her personal life.

"But I can't ignore this. You need to stay away from Connor Duffy."

The use of Connor's full name startled her. She'd never told Aiden his last name.

In answer to her surprise, he continued, "How hard do you think it is for me to use my resources to dig up whom you're involved with?"

She was well aware of how he used his resources; every date she'd had in high school had to pass a background check. "You have no business digging into my life. I'm not you. I don't want people ripping into my life all the time as if it's their right. I shouldn't have to suffer because of who you are." She shoved away from the table. "I've had to live in your shadow for so long. Every relationship I've had was tainted by who my family is. Except this one. Until tonight, Connor had no idea who I was. I used Mom's maiden name. He knew me as Fiona Wells, at least until he saw me standing beside you on TV tonight."

"Are you sure about that?"

"Yes."

He stood now, shaking his head at her as if she was too naïve for her own good.

"Dad, I know you think you're looking out for me. But my

relationship with Connor is between me and him. I don't want to know what you think you know about him. If he wants to share something, he'll tell me. Until then, I don't care."

She walked over to the door and opened it. Her father followed.

At the door, he said quietly, "I don't want you to get hurt. This man will hurt you."

He kissed her forehead and walked down the hall. Fiona closed the door and leaned against it. Nagging feelings tugged at her. It wasn't like her father to confront her about her choices in men. Since she turned eighteen, he'd been good at staying out of her business, unlike her mother.

It made Fiona wonder what her father had found out about Connor. Maybe she should've heard him out. How bad could it be, though? If Connor were a rapist or something, surely her dad would've led the conversation with such information instead of saying Connor would hurt her. Those thoughts were crazy. She knew Connor wasn't anything bad. She went to the bathroom and filled the tub with hot water and scented bubbles.

Her emotions had been battered enough for one night. She'd soak and wash away the doubts. Connor was a good man. She knew it like she knew her father was a good man despite what the press printed on a regular basis. Connor had secrets, but so had she until tonight. He never pressured her to reveal them.

What if Dad was right and the reason Connor hadn't pushed was because he did know her real name? She sank into fragrant hot water. Being with him hadn't felt like he wanted something from her, but what if? What if he was biding his time to see if her dad won the election? Could he be that deceitful?

She closed her eyes and remembered the man who cradled her while they made love. The man who called tonight to check on her. He didn't sound angry when they spoke. Maybe that was because he hadn't been surprised to see her on TV or maybe Connor was just that even-tempered. She wanted to believe the latter.

∞

A full week had gone by without seeing Fiona. They spoke briefly on the phone in rushed conversations. She'd apologized again for lying about her name and Connor asked careful questions about her family. She revealed so little. He learned more from the newspaper than from her. Although she'd come clean about her name, she still kept him at a distance. He wanted her to open up, let him in. He didn't have the right since he hadn't offered her the same, but if they were going to pursue this thing between them, something had to give.

Campaign press was about finished and Fiona seemed excited about her cousin's wedding. He attributed it to wanting to be with him. He'd gotten fitted for a rented tux. He saw no reason to buy something he probably wouldn't wear again. No matter what happened between him and Fiona, he would never be welcome at her family's functions and he had no other reason to own a tuxedo. Shit, he didn't even own a suit.

As much as spending the evening surrounded by strangers didn't appeal to him, the thought of having Fiona in his arms again did. She might even convince him to dance with her. He began to feel like a kid going to the prom. He'd never made it to his. More important things to do, like get high and screw any available girl. Connor wondered what it would've been like if he'd had a real girlfriend in high school. Or if his father had lived to keep him in line. Things would've turned out differently. He'd be a different person.

His doorbell rang and he checked the time. Max barked, and he shushed him. Connor wasn't expecting anyone and it was earlier than Fiona's usual late-night visits. Maybe she couldn't wait any more than he could. Max stood by his side as he opened his front door with a smile on his face.

Once the door opened, his happiness vanished because the face staring at him wasn't Fiona's but Brady Cavanagh's. *Fuck!*

Max growled. Connor stiffened his back and tightened his grip on the door, blocking Max from attack. "What do you want?"

One of Brady's gray eyebrows rose and Connor was struck by the fact that the man always looked dignified, no matter what he did.

"I'd like to speak with you."

"Last time I let you speak to me, I ended up in prison."

"You were well-compensated for it."

His mother had been well-compensated, for which he was grateful, but he'd barely been tipped.

"This is not a conversation I wish to have out on your porch. Hear me out and I'll leave."

Connor wanted to slam the door in his face, but he thought of Fiona and the fact that he would have to spend time with her entire family tomorrow at the wedding. Starting a fight tonight would not be a smart move.

He opened the door wider. Brady eyed Max and hesitated.

"He won't attack until I tell him to." Connor would never admit Max wasn't a watchdog. Pet him once and he was a friend for life.

Brady sidestepped Max and walked into the empty living room. At least he'd finally gotten it painted. It couldn't compare to what the Cavanaghs were used to. Brady Cavanagh was completely out of place standing in the stark room. Fiona never was though. He held onto that thought while he waited for Brady to start talking.

"Looks like you've done all right for yourself in spite of everything."

"In spite of you, yes."

A muscle in Brady's jaw twitched. "I know you've been seeing Fiona."

Connor didn't respond. If Aiden knew, of course he would've told his father. He was surprised it took so long for Brady to interfere.

"What do you want?"

"I don't want anything you'd offer." Connor knew where this was headed and his stomach clenched.

"Let's not play this game. Everyone wants something and there are plenty of women for you to get involved with. Since you've chosen Fiona, you're looking for something."

"I want my name cleared. I want the felony on my record erased."

"I can't do any of that. We had an agreement which we both honored."

"I was nineteen. I had no idea what I was getting into or how it would affect the rest of my life. Do you have any idea how hard it is to find a job when you're an ex-con? I can never apply for any decent job because I can't pass a background check." No one ever warned him the past would haunt his every move.

"What do you expect to happen now?"

Connor shrugged. He didn't have an answer because everything had changed for him. He thought he could use Fiona to get at Brady, but he no longer wanted to. He just wanted Fiona.

The acknowledgement bolted through him, startling his brain. He retrained his focus on Brady.

"How much will it take for you to leave Fiona alone?" Brady reached into his coat and withdrew a checkbook.

"I don't want your money. Lesson learned. You can't bribe me to stay away from Fiona."

"You can't possibly think it will ever be a serious relationship given our history. There are far too many skeletons between us."

"Those are your skeletons to deal with."

Brady tucked the checkbook back into his pocket. "So you've told Fiona about your past?" He waited a beat. "No, I didn't think so because she would've said something to me when I spoke to her. Do you think she'll have anything to do with you once she finds out?"

"You have more to lose than I do if she finds out. It was your plan and your money that paid for it. I was a nobody suckered into your mess."

Brady stepped closer and Connor shoved his hands into his pockets. No matter what, he refused to hit the old man.

"You brought my son into trouble. You were always the problem with the drugs and alcohol. He followed your lead."

A bark of laughter burst from Connor's chest. "You seriously believe that? Is that the story you created or one Aiden told? I was far from an angel, but Aiden never needed any coaxing. He usually led the way to the party."

Connor suddenly realized that back then, Aiden had partied as a means to escape. Just like Fiona. Aiden had used drugs and Fiona used sex with Connor to escape being a Cavanagh. Too bad he couldn't have seen it back then. "I think it's time for you to go. You've said your piece."

"You're making a mistake. I can make your life hell as much

as I can make your life easy. You want a better job? I can make that happen. Continue to provoke my family and you'll have nothing."

Connor swung the front door open and Brady left without another word.

Maybe it was time to finally forget the Cavanaghs. He might not be able to clear his name, but he could use Brady to get a better job and move on. But he'd already allowed the Cavanaghs to eat up too much of his life.

What about Fiona? A little voice in his head jabbed.

He'd known all along that she'd been using him, but he hadn't understood why. Although she'd said she was looking for sex, he knew it was more. She sought him out for escape, for normalcy. Having Brady Cavanagh in his house reminded him that Fiona would never be normal. She would always be a Cavanagh.

There was no hope for him. For them.

Fiona dabbed at her eyes in the bathroom mirror. Happy tears were the worst part of a wedding and they happened to her every time. The banquet hall filled as people made their way through the reception line. Fiona wanted to fix her makeup before Connor arrived. She knew he wouldn't show for the cocktails before dinner. It would be too much to ask him to mingle and make small talk with all of her parents' friends.

But the anticipation of seeing him tingled her nerves.

They'd spoken multiple times since the election and with each conversation, she became more certain Connor was just who he'd always been. He wasn't after anything from her. And she'd been right in telling her father to stay out of it. If Connor wanted to tell her something about his past, he'd do it in his own time.

Just hearing his voice soothed whatever nagging ideas her father had planted.

Tonight they would have a good time. She'd walk in front of her family with Connor and then they would leave and get reacquainted. She'd needed little doses of him to make it through the tedium of dealing with her family. Tonight, a small dose wouldn't do; she planned to splurge. She might even get him to spend the night. His house, hers, it didn't matter, as long as she could get her fill of him.

Fiona left the bathroom and went to the bar for a glass of wine. Aiden watched her coming toward him as he leaned his back against the bar. She half expected him to leave at the sight of her. She'd been pretty cold and nasty to him for getting Dad to stick his nose in her relationship. But Aiden didn't move. He simply sipped from his drink.

She eyed the glass.

He lifted it. "Coke. No rum, no vodka."

"I didn't say anything."

"You didn't have to. Your look said it all. I'm clean. I haven't had a drink in years. If I made it through election night without taking a drink, while all of Dad's cronies poked at me to run in the next race, I'm sure I can handle a simple wedding." He sipped again.

She ordered her wine and although he tried to hide it, she noticed Aiden staring at her as she drank. She probably should've been more supportive and ordered a soda, but she still wasn't feeling amiable toward him. He was right. He'd been sober for years. If he couldn't handle being at a wedding, he shouldn't be here. In the past, he would've skipped it.

"When are you going to stop being pissed at me?"

"When are you going to stop telling me how to live my life?"

He set his glass on the bar. "You know I don't try to, but—"

"But nothing. I get enough of that from Mom. When you and Dad start in, I can't handle it."

"Forget Connor and I'll never bother you again."

Fiona looked up from her drink. He was serious. "Why Connor? I've dated some real deadbeats in the past and you never even blinked. How can you decide he's the worst man on the planet after only talking to him for what, five minutes?"

"Because I know."

As much as she wanted to ask how he knew, she didn't. The possible answers frightened her. She wanted to believe Aiden and her dad were wrong, but something in their conviction about Connor left her unsettled.

Aiden stared at her, almost willing her to ask, she could feel it, but instead, she smiled and walked away. She wouldn't let Aiden or anyone take tonight from her. She'd talk to Connor. She'd get answers from him.

Back at her table, she was glad she'd had the foresight to call her cousin and ask not to be seated at the same table as her parents. Being stuck between her parents and Aiden would suck every ounce of fun out of the night. Instead, she sat at a table with some of her cousin's college friends.

She sat and introduced herself. Plenty of friendly conversation to keep her mind occupied, even as she kept an eye on the door looking for the one man she wanted to see. As cocktail hour wrapped up, more people filtered into the banquet hall and to their tables, but still no sign of Connor. The band announced the bridal party and the bride and groom. Once the head table was seated, salads were brought out.

Fiona discreetly pulled her phone from her purse. Connor hadn't called, so she shot him a text. **SALAD COMING**

OUT NOW.

Then she thought maybe he'd lost the address and like a typical man, wouldn't call for help, so she texted him the address again. She picked at her salad, waiting for a response.

"It's only salad. There's no way to screw it up, so it's gotta be safe to eat," the man sitting on her left said.

She smiled at him. "Maybe you should be the guinea pig."

He returned her smile and shoved a forkful of lettuce in his mouth. He chewed, swallowed, and then said, "See? Totally safe. I make no guarantees about whatever meat they bring out for the main course though."

"I'll keep that in mind." She wiped her hand on her napkin and extended it to him. "Fiona."

He took her hand. "John. Friend of bride or groom?"

"Bride's cousin. You?"

"Groom's colleague." "Which would mean you do what?" She felt kind of bad she knew so little about her cousin's fiancé—husband—that she didn't even know his occupation.

"Accountant."

They ate their salads in silence and Fiona grew more uncomfortable. She had a bad feeling about Connor not answering his phone. "I'd kill for another glass of wine, but the bar's closed until after dinner, isn't it?"

John smiled again and she caught a glimpse of dimples. "I can't help with wine, but I do have an extra beer."

"I don't want to take your drink."

"I always grab a backup before dinner is served at a wedding. People always underestimate how long the meal and speeches will last before they can get another drink." He put a bottle of beer in front of her.

She moved it back. "You shouldn't lose your beer because I didn't plan ahead."

He put it back in front of her. "You look like you can use it. Bad day?"

"I think my date is standing me up."

"Oh. Then I definitely insist."

"Are you here alone?"

"Yep." They looked around the table. Most of the other people sitting with them were paired off.

The wait staff cleared their plates and brought out the main course.

John nudged her with his elbow. "I tried the salad. It's only fair if you try the meat first."

"Doesn't seem like a fair tradeoff. Like you said, it's difficult to screw up salad. Meat opens up so many more possibilities." But she cut into the small slab of beef and tasted. Bland and slightly tough, but not unbearable. She took a swig of beer to wash it down. "Not horrible, but I'd trade it for a cheeseburger in a heartbeat."

"We could always cut out of here and go grab a burger." He flashed another smile, this time a hint of white teeth gleamed at her and full dimples winked in his cheeks.

Cute charm on a platter.

"I think that would be a little rude. Plus, my whole family is here and they'd notice. I can't leave until after the dancing starts." She scooped some mashed potatoes and tried them. Better than the meat, but still not stellar.

"I can understand. Save a dance for me?"

"Sure."

"Tell me about yourself."

In between small bites of food, Fiona told John about her jewelry and the outreach center and he seemed genuinely interested. At least as interested as any man who thought he might get some no-strings wedding sex.

But he was cute. And he was here, unlike Connor. As soon as the speeches finished and the bar reopened, John stood. "Would you prefer a wine or another beer?"

"I think I'll stick with beer, thanks."

She watched him walk away and texted Connor again. This time, she let him know how angry she was. He'd had plenty of opportunities to back out. She'd been prepared to go to the wedding alone. But when he volunteered to be her date, she felt so relieved. Word had spread through the family that she was bringing a new date to the wedding. Her cousins had all asked about him and she could feel their stares at the empty seat beside her during dinner. Luckily, her parents were at a table at the far end of the room, close to the head table. She sat near the back, which would allow her to make an early escape.

Before, she thought her early escape would be with Connor, so they would have more time together, but now, she just wanted to be gone. She needed to get away from the prying eyes of her family. At least the people at her table didn't know she'd been stood up. Except John, and since he was flying solo for the evening, he was happy for her loss.

John made his way back through the crowd with two bottles of beer and she checked her phone. Still no response from Connor. Asshole. She dropped the phone back in her purse and accepted the bottle from John.

"Boyfriend call?"

"No, I was letting him know he's an asshole for blowing me off. Want to dance?"

"Sure."

They set their drinks on the table and walked to the dance floor. The band had already played a few waltzes for the older people in the crowd, and now they started to play more upbeat music. The beat thumped and Fiona started moving. John wasn't much of a dancer, but he obviously wanted to be with her.

After returning to their table, they finished their drinks and then went back to the dance floor. They danced through three or four songs, with each one, John moving closer and getting bolder with touching her. She didn't rebuff his advances. She liked the attention.

As the band took a break, she grabbed John's hand to lead him from the dance floor. "I'm thirsty."

On the way to the bar, her mother stood in their path. "Fiona, darling, have you been avoiding me?"

Yes almost slipped from her lips before she bit her tongue. "Of course not, Mom." She leaned in and brushed a kiss on her mom's cheek.

"Are you going to introduce me to your date?"

"Uh…" Fiona didn't know how to respond. How could her mother not know that John wasn't supposed to be her date? Was it possible Aiden and her father had left Mom out of the loop? "This is John." She shifted slightly. "John, my mother, Sheila Cavanagh."

"John, so nice to meet you," she extended her hand in her usual limp shake.

Not wanting to give her mother a chance to do too much talking, she took John's hand again. "We were on our way to the bar for a drink."

She tried to curve around her mother, but Sheila wasn't having it. "What's your hurry? I could use another glass of wine myself."

Fiona dropped John's hand and headed to the bar, hating that her mom invited herself. Sheila either didn't notice, or ignored, Fiona's irritation as usual, and tucked her arm around

John's elbow. "Tell me about yourself," she started, and Fiona picked up the pace to reach the bar. She needed a drink now more than ever.

Her cousin Stacy, younger sister to the bride, swirled a straw in her glass and smiled at Fiona's approach. Fiona had wanted to avoid this most of all.

"Hey, Fi. Good to see you." She pulled Fiona into a one-armed hug, careful not to spill her drink. Before pulling away, she whispered, "Where's the new boyfriend?"

Fiona's jaw tightened, but she forced a smile. "He got hung up doing something and isn't going to make it."

"Oh, you poor thing. You really aren't having any luck in the man department, are you?"

Moments of being naked with Connor flashed in her head and she almost said she'd been plenty lucky. Instead, she offered, "I'm in no hurry to find the perfect guy. There are plenty to sample."

Just then, Sheila and John pulled up behind her. Stacey checked John out and gave Fiona an appreciative smile. "Your mom seems to be doing okay."

Fiona rolled her eyes. "She only nabbed John because I was dancing with him and having a good time."

She ordered another beer and headed back to her table to avoid engaging with her mother. Once seated, she gulped her beer and tapped her foot to the music. Her tablemates had left, some gone to dance, others to chat and mingle. She sat alone at a table for ten. Just when she'd about given up on John ever joining her, she saw him weaving around guests, carrying two bottles of beer. The man was a lifesaver.

"Thought you might be ready for another." He set a fresh bottle in front of the one she'd almost finished.

"You thought correctly." She was pleasantly buzzed and saw

no reason to stop. She chugged the remainder of her first beer and started on the one John brought. "Did you have a nice conversation with my mother?"

He laughed. "I think she was vetting me. Her main concerns were that I had a stable job and no wife at home."

"Since you're back here sitting with me, you must've passed. Congratulations." She tipped her bottle in his direction. "Do you have a car?"

"Yeah."

"I mean, do you have one here or did you carpool with someone?"

"I drove myself."

"You want to get out of here?"

"Say the word."

"Word." She stood, possibly a tad wobbly. "Let's find a better place to drink."

Fiona looked around and debated saying good-bye to people. She ultimately decided that doing so would ruin her buzz.

Chapter 9

CONNOR REACHED FOR HIS PHONE again, wanting to call and apologize to Fiona. Standing her up had been a dick move. But after listening to her father, he knew he couldn't show his face at a family wedding without doing a whole lot of explaining. Part of him wanted to show up and cause a scene, tell everyone the truth, but he couldn't ruin the wedding of some woman he'd never even met. Fiona would definitely hate him then. Now, however, it seemed as though she hated him anyway for blowing her off.

He toyed with his phone and studied the last text from her. **YOU'RE AN ASSHOLE. IF YOU DIDN'T WANT TO COME TO THE WEDDING YOU SHOULDN'T HAVE OFFERED.**

Connor slugged back a shot. Dermott simply shook his head. Connor spent the day finishing the cabinet he'd created for Fiona. He didn't know why he continued to work on it. It wasn't not like he thought she wouldn't care if he blew her off. Somehow, it was important that he finished it. The whole time, he'd put the wedding out of his mind and along with it, the possible ramifications of not showing. He hadn't learned all that much over the years. The same fucking thing he'd done when Cavanagh approached him years ago. Act without thinking it through.

He drained his beer and then dialed her number. He wasn't sure what he wanted to say, but he wanted to hear her voice, even if she just called him an asshole.

"What do you want?"

Yeah, she was pissed. Not even a hello. "I'm sorry. I should've called you to cancel."

"Damn straight."

Her voice held an odd quality, but he couldn't quite put his finger on it. "Can I stop by when you're done at the wedding?"

"We're already done. Moving on to the next drinking establishment."

We? Who was she with? Aiden?

Before he could ask, she continued, "No need to worry about me. I met John, who wasn't afraid to attend the wedding. We're heading out for drinks."

She picked up a guy at the wedding. Connor's gut began to churn, a mixture of alcohol and regret. Then his stupidity got the better of him. "I'm at Dermott's. Come have a drink with me."

She snorted. "You had your chance."

Then he recognized the odd quality to her voice—she was drunk, or at least well on her way. Drunk and with a strange man. "At least call me when you get home so I know you got there safely."

"I might be too preoccupied to call." Then she disconnected.

Connor felt like shit, both because Fiona was really upset and because she was talking about fucking some other guy. He drank another beer to put Fiona Cavanagh out of his mind, but knew it wouldn't work because he hadn't been able to accomplish that in weeks.

Fiona hung up and looked at John. He was a good-looking guy. Short hair, precisely cut, probably for the wedding. Clean-shaven. His hands were smooth, unlike Connor's rough calloused palms. John's lips were full, like they would be comfortable to kiss and when he smiled, his whole mouth widened and brightened his face.

He caught her staring at him. "Boyfriend?"

"He's not my boyfriend. We had a casual thing going. Until he blew me off. He just invited me for a drink. Want to go?"

"You want me to take you to have a drink with your boyfriend?"

"Not with him. But you could go with me and show him what he missed out on."

"So you want to use me to make him jealous."

"If you're game."

He shot her a look from the corner of his eye. She was being adolescent and the alcohol clouded her judgment. She was aware of that much. But she wanted Connor to feel a hint of the hurt she'd been feeling all night.

"How big is this guy?"

"Not huge. But strong."

"Violent?"

She shook her head. "Not that I know of."

"You seriously want me to make a guy jealous and risk getting my ass kicked."

"He won't start anything." She was pretty sure anyway.

"What's in it for me?"

"A good night kiss?"

"You're asking for a lot of risk for very little reward. I think I'd get a kiss no matter what."

"Whatever. I thought it would be worth a shot." She inhaled deeply. "I want him to hurt a little. I believed he was coming as my date tonight and I was excited about it. It's disappointing, that's all."

John sighed. "Where are we going?"

"You don't have to do this. I know I'm acting childish."

"So was he. He deserves a little of his own medicine."

Fiona gave him directions to Dermott's and hoped Connor would still be there. When they parked on the street alongside the bar, Fiona became nervous. She turned to John. "Are you sure about this?"

"I've got nothing else going on tonight."

She reached across and tugged at his tie, then unbuttoned the first couple of buttons on his shirt. "This isn't very upscale. More neighborhood bar, so you might want to lose the jacket."

"Why don't you take the jacket? It's a chilly out."

They stepped from the car and he laid his jacket across her shoulders. Fiona's mind flashed back to when Connor had done the same the first night they met. John's cologne swirled around her. It smelled expensive and a little too strong. But the coat warmed her and warded off the shivers.

John walked beside her with his hand on her lower back. When they entered the bar, it was darker than Fiona remembered. Then again, it had been full of soccer-loving men last time she'd been here. It wasn't overly crowded for a Saturday night. A row guys sat on stools at the bar and couples sat at a few scattered tables. Fiona felt infinitely overdressed, but she refused to feel out of place. She grabbed John's hand and led him to a table.

As they walked, she scanned the room for Connor, but saw no sign of him. He would've been at the bar if he were still there. He wouldn't sit at a table alone. She didn't know how she knew that, but she did. She studied the backs of the men at the bar. Connor's broad shoulders would've called to her.

John pulled out the chair for her. "Thank you." She took the seat and when he was settled across from her, she said, "I think he's already gone. Sorry to have dragged you here."

"No big deal. We were planning on stopping for another drink. Might as well be here. What'll you have?"

"Beer is fine."

He stood to go to the bar to order their drinks and she caught him by the hand and pulled him toward her. "Most guys would've dumped me off as soon as I suggested this. I appreciate you being a good sport."

She tilted her head up and moistened her lips to hint that she planned to kiss him. John lowered himself to her and pressed his lips to hers.

His lips were soft and comfortable. He opened them slightly and deepened the kiss. It was a nice kiss. But that was it. Nice. No sparks. No real chemistry.

John pulled away with a smile. "I'll be right back with our drinks."

She saw it in his eyes. He felt it too, or rather, didn't feel it. Damn Connor. Now he was ruining her for other men.

Connor rounded the corner from the bathroom and froze. A man bent and kissed a woman he knew had to be Fiona. He didn't need to see her face; the mass of red curls would forever give her away. Every muscle in his body tightened and flexed. His hands fisted. Why the fuck would she bring her date here?

Because you invited her, idiot.

As the man backed away and walked toward the bar, Fiona stared after him. Connor focused on her, his brain scrambling to create his next move. The man returned quickly with two bottles of beer. Then she realized Connor was there. It was a subtle shift at first.

She'd been smiling at the guy carrying drinks. Then she rolled her shoulder and accepted the bottle. She glanced at Connor without turning her head and tilted her bottle toward him. Her focus returned to the man across from her, dismissing Connor.

His blood boiled seeing her smile at another man.

How could she so easily brush aside what they had? He didn't go to a wedding, so she found his replacement? Fuck that. If she wanted to play games, she could play by herself. He wouldn't give her the satisfaction of seeing him crazy. Connor went back to the bar and reclaimed his seat. Unfortunately, it put Fiona and her date in his line of sight. He looked up and down the bar. Every stool was filled, so he couldn't move.

He waved his hand to get another shot and beer. Doing his best to ignore Fiona and her date, Connor questioned his sanity. What had he hoped would happen by inviting her to Dermott's? Hadn't he already decided they didn't have a chance? At least as long as she remained a Cavanagh.

Yet watching her smile and laugh with someone else gutted him.

He was glad Dermott had left and couldn't witness this. He'd be the first to point out that Connor had lost his focus. He was supposed to be ruining the Cavanaghs, not climbing into bed with them. But being in bed with Fiona was exactly what he craved. Connor shook his head, berating himself, and downed the shot.

Laughter curled around him and Connor knew he couldn't stomach Fiona's game. She won. He drank his beer quickly to end the misery. Then he saw Fiona walk toward the bathroom. Without thinking, he followed.

He stood outside the bathroom door and waited for her exit. When she did, she started and blinked, as if surprised he was there. As if.

"Having fun on your date?"

"Yes, I am. Thanks for asking." Her syrupy sweet voice made his teeth ache.

"You shouldn't have brought him here."

"What do you care? You decided to blow me off. What are you going to do, start a fight?"

"I'd start and end it, and we both know that. The poor schmuck wouldn't even see it coming. Doesn't seem fair." He edged closer to her.

She spoke quietly. "What do you want, Connor?"

"You know what I want."

"I'm here with someone else."

Her eyes darted everywhere but where he wanted them, needed them. He tilted her chin up to catch her attention. "I don't give a fuck who you're here with."

He leaned down and captured her mouth. Her gasp sucked the breath from his lungs and he pushed against her. A moan rose in her throat and he swallowed it as her hands grabbed at his shirt. He waited for her to push him away, but they twisted in the cotton. She tasted of beer and the same sweetness that was always Fiona. Connor thrust his hands into her hair and shifted to take more from her, to make her want him.

As if suddenly realizing what they were doing, she pushed him. He inched his chest from her body, but they were still rubbing pelvises, his fingers tangled in her curls. He simply raised an eyebrow at her, waiting explanation.

"Get off me. You can't do this. You can't decide to stand me up and then make out with me in the hallway of a bar. Who the hell do you think you are?"

"I'm the guy you've been taunting. I'm the one who gets you hot and bothered. The one who can kiss you the way you beg to be kissed." He released her hair and stepped back. "Don't tell me you don't feel it too. After that kiss, I'd venture to say your *date* doesn't have what it takes."

"My date is none of your business." She swiped her fingers over her lips and he saw the slight tremble.

"Is there a problem here?" A voice asked from behind them.

Fiona shoved past Connor. "Not at all. I'm ready to go. Please take me home."

The man threw a glare at Connor over Fiona's shoulder, but asked her, "You okay?"

"Yes, I'm fine."

Connor saw her try to shake off the effect of their kiss as he leaned against the wall to watch her walk away. When she reached for the guy's hand, Connor had to stop himself from lunging forward. He had no right to prevent her from leaving with someone else. He pressed his feet to the floor willing himself not to move. After a few minutes, he shuffled forward, certain Fiona had had enough time to escape. Enough time had passed so he couldn't pull her back into his arms where he wanted her, but where she didn't belong.

Once they were settled in John's car and Fiona had given him directions to get her home, he finally asked, "How did your plan work?"

"Better than expected." She'd felt Connor's jealousy in his searing kiss, in the way he possessively held her head, in the way he'd taken her despite the fact she was with another man. "I'm sorry I dragged you into this. I don't know what I was thinking. It might've been the alcohol making decisions."

"I think alcohol played an important role, but don't apologize. You made my evening interesting. I'm almost never used to make a guy jealous."

"Really?" she asked playfully. "You did such a great job I figured you had ample experience."

He laughed and it was a warm, easy sound. Which described John. Comfortable. Why couldn't she be more attracted to him? They drove in silence the rest of the trip to her condo and as Fiona's buzz wore off, she began to drag and wanted nothing more than to curl up and go to sleep.

John parked and jumped out of the car to open her door for her. She stood awkwardly looking at him, knowing she wouldn't invite him up, but not sure if she wanted to exchange numbers. He was a nice guy. Her mother already approved.

"Thank you for a great night, Fiona." He leaned in and kissed her cheek.

"Don't you want to collect on our deal? A goodnight kiss?"

"We tried at the bar. I think we both know that although we enjoyed each other's company, it's not going to turn into anything else." He pulled a business card from his pocket. "Here's my number, though, if you ever want to get together to hang out. I have a feeling that spending time with you would be a blast."

She smiled and took the card. "Thanks. You saved my night."

She pushed away from the car and walked toward her building. John watched her walk away and although she was conscious of it, she didn't feel it. Not the way she felt Connor's hot glare on her back as she'd held John's hand to leave Dermott's. Inside, she kicked off her shoes and grabbed her phone to call Sarah. No one bitched about men like Sarah could.

A healthy dose of girlfriend trash talk would straighten her out. Who needed a man like Connor?

If her hormones answered the question, they would say she did. She sighed and dialed Sarah's number.

Sarah answered on the second ring. And here Fiona thought Sarah had a more engaging social life than she did.

"How'd it go?"

"The wedding was beautiful. Connor stood me up. I met a guy who I convinced to take me to drink at the bar where Connor hangs out to make him jealous. I'm coming down off my buzz and home alone."

"Wow. Where to start? Connor's an ass, at least you drank for free, and tell me about the new guy. Did he fight with Connor over you?"

Fiona laughed. "No fights. I don't know what I was thinking. I was with John, who's a nice guy, gainfully employed, and cute. Unfortunately, no sparks. But he was fun. We ditched the wedding after my mother decided to hound John, and Connor called when we got to the car. I shouldn't have answered, but I was pissed, you know? I didn't *expect* him to go to the wedding with me, he volunteered."

"I think you did expect him to go."

"Well, sure, after he volunteered."

"No, before that. You told me you asked him and he dodged it. I know you. In the back of your head you were clinging to the hope that he'd change his mind and when he did, you probably started hearing wedding bells."

"I did not." Not the wedding bells anyway. So she was falling for him. Where was the harm in that?

"As soon as you fall for a guy, you start imagining the future. It's not a bad thing, but you keep doing it with the wrong guys. Connor isn't your future."

Fiona knew it. Hadn't she told herself the same thing a bunch of times? But hearing the harshness of the reality stung. "What's wrong with me?"

"Nothing's wrong with you. You're a romantic. You love being in love. It's a great place to be, but you have to be realistic, too. Why Connor? I picked him out of the crowd because he screamed *temporary*. And you told me earlier this week that both Aiden and your dad don't like him. What does that say?"

Fiona rubbed the spot between her eyebrows that had begun to ache. "He's different, Sarah. He doesn't expect anything from me. He likes me, not my last name." Guilt still weighed on her for lying about her name even though Connor now knew the truth. But she still hadn't gotten the chance to explain to him.

"Maybe him not showing was supposed to be a clear message."

"But it wasn't. He called me to apologize. He could've ignored my nasty messages. After I lied about who I am, shouldn't I at least give him the chance to explain?"

"How deep are you into this guy, Fi?"

"I think I love him."

"I knew it. Didn't I tell you not to let that happen?"

"You know I can't control it. Especially when it comes to guys I shouldn't fall in love with. I feel good when I'm with him, Sarah, different than with other guys. Ever. I can be me. Why shouldn't I love him if that's the way he makes me feel?" Antsiness struck, so she paced her living room.

"I can't help but feel Aiden and your dad know something

about this guy. If it were your mother saying you should stay away from him, I'd tell you to ignore it. But Aiden? When has he ever cared about who you date? I can say a lot of nasty shit about your brother, but I don't think he's pulling anything. What do you really know about Connor?"

In truth, she didn't know much. He kept his personal life distant from whatever they shared. Except for when he looked at her while they made love. He was open then and she saw into him. He carried deep pain and he was a little lost, but he cared for her. She knew it.

"Fi?"

"I'm still here. You have a point. I don't know much about Connor. He makes great furniture. He's all alone, except for his dog. He's searching for something." Why couldn't it be her?

"Can you at least try to slow it down before you declare your undying love? Take some time to get to know him. Find out who he is. Maybe even talk to Aiden."

The thought of talking to Aiden and giving credence to whatever he thought he knew about Connor turned her stomach into a pretzel. "I'll try."

"You're going to call him now, aren't you?"

"No." She was already shimmying out of her dress and searching for her yoga pants.

"Be careful." Sarah always knew when she was lying.

She disconnected and called for a cab. She hadn't really lied to Sarah. She wasn't going to call Connor. She needed to see him. The alcohol haze had worn off and she vividly remembered the kiss they shared at the bar. She was too angry to realize it at the time, but it had been possessive more than jealous.

He knew what effect he had on her and he'd used it to his

advantage. Well, he wasn't unaffected by their chemistry. She'd use it to her advantage to get him to open up. If he wanted to talk, this would be his chance.

Chapter 10

CONNOR LAY IN BED STARING at the page of the thriller he'd tried to read. He blamed his lack of page turning on his blood-alcohol level, but the truth was, he couldn't stop thinking about Fiona. The damn woman wouldn't let him go. Max jolted from his spot on the floor and growled. Then he ran downstairs barking.

Connor followed his dog, hoping Max hadn't been imagining a guest on their doorstep. By the time he reached the bottom of the stairs, the knock sounded. Max jumped excitedly. Fiona stood on his porch gripping two cups of coffee.

"Hey."

"Hi," she said with a forced smile.

He'd seen the same smile on TV while she stood next to her family. He hoped he hadn't been relegated to the same position.

"I thought we could both use a cup of coffee. Can I come in?"

He stepped back and reined in his need to pull her to him and kiss her, to know she was really there, to know he hadn't scared her off.

"Why are you here?" he asked and immediately regretted the accusation in the question.

Luckily, she didn't seem bothered.

"You said you wanted to talk and I thought I owed you that."

She owed him? She had no idea. This was his chance. He could tell her everything, lay out his life and her family's involvement, and let the things fall wherever.

He closed the door against the cold night air and Max danced between them. Fiona looked awkwardly around his empty living room as if just remembering he didn't have any furniture. He suddenly found it funny given his occupation.

"You want to go upstairs and talk, or would you feel better in the kitchen?"

She weighed the question and he hoped she'd opt for the kitchen. If they went to his bedroom, they might not get around to talking. She wore those thin pants again and he was sure if he took her jacket, her nipples would greet him through an equally thin shirt. Kitchen was definitely the way to go.

"Let's go upstairs."

Shit. She turned and headed up, giving him an eyeful of swaying hips and grabbable ass. He swallowed hard and stared at his feet.

In his room, she set the coffee on the nightstand and tossed her coat on the chair. Max returned to his pillow on the floor, ignoring them. Fiona kicked off her sneakers and grabbed a cup of coffee before settling on his bed. She crossed her legs like a little kid and cradled her cup as if stealing its warmth.

Connor stood awkwardly, not knowing where to go or what to say. She finally looked up and he saw she wasn't nearly as drunk as she had been earlier in the evening, which meant that after leaving Dermott's she didn't continue to drink. What if she was busy doing other things, like her date? A flash of anger sucker-punched him.

"You can sit. I won't bite."

He stared at the chair and tried to make his feet move in that direction, but his dick won out again and he headed for the bed. The mattress dipped under his weight, tilting her body toward him. When he sat, Fiona looked at the tux hanging on the back of his door.

The expression on her face was a cross between bewilderment and hurt. "Why didn't you come to the wedding?" She pointed her cup at the tux. "At some point, you must've planned to."

"I was going to. But then..." He didn't know what to say. Why had he chosen not to? Because of Brady? No, Brady had been the final push. He could use that information to drive a wedge between her and her family, but he couldn't follow through. "I saw you on TV Tuesday and I realized we don't belong together."

She pressed her lips together and continued to stare across the room. When she finally turned to face him, her eyes were glassy and pain speared his chest. "Was that when you realized I lied about my name?"

Instinct made him want to lie, but he couldn't. He shook his head.

"How long did you know?"

"From the beginning." There. Telling the truth wasn't so hard. Maybe he could do this.

"Why didn't you say anything?"

"At first I didn't think about it. But then I figured you probably had a good reason for lying. I thought you'd tell me when you were ready, but it never seemed to happen." He reached for his cup of coffee to have something to do with his hands.

If he held a cup, he wouldn't reach for her.

"I lied because of the election and needing to get away from being a Cavanagh. Being my father's daughter is hard. You and I were supposed to be a one-night thing. And if the sex had sucked, that's all it would've been." She offered him a half-smile.

"I'll keep that in mind. When I want a one-night stand, make the sex mediocre."

She shifted to fully face him. "I'm not sure you have the ability." She pushed her hair behind her shoulders. "Anyway, it started out as sex, and it was okay to be anonymous. But then I realized I enjoyed being with you. Fully clothed. Like I said on Tuesday, you offer me some normal. In an election year especially, I crave normal."

She reached across to put her untouched coffee back on the nightstand. The movement made her hair tickle his forearm and her scent drift to his nose. He inched back to be able to focus because he craved her.

"Most of the time, my life is normal. I see my family on a regular basis, but I avoid the political crap. Except when I want money from them for the outreach center. It's kind of a quid pro quo thing. My mother wants my face for something, she pays the outreach center. We both get what we want. Other than that, I'm kind of the black sheep of the family."

He smiled. She had no idea what a black sheep really was.

"So I'm your non-family quid pro quo. I give you normal, you give me sex." He'd meant it as a joke, to lighten the mood, but he should've known better. It sounded like another accusation and she flinched.

He fumbled to put his coffee down and then he did reach for her. His large palms cradled her face. "I didn't mean anything. A joke. You should know by now I'm not very funny."

"What are we doing here?" she whispered.

Fuck if he had an answer. He only knew he wanted to feel her pressed up against him, her lips saying his name. In those moments, he could forget the past and who he was. Maybe they weren't so different after all.

He leaned closer and brought her lips to his. Their breath mingled, the air around them charged. He kissed her softly, swiping his tongue across hers. Every time they did this, she melted and became his.

She gently disengaged and sat back. "Why do my father and brother want you out of my life?"

This was it. "I'm a felon."

Again, she flinched, but tried to cover it.

"I went to prison for hit-and-run. I was drunk and high and a woman was injured. Being young and stupid, I fled the scene." He couldn't bring himself to tell her about Aiden. It ultimately wasn't his place. As much as he wanted the world to know the truth, he couldn't tell her. He didn't want to hurt her. The story was Aiden's to tell.

Fiona didn't speak, but she didn't look away from him either. He couldn't bear her scrutiny, so he moved to the edge of the bed. He braced his elbows on his knees and tried to think of a way to tell her the rest.

"It's in the past. What does that have to do with you being with me now?" She rubbed his back.

The touch comforted him. He didn't deserve any comfort. "I spent three years in prison. When I got out, I had no one. My mother had left the country, so I went back to my old stomping grounds. I got a job working for a bookie collecting debts."

Her hand paused on its circuitous path on his back.

"I beat people up for money. It was pretty good money too.

I tried to get a decent job, but no one wants to hire a felon. That's why I'm not good enough for you. I'll never pass the test."

"What test?"

"The test of being in the public eye. I run my own business because I can ignore my past. The press will never ignore my past when it comes to your family. If my past was publicized and my business went belly-up, I couldn't promise not to end up back in prison. I'd like to think I wouldn't, that I could find a different way, but desperate people do desperate things." The air around him pressed down heavily. He couldn't look at Fiona, didn't want to see the disappointment in her eyes.

But part of him felt relieved. He'd never talked about any of this before and it was freeing. Hearing his own words shored his resolve. He and Fiona didn't belong together. He'd drag her down, and he couldn't live with himself if that happened. And it had nothing to do with her being a Cavanagh.

He felt her move and knew she'd leave. He covered his face with his hands to avoid watching her walk out, knowing it would crush him. Her cool fingers peeled his hands away and held them. Connor looked up, fighting to keep his raw emotions in check.

Fiona still didn't talk, but moved closer and straddled him. He wrapped his arms around her, anchored himself to her as she leaned in and kissed him.

This. His mind screamed. Fiona filled him with whatever acceptance she offered and for the first time in years, Connor experienced peace.

Fiona kissed Connor with all she had. She felt tears clawing at the back of her throat, but she wouldn't give in. He didn't need or want her tears, but she could give him this. Herself, her body. She could comfort him the same way he had her.

She leaned back and peeled off her shirt and then tugged at his. She ran her hands across his chest, down his torso, and around to his back. His muscles bunched and flexed beneath her fingers, almost rejecting her touch. She continued to stroke his skin as her hips rocked against him.

His eyes closed and she was grateful because the soul-crushing pain she'd glimpsed would bring her to tears. She eased off him to remove her pants and gently pushed him back to lie on the bed. When he finally looked at her, she saw nothing but desire. The man was a master at masking everything he felt.

Climbing back on the bed, Fiona straddled Connor's prone body. His erection strained against the sweatpants he wore. She rubbed against him, loving the friction, and kissed her way up his body to his face. He reached for her, his rough hands caressing her, turning her on even more. He gripped her hips and held her tight against his cock. She whimpered.

Stretching closer, she nipped his earlobe and whispered, "Let me love you."

He growled deep in his chest and flipped her over. Before she could focus, he was kneeling in front of her, naked and sliding a condom on. He ran his fingers over her to test for her readiness, as if her gyrating and moaning hadn't been clue enough.

She trembled at his touch. She hated always being at his mercy. She wanted to make him feel better, yet he'd turned this back on her. Again.

Connor covered her body and continued to stroke her while he sucked at her nipples. Her hips matched his rhythm. She was on the edge, gripping his shoulders, his scalp, pulling at him to join her. "Connor," she said with the little breath remaining in her lungs.

He rose up and slid his entire length into her. He curled his arms under and around her, surrounding every inch of her. He buried his face in her neck and inched out of her body. His movements were slow and precise as he drew out her pleasure. As always, Connor took the lead, taking her where he wanted, in his time. But somehow, this was different. She recognized it even as she spiraled out of control.

Their slick bodies rubbed and slid against each other. Her muscles clenched around him and he froze. She pulled and pushed wanting to ride the pleasure but he pinned her down. She hung there for what seemed like hours, dangling on the edge of orgasm, her nerves tingling, her breath hitching. Finally, finally, Connor began to thrust, and everything in her exploded.

His muscles strained on top of her and his body was rigid, but he whispered one word, "Mine."

Fiona had barely heard the word in the haze of oblivion. But as they lay panting and sweaty, she replayed the moment and wondered. Was he just controlling her pleasure, making sure she knew her orgasm was his? Or—and her heart gave a little leap at the thought—was he claiming her as his? Her lungs still struggled for air, but now the cause was unclear. Did the rampant thoughts running in her head or Connor's weight pressing down her steal her breath?

He shifted, pulling out of her, but not letting her go. Why wouldn't he say something? Anything. Whatever connection she'd thought they'd had before the election had been magnified tonight. She knew he felt it too. He groaned and pulled away long enough to dispose of the condom. Fiona shivered with his momentary absence. When he returned to the bed, he stretched out beside her and pulled her close once again.

Connor's heart beat steady and sure beneath her ear. His muscles were relaxed under her hands. The tension that had clung to him disappeared. She'd accomplished something tonight. She sat up and looked into his eyes, searching for the past that haunted him, made him believe he wasn't good enough. He smiled and it stole her breath.

It was not his corner-lifted, half-smirk that she'd come to love. This smile transformed his face and broke her heart. She leaned down and pressed her lips to his. Then she stood to leave, the way she always did. If this was the best relationship she'd get, she'd learn to live with it.

With her back to him, she straightened her shirt and pulled it on quickly, feeling more naked than ever.

"Fiona." His voice was craggy, like he hadn't used it in years.

She licked her lips and faced him.

He searched her face like she'd done to him, but she had no idea what he was looking for. He lifted his hand and said the most important word she'd heard in a long time. "Stay."

She swallowed hard and tried not to read too much into the gesture. When her hand met his, he curled his fingers around hers and stood. He released her for a moment and removed her shirt again. The only explanation he offered was his half-smile. They crawled under the covers and Connor pulled her to him. The quiet of the room added to their intimacy. She closed her eyes and began to paint the feeling in her mind's eye.

This feeling needed something, required exposure. She wanted the world to experience what she felt at this moment. She could accomplish that through paint. Lying on her side, her head pillowed on Connor's bicep and with his arms circling her, he sandwiched her hand between his palms.

"I have another confession to make and I think after this one, you might hate me. I should've finished before we got naked." His voice had changed again, still heartbreaking.

Fiona tried to turn to face him, but he held her tight.

"No. I can't look at you when I say this."

She stilled and waited. His breath blew against her hair. Minutes ticked by.

"The Halloween party wasn't the first time I met Aiden."

She couldn't stop the tension in her shoulders, but she wanted to give him the benefit of the doubt.

"When I told you I worked for a bookie and I did collections...I don't know if you know this, but Aiden gambled. Often. Don't know if he still does, but...he owed a lot of money. He probably could've gotten it from your father, but he refused. I beat the crap out of him."

Fiona couldn't move. She didn't know what she'd expected, but it wasn't this. She didn't know how she was supposed to feel about Connor's admission. She waited to feel something, but nothing came.

She wasn't quite numb, but she no longer knew how to name her emotions. Aiden had done a lot of things to screw up his life. She knew because she'd covered for him and watched her father clean up after him too many times. Connor's admission wasn't too surprising.

Connor's heart raced against her back. Long gone was the calm thump she'd been comforted by.

"I don't want you to go," he said, "but I understand if you need to."

Fiona still couldn't move. It was like a glitch in her processing. While she didn't know if Aiden deserved to get beaten, she was certain he knew exactly what he had gotten himself into. She stared at Connor's hands still holding hers. They were big hands. Rough and scarred. Definitely capable of causing pain and destruction. But with her, they'd always been gentle and loving. Even when he was hurt and angry.

"Fiona? Say something."

God, how she loved the way he said her name. Each time, it was like it held new meaning.

"You don't do this anymore, right?"

"What? Collections?"

She nodded.

"No. I stopped four years ago."

"Okay."

His grip on her loosened, allowing her to turn in his arms. "What does that mean?"

She touched his cheek. "I believe everyone can change and deserves a second chance. Hell, Aiden's gotten more second chances than anyone I know."

"Everything I said before still holds true. I can never be what you need."

"You're what I need right now. We can worry about the rest later." She threw her leg over his hip and kissed him again. The rightness of their bodies together erased all confusion. Lying in Connor's embrace for the night filled her with all she needed to know. As much as she'd tried not to be, she was in love.

Connor laid awake for hours while Fiona slept in his arms. She was too good for him. He'd admitted to beating the crap out of her brother, and she'd forgiven him. After that, he couldn't tell her the rest. Not when she looked up at him with those bright blue eyes filled with understanding.

She didn't understand anything about him, but she thought

she did. She believed she saw something in him that didn't exist. He tried to show her, but she refused to see. And he wasn't strong enough to push her away for good.

He spent the night holding her, afraid it had been a dream, that he'd wake up and she'd be gone again, but in the morning sunshine, she still lay in his arms. He'd never been more grateful for anything. The bright light illuminated her pale skin and he stared at every visible inch of porcelain, interrupted only by scattered freckles across her shoulders.

Thoughts of her last name clawed at him. How could they forge any kind of relationship with her being a Cavanagh? But she wasn't one of them, not really, the sneaky little voice in his head reminded him. He'd known that from the start. No one got to choose the family they were born into. He wondered how they managed to keep Aiden's past from her. She knew Aiden had had problems, but when he mentioned the accident, she showed no sign of recognition. Knowing the Cavanaghs, they probably pretended none of it ever happened.

Could he do the same?

If he pretended he never had a relationship with Aiden and the Cavanaghs, he could have Fiona. He tried to live his life like prison never happened, except when something reminded him. If he let go of his disgust for Brady Cavanagh, could he and Fiona have peace?

Fiona stirred next to him. "I hear your brain spinning. It's so loud it woke me up. What are you thinking about?"

"Nothing." He traced lines down her arm until she turned to face him.

"Regretting last night?"

He froze. "Are you?"

"Never. You were honest and open with me. How could

I possibly regret that?" She tossed her leg over his hip and tugged him closer to her.

He didn't know if he would be able to pretend the past didn't exist, but for more time with her, he was willing to try. "What are your plans for the day?"

She pushed against him, showing him at least part of what she had planned. He wouldn't mind spending the day right there.

"I have to go shopping. I need some more supplies. Want to join me?"

Shopping? He'd rather eat a rat.

She cupped his ass. "It'll be fun."

"I hate malls."

"Not that kind of shopping. I need to hit the flea market. It's where I get my best stuff."

Her nipples rubbed against his chest and his brain clouded. "Let's stay here."

"I can't. The market's only open on the weekend. I can't wait another week." She tilted her hips into him.

His hard-on raged and he couldn't effectively negotiate in that condition. She reached over his shoulder, grabbed a condom, and covered him. Her cool fingers gliding over his heated flesh offered little relief. He rolled her under him and rubbed against her already-wet entrance.

She smiled playfully. "I'll let you feel me up in the truck at red lights."

"Maybe I'll just chain you up here and have you whenever I want."

Her eyes danced as she readied another quip, but he thrust into her. Her breath hitched and then she sighed as he sank the rest of the way in. As her warmth surrounded him, he knew he'd be spending his day at the flea market. In that moment, he would've given anything she asked.

Five hours and miles of walking later, Connor could barely remember why he had agreed to join Fiona. Part of him understood her excitement over finding the perfect piece of junk—and it was crap: broken dishes, old buttons, antique pins—because he knew the feeling when he discovered just the right hunk of wood for building something. He looked at her bags of unwanted material the same way some people saw a tree stump.

But he knew she'd make something beautiful from it. He'd seen enough of her work to know she was talented. He piled the bags into the back seat of the truck and prayed she was done.

"Sorry it took so long. I'm usually done in an hour or two. Sometimes, there's so much to look at though…" She ran a finger from his shoulder down the center of his shirt to the button on his jeans. "I'll make it up to you. I'm promise."

He leaned against the door and brought her with him. He really liked the way their bodies aligned. With his hands on her ass, he lowered his head to kiss her. He brushed his lips against hers and asked, "What did you have in mind?"

"We could pick up some dinner and head back to your place to eat. Naked. Then we can watch TV. Naked. Then we can go to bed—"

"Naked," he growled, getting harder at the thought. He looked around and wondered if they could get naked in the parking lot. But a security guard drove by, ruining the plan.

Fiona wiggled against him. She opened her mouth the say something, but her phone rang. She stepped away from him to answer it, and he took that as his cue to get in the truck. His dick was so hard he was afraid he wouldn't be able to walk. He adjusted himself as discreetly as possible and Fiona snickered into her phone as she answered, "Hello."

"Hi, Aiden. If you're calling on Mom's behalf to yell at me, don't bother."

Connor stopped and listened. He wasn't sure how to feel about her talking to her brother. How could he pretend she wasn't a Cavanagh when they were around so often?

"Yes, I left the wedding early with John, but we went our separate ways." She climbed into the seat and shut the door. "No. I'll call you later. Better yet, I'll meet you for coffee in the morning."

She disconnected and Connor started the engine. He wanted to ask about the conversation, but didn't. Part of accepting who Fiona was meant ignoring things like phone calls from her brother. Knowing that didn't prevent the tension from taking hold in his shoulders.

"Something wrong?"

Connor focused on pulling into traffic. "No."

"You seem a little tense."

He drove, keenly aware of her staring at him.

"Don't tell me nothing's wrong. Don't shut me out. Not after last night."

He stole a peek at her. Her words tugged at his guilt. "Look, Fiona, I'm not a sharer. Don't expect me to pour my heart out at every turn. It's not going to happen. But right now, I can't help but wonder what's supposed to happen here."

"What do you mean?"

"I mean with your brother. I explained our past. We both know he doesn't like me, and he wants to keep you as far from me as possible. How to you see that playing out?" His grip on the steering wheel tightened.

She scooted closer to him on the bench seat. Her hand

rubbed his thigh. "My brother doesn't choose who I date."

Connor didn't respond. There was nothing else to say. Maybe she believed that line of bullshit, but her family had more control over her life than she wanted to admit.

"They're my family. That's not going to change, and I do talk to Aiden often. He's not the same guy you beat up years ago. He turned his life around. I don't expect you to be friends with him, but you need to accept he's in my life."

Connor understood, but a small part of him hoped Aiden wasn't in her life regularly. She kissed his neck, in the spot that drove his crazy, and all of his focus turned to not crashing the truck. She inched away.

"How about dinner?" she asked.

"I was thinking we'd go straight for dessert."

"What kind of girl do you think I am? You should ply me with food and drink before you get in my pants."

Her joke lightened the mood of the truck, and the tension left him along with thoughts of Aiden. "I think I see a drive-thru up ahead. You want a Happy Meal?"

Chapter 11

THE FOLLOWING MORNING, FIONA PUSHED through the coffee shop door to see Aiden already waiting. Not surprising since he'd always been a morning person. She shoved her gloves into her coat pocket and hung her coat on the rack in the corner.

"What's up? This is an early start for you."

"I had a great weekend."

He sipped his coffee, but she just wrapped her hands around her cup to warm herself.

"What did you want to meet for?" he prompted.

"I wanted to tell you—so you can pass the word onto Mom and Dad—Connor and I are officially a couple." She raised a hand before he had a chance to argue. "I know you don't like him and I know why."

He bobbled his cup. A look of guilt stole across his face. It had been so long since she'd seen such an expression on him that she'd almost missed it. She reached across the table and placed her hand over his. "He doesn't do that anymore. He told me about his past. He spent time in prison, and when he got out his options for work were limited."

Aiden looked confused. "What are you saying?"

"He doesn't beat people up for money anymore. He builds furniture. It's beautiful furniture too."

Aiden's hand steadied beneath hers.

"I can understand why you wouldn't like him. Who would befriend some guy who beat the crap out of him? But you got yourself into the mess. And while a horrible job, it was Connor's job. Nothing more. I wouldn't go so far to say you had it coming, but it's not like you were some stellar citizen back then."

He slid his hand away from hers. "I'm very aware of the person I was. I've changed."

"So has Connor. I wish you could see that. He's kind and gentle and protective. You've been able to experience a clean slate because the Cavanagh name bought you forgiveness for your transgressions."

She stared into her brother's eyes, but couldn't read them. He was almost as good as Connor at masking his emotion. "All I'm asking is for you to give Connor a chance. I don't expect you to be friends, but like I told him, you need to find a way to accept you're both part of my life."

Aiden shook his head. "I don't know if I can, Fi. And what about Mom and Dad? Do you think they'll ever be okay with this?"

She straightened in her seat. "You know what? I don't care. I love him, Aiden. If you can't accept that, then you'll have to accept losing me."

"I don't understand what you expect from me."

"I want you to keep an open mind. Mom and Dad fixed your life. They taught you it was okay to skirt the law without consequence. How does that make you, or them, better than a man like Connor who served his time and still managed to make a decent life for himself?"

Aiden swallowed hard. "You're right. But I don't know if I can look at him and not think about the past."

"Well, you have about a week to figure it out. I'm bringing him to Thanksgiving dinner. If Mom and Dad have a problem with it, tell them to shoot me a text, and we won't come. Make sure they understand that if they lock Connor out, I'll be with him."

He nodded, but didn't say anything. He stared into his cup of coffee. She stood and patted Aiden's shoulder before gathering her things to leave. She'd given him plenty to think about. For the first time, she felt lighter after dealing with a member of her family.

She didn't know what she'd expected, but she felt sure and strong while talking to him. Then again, Aiden had never been the source of conflict in her life. She couldn't wait to tell Connor. She hoped he wouldn't say no. She wanted him to come to Thanksgiving dinner even though it was a family thing and they'd spend it with her family.

She'd spent the remainder of the day working on jewelry for her online shop. By the time the sky darkened outside, she'd finished three sets of earrings and two necklaces. It had been a productive day even though thoughts of Connor kept distracting her.

Her bell rang, stopping more images of Connor. She asked into the call box, "Who is it?"

"It's me."

Connor. She hadn't expected him since they hadn't made plans. She buzzed him up and waited by her door. When the elevator slid open, all she saw was his head poking above the cabinet he held. "What is that?"

He moved past her into her condo and straight for her

workroom. "Hold on. This is heavy."

She followed him and he set the thing on her table near the window.

He wiped his hands on his jeans. "After I watched you work, I noticed you didn't have any storage for your supplies, so I made you cabinet."

He turned and drew open drawers. "I think this'll be enough room for your pieces of china and chains and whatever else you have."

She was speechless. He'd made her a piece of furniture to help organize her junk. It was a beautiful cabinet, bare wood with pretty little mismatched handles on the drawers.

"I figured you'd want to paint it. Make it your own."

Fiona continued to stare at the cabinet, but she felt him shift uncomfortably. Connor was nervous? She ran her fingers over the smooth wood and looked into the empty drawers. "Wow." She had no better word.

His mention of paint made her remember her idea to paint the other night. The feeling she wanted to capture while lying in Connor's arms. Her heart swelled and she knew she'd be up all night painting. As soon as she dug out her paints and found a canvas.

She turned and jumped into his arms. "Thank you. It's awesome."

His chest fell in a heavy exhale. He *had* been nervous.

"Were you actually worried I wouldn't like it?" She pulled back from him embrace.

"No. It's a piece of furniture. If you didn't like it, I could sell it somewhere." He rubbed a hand over his head. "I didn't want you to think I was telling you what to do with your space." He glanced around the room and the perpetual mess scattered around. "I could never work like this, but you seem to like it. I didn't want you to think I made you a cabinet because you—"

"I get it." He didn't want to be like her parents who told her what to do. "You wanted to be helpful. I love the cabinet, but the mess will still be here. Having drawers to slide some of it into means I'll be able to find what I need a little faster. Hopefully. Plus, it'll save space for more stuff."

She moved back to the cabinet and started to think about how to decorate it. Simple paint wouldn't do. This needed something more. Maybe decoupage.

Connor hadn't said anything, but she'd felt him get closer. His hands ran down her back from her shoulders to her hips. He leaned forward and kissed the back of her neck. "I love seeing you in this room. So intent. Focused. Hot." He nipped at her neck again. "Want to go out and grab some dinner?"

She tore her eyes from the cabinet as her mind raced to find the right images to plaster to it. "Sure. What'd you have in mind?"

He stepped back and grabbed her hand. "You pick. Someplace with beer. I've had a crazy day."

They walked into her living room and she caught sight of herself in the mirror above the couch. She was a mess. "Wait." She pulled her hand back. "Let me go change and fix myself."

His eyebrows furrowed. "You look fine." He tucked a loose curl behind her ear. "Better than fine."

In the back of her head, whispering quietly, she heard her mother's voice. *Can't you put in some effort, Fiona? People will stare.*

But then she saw the heat in Connor's eyes and she knew she didn't care who stared as long as he was one of them. "Are you sure?"

"Yes."

She grabbed her purse and followed him out the door. Things had changed between them. The sharing of secrets opened them up and she hoped they didn't lose that. Being with Connor made her feel good.

Connor drove to the restaurant Fiona had picked. He hadn't asked about a dress code, but since she'd seen him walk in wearing jeans and a T-shirt, he figured he was safe. Hopefully they wouldn't have more than one fork on the table. He wasn't in the mood to have to think.

"Tell me about your day."

"A whiny customer. No big deal. Just tense." He'd been tense all day, worried about his confession to Fiona, terrified of her brother scaring her from his arms. The customer bitched about him fucking up a door. He was at fault because he'd been distracted.

So when he left the job site, he had to see Fiona. He used the cabinet as an excuse. The moment he looked into her eyes from across the hall, he felt settled. Calm stole through his body and he wanted to hold onto it forever.

They got to the restaurant, sat, and ordered. It was a family restaurant, but quiet. They tucked into a booth and shared some bread before their meals arrived.

"I saw Aiden this morning."

The sentence held no surprise, yet he choked on the bread. He gulped water to clear his throat.

She waited for him to breathe normally and look at her. "It was great." Her face brightened. "I told him about us, about you telling me about your past."

Aiden probably had a near-heart attack. Letting the secret slip would crush Aiden's carefully constructed life.

"I told him we're a couple and he needed to accept it."

"How did that go over?" He crumbled the rest of the crust

lying in front of him while picturing Aiden's outrage over how his sister could pick such a loser.

Fiona reached across the table and held his hand. "I went to Aiden instead of my parents for a couple of reasons. First, he'll at least listen to me. Second, if anyone can understand about changing and second chances, it's Aiden. That's what I told him."

"What?"

"I told him he had to give you a chance and he needed to pass the message on to my parents. I want you to come to Thanksgiving dinner with me."

His stomach lurched. He couldn't pretend the Cavanaghs didn't exist if they were face to face. "I don't think that's a good idea."

"It's the best idea. I need my family to understand that you're not going anywhere. If they don't like it, too bad. If you're not welcome, I won't be going."

He watched as her face became fierce. She was so open and honest; it hurt to look at her. She was willing to walk away from her family to be with him. For a brief moment, he imagined a life where he and Fiona were together without a single thought spared for the Cavanaghs.

But they were her family. It wouldn't be fair to make her choose. "I don't want to come between you and your family."

"It wouldn't be your fault. It's up to them. It's about time I stood on my own and made them, specifically my mother, realize I'm not a little girl anymore and I get to make my own choices." Her thumb stroked over his rough knuckles. "I choose you."

His heart stopped. It was the only explanation for the feeling of lightheadedness he experienced. Fiona's bright blue eyes focused on him and although she hadn't said the words, he knew what she meant. She chose him because she loved him. *Fuck.*

He stood abruptly. "Excuse me."

She jerked back. "Is everything okay?"

"Yeah, just going to the bathroom." He wandered the restaurant in search of the bathroom.

She loved him.

The knowledge clanged around in his head as a vice gripped his heart. She shouldn't love him. She had no idea who he really was.

But she believed she did.

He found the bar before he found the bathroom. He ordered a shot of whiskey and downed it quickly. The burn stung his throat and warmed his belly. The smooth sensation calmed his nerves. He wanted to believe he misread the signals. It wasn't like he'd had any experience with a woman falling in love with him. He closed his eyes and Fiona's face came to him.

In his mind, he saw it in her eyes. They didn't hide anything. Even when she tried, she did a horrible job. What else could it be?

Connor pushed off the bar and walked to the bathroom. He splashed water on his face and returned his breathing to normal.

Normal? How would anything be normal again?

He stared at himself in the mirror and smiled. Fiona loved him.

Fiona sat at the table and fiddled with the napkin on her lap. She'd screwed up. She wasn't sure how, but she knew she had. How much worse would his reaction have been if she blurted out the words that scrambled on her tongue?

I love you.

She wanted to say it. The need burned in her every time she touched him and he looked at her. But she knew it was too early. And now she spooked him with a Thanksgiving dinner invitation. She'd play it off like it was no big deal.

That's what Connor would need. He had a week to get used to the concept. She had a week to convince him it wasn't a horrible idea. What better way for her family to see that he was a good guy? If they saw them together, they'd be able to accept the relationship.

She looked over her shoulder, wondering where Connor had gone.

Sipping from her wine, she tried to develop her response for when he returned. A joke, a light comment. But what?

"Hey," his rough voice sounded at her ear as he leaned over and kissed the top of her head. His hand toyed with her hair.

She turned to face him and his kiss moved to her mouth. She tasted the bite of whiskey, and briefly wondered where it had come from, but it didn't matter. They didn't need words, not when a kiss put them on the same page. Whatever tension or uncertainty existed before disappeared.

He pulled away and reclaimed his seat across from her.

She stared at him, but before either could speak, the waitress arrived with their food. They mumbled a thank you, but didn't look at the server or the food. Just each other.

Then Connor smiled his oh-so-rare full-on smile, and she couldn't help but return it. "So, Thanksgiving. Should I have held on to the tux?"

"We're not formal, but my mom might have a coronary if you show up in your jeans and work boots."

With a nod, Connor turned his attention to the plate in front of him and attacked it. She didn't need to discuss her invitation. The moment had passed and Connor was dealing with it the way he needed to.

She wished she could have a moment, a brief glimpse into how he felt about it. He cared for her, desired her, but she felt like they had more. Or at least *could* have more. But Connor wasn't a sharer. And she didn't know how much longer she could tamp down her need to tell him. She knew she blurted out her feelings. Often.

Plenty of men in her past were annoyed by it. Some even broke up with her over it. She fell in love hard and fast. It was who she was, and she didn't regret it. Love made life worth living.

Being with Connor was different. Somehow, if he walked away because he wasn't ready for her love, or he didn't feel the same, she wasn't sure she could handle it. With him, she felt like she stood on the edge of a cliff. As much as she wanted to jump and feel the sheer joy of the fall, she wanted to cling to the edge, where he would keep her safe. She wasn't used to playing it safe.

"Something wrong with the food?"

Fiona blinked. She hadn't touched her food because her thoughts had taken over. She blinked again and smiled. "No, everything's good."

After dropping Fiona off at home, Connor went to Dermott's as much for another drink as for conversation with his friend. Dermott was the only confidante he had since prison. Before that, Aiden had held the spot. Now he couldn't think about Aiden without being assaulted with images of Fiona.

Surprisingly, though, he'd been able to think of her without thinking of Aiden.

He sat at the bar and waited for Dermott to be free. A good-sized crowd filled the bar, but not enough to warrant having an extra bartender on duty. Dermott poured him a Guinness without asking and Connor nodded his thanks.

With the first sip, he knew it wouldn't be a strong enough. "Get me a shot," he called out.

Dermott poured and leaned against the bar when he delivered it. "What's the problem?"

"What isn't?"

Dermott poured himself water and waited.

"Fiona's in love with me."

"Did she tell you that?"

Connor shook his head. "Didn't need to."

"That ought to be worth some leverage, huh? To get information on her daddy."

He slugged back the shot and chased it with a drink of beer. "Thing is, I don't want the leverage anymore. She's not like the rest of them."

"You sure? They're a wily bunch."

"Yeah, I'm sure." He turned the glass of beer in his hand. "What do I do?"

"If she's clean, then leave her be. Find some other way to make your story happen."

Story. He hadn't thought about his book. Even when he poked around Fiona's condo looking for information, or scrolled through stories on the Internet, it felt half-hearted. He'd expended so much energy to keep his secrets, there'd been little left for writing.

"You can't give up. The Cavanaghs should be exposed for the shit they do. For what they've always done. They act like they're better than everyone."

Connor's stomach tumbled. He didn't want to disappoint

Dermott, but the book wasn't going to happen. He was finally ready to move on. Dermott just wasn't aware yet. He turned his glass in a slow circle. "No one can touch the Cavanaghs. If I've learned nothing else over the years, it's that."

"But you can. You can show them they're touchable."

"I don't think I want to. It's not worth it. They're better at this game than I am." And Fiona would be crushed in the middle.

"After all the work and effort, you're going to walk away as if none of it matters?"

Connor sipped from his beer, glancing at Dermott over the rim. He never understood why this was so important to Dermott. The Cavanaghs hadn't done anything to him directly. He still had the ability to live whatever life he wanted.

Now was the first time Connor felt like he had the same chance.

"Shit, boy. What the hell?"

Connor set down the beer and looked at Dermott, confused.

"You're in love with her."

Love? "I didn't say that."

"No, but you got a stupid puppy-dog look on your face."

"What do you know about love?" To his knowledge, Dermott hadn't ever been in love. Unless you counted Connor's mother and he didn't think that relationship had gone anywhere, mostly because Connor had been arrested. He wondered if Dermott had kept in touch with his mom. Connor hadn't, wanting her and Danny to have a fresh start without his actions weighing them down.

"I know it makes you stupid." He sighed and shook his head. "But when it's right, it's worth every bit of trouble. Is she right?"

Connor shrugged. "I don't even know if it's love. She makes

me feel like a teenager, not wanting to worry about work or anything else. When I'm with her, nothing else matters. Not even the Cavanaghs. Shit, if her last name wasn't Cavanagh I wouldn't be having this conversation now. I'd let the relationship ride its course."

"But she is a Cavanagh."

Connor blew out a heavy breath. Talking to Dermott didn't help, but at least Dermott didn't seem mad about Connor not pursuing the book.

"If you care about her, you need to tell her the truth. About prison, her brother, the book, everything."

"If I tell her everything, she'll hate me. I don't know if I can handle that."

"She'll hate you more if you don't."

"I told her the important parts."

"What do you consider important?"

"I told her I went to prison. And that I beat the shit out of Aiden."

"That's only about half."

"It's the half that lets her know who I am, what she can expect."

"What about how you took the rap for a friend?"

"Who are you kidding? I did a stint in prison for money, not for Aiden."

Dermott dumped his water in the sink. "We both know money was only part of it. You wanted a better life for your mom and Danny. You knew prison would be harder for Aiden. You're loyal. She should know that about you. You're more loyal than all the Cavanaghs put together."

"They're pretty loyal to each other." Too bad their loyalty didn't extend outside the family. Aiden had been his friend. One who he'd expected to care while he was in prison. As soon as they'd been picked up, Aiden distanced himself, as if they'd never even known each other.

If he told Fiona everything, would she do the same? Would she pretend they'd never met?

"It'll never be real without honesty," Dermott said and walked away to serve other customers.

The alcohol wasn't making anything clearer for Connor. Every time he blinked, he saw the *I love you* look in Fiona's eyes. She hadn't said the words, but he could tell she struggled to hold them in.

He never wanted her to be afraid to tell him anything, but he couldn't quite wrap his head around the idea that she could love him.

Even after his confessions, and telling her about his past, she held fast. Nothing made her waver.

He didn't know if he could offer her the same.

Fiona didn't know what was wrong with her. The election was over. Her father's position was secure. She could fade back into relative anonymity. But she found herself checking in and reading Weston's blog a few times a week.

Something about it fascinated her. After she'd starred in the one post, she'd read the archives to better understand this guy. For the most part, he didn't sound like the nutjob she'd assumed. The archives revealed a man who fought corruption in the city the best way he knew how. The gossipy post about her and Patrick had been an anomaly she couldn't explain.

Which was why the post two days ago made her blood run cold. Weston had written about her father again, the first time in the week and a half since the election results. He accused her father of taking bribes to award construction contracts.

Fiona stressed over the bad press. Weston said he had a source, an anonymous insider. Once again, she questioned the rumors about her father's political dealings. Her father cared about his job, his position, and most important, the city. Every politician engaged in wheeling and dealing, and she was sure there was no way around it in a city like Chicago. For all the changes and reform, things ran the same.

She'd called her father after reading the post, hoping for reassurance.

"Fiona, it's after eleven. What's wrong?"

Shit. She hadn't thought about the time. "Sorry I'm calling so late, but have you read Weston's blog?"

Rustling greeted her question. She pictured her dad getting out of bed so he wouldn't disturb Mom. "Sweetheart, I told you not to read that trash."

"But Dad, this feels like he's on a hunt, coming after you specifically."

"He usually is."

"Have you read his posts beyond the ones about you?"

"Honestly, I haven't even read those."

She sighed. Of course he hadn't. He had people to do it for him. She wished she could explain why this post bothered her, why it made her question her father.

"Fiona, don't worry yourself over my career. We won the election. The people have spoken. They trust me. The naysayers will always attempt to knock me down."

"Okay." It wasn't quite the reassurance she'd hoped for, but he was right. She'd always avoided reading articles about him in the past. Why was she compelled to read them now?

Fiona disconnected and deleted the bookmark for Weston's blog.

She worked through the night and slept most of the day.

When she woke, she read the newspaper and wished she'd pushed harder to make Dad understand. The *Sun-Times* had picked up the accusations and Fiona felt her eyes fill as she read. If only she'd caught Weston's blog when it had posted instead of two days later. Then she could've pressed her dad, or worst case, talked to her mom.

The *Times* reported the Legislative Inspector General, a post her father helped create to fight corruption in the city council, was allegedly investigating her father. This was a legitimate paper, not some blogger with a grudge. They wouldn't print something without evidence to back it up.

Of course her father's only response had been his favorite: no comment.

Fortunately, the Inspector General didn't comment either. Maybe the sources being used for the story were misinformed.

Fiona spent the afternoon at the outreach center, knowledge of the accusations weighing her down. Her students showed no indication that they'd read the paper and made the connection between Fiona and her father. Sarah met parents at pick-up time, so Fiona avoided any questions.

As soon as the kids were gone, she drove to her parents' house, but when she saw the flock of reporters standing out front, she kept driving. She didn't know how long she drove around, but she didn't want to go home. Her nerves were frazzled and her worry about her dad gnawed at her, so she called Connor. "Hey. Are you at home?"

"Almost. What's up?"

"Have you seen today's paper?"

"No, I've been in Lake Forest finishing up some book-shelves."

"Can I come over?"

"Since when do you need permission? I've gotten kind of

used to you just popping up."

His tone was light, but she couldn't make herself go along. "I'm cranky and miserable and I need to hide out. I won't be good company."

"What happened?" His tone had shifted and she imagined his face becoming that cold distant stone she hated.

"I'll explain when I get there. You want me to bring dinner?"

"Sure."

"See you soon."

Fiona grabbed some Chinese food near Connor's house and breathed a sigh of relief when she saw no suspicious activity in the neighborhood. In the back of her mind, she'd feared someone would've ferreted out their relationship and she'd lose this refuge. It didn't matter that the entire concept was ridiculous. She only heard the echoes of Connor telling her that he'd never pass the test to be in the public eye.

Connor opened the door before she even knocked. The concern on his face undid her, and the entirety of the stress she'd smashed down all day bubbled up. He didn't say a word, just opened his arms and pulled her close. She sagged against him and let go.

Chapter 12

CONNOR HELD FIONA AND TRIED to figure out his next move. They couldn't stand in his doorway all night. It was getting damn cold out. He'd just gotten home a few minutes ago and hadn't had a chance to take a shower or look at the newspaper to see what had Fiona so upset. He inched away from the door so he could close it. Fiona sobbed silently, but her shoulders shook and his shirt became damp. Max whined beside them, knowing something was wrong.

"Come on, let's sit down and you can tell me about it." He led her to his new couch.

She sat before looking up, startled. Her eyes were red-rimmed and her cheeks were ruddy. "Where did this come from?"

Max plopped down on her feet, as if to make sure she couldn't go anywhere.

"I finally bought a couch. It was overdue." Besides, he needed to do something besides drink, which was how he'd spent his time without Fiona over the last few days. Every time he thought of her loving him, he sought out another drink.

He didn't have that problem now. When she was in his arms, it felt right, like the words didn't matter. He didn't know how to keep the doubt at bay when she went home.

Unless she didn't.

He forced the thought away and said, "What's wrong?"

She inhaled deeply and released a shuddering breath. "An article appeared today about my dad."

Of course. He should've figured as much.

"The damn political blogger is at it again. This time, he's saying my dad took a bribe from some construction company. The details are fuzzy. He says he has a source with information. Then the *Sun-Times* ran a similar story saying the Legislative Inspector General is investigating my dad."

He already knew most of what the Cavanaghs did had to do with money. "Is it true?"

She shrugged and fresh tears streaked down her face. "I know my parents aren't perfect. But this...this is my dad going against everything I really thought he believed in. There have always been accusations, but he swore they were false. I haven't spoken to him since last night, before the *Times* article. He told me not to concern myself with the naysayers."

She was more naïve than he'd suspected. Talk about living life wearing rose-colored glasses. She curled next to him and settled her cheek against his chest. It was much easier to comfort her when he didn't have to look into her eyes.

"I'm not totally naïve, but I want to trust my parents, especially my dad. When rumors spread about my dad and he dismisses them, I want to believe him. I should be able to trust my parents. Every politician faces rumors and allegations. I never saw any proof not to believe my dad. Something feels different this time."

Connor didn't know how to respond. As much as he despised

her parents, he wanted to comfort Fiona. He hated them even more because now they'd hurt her. Instead of talking, he simply stroked her back to help her calm down and relax.

Fiona pushed away from his chest and used the bottom of her shirt to wipe her face. Her bright blue eyes glistened and still held a look of hope even in spite of her parents.

Connor held her hand and kept his mouth shut. Anything he said would come out as criticism, and she didn't need to hear that.

She pulled her hand free. "Let's eat before the food gets any colder. I'm sorry I rambled on so long. You're probably starving."

"It's fine. That's what I have a microwave for." He sat and held her until she calmed.

The quiet was a reminder for Connor to get a TV for the living room. Having the mindless noise in the background would've helped. He still didn't know what to say to make her feel better. His words would either be filled with hate or they'd be lies. He'd had enough of lying to Fiona. From this disaster, though, came the reassurance that she could never find out about her parents paying him to go to prison for Aiden.

Although he couldn't imagine her holding it against him, it would definitely drive a wedge between her and Aiden, and the more he found out about Aiden, the more he began to believe the man truly had changed. Aiden wasn't the spoiled rich kid he'd been. And he was Fiona's ally, one who understood their fucked-up family.

After a long time, Fiona pushed up and looked into his eyes. "Thank you for everything."

"I haven't done a damn thing. I didn't even buy you dinner."

"You were here for me. And you're letting me hide out here to avoid my family and the press."

"It's no hardship. I like having you here, and so does Max." The dog had followed Fiona's every move. Connor had never seen him so attached to anyone.

"Max is good for sadness. It's no wonder you love him." She lowered herself and gave Max a hug. When she straightened, she rubbed her eyes. "If it's okay with you, I'm going to take a shower."

"Whatever you want." He cupped her jaw and kissed her, hoping it would offer her some comfort.

After the kiss, she hugged him tightly and whispered, "I love you," before running up the stairs.

Connor sat, stunned, unable to move until he heard the bathroom door close and the shower start. His heart hammered at hearing the words.

He'd known. He'd known, but he'd been trying to block it out for days. Not knowing what to do, he went to the kitchen and popped open another beer. Alcohol wouldn't fix anything, but he might feel better on his way to finding some answers.

Love was a step he'd tried to ignore with Fiona. He cared about her more than he thought possible, but *love*? He'd never loved a woman before, so he didn't know what it was. All he knew for sure was that Fiona had taken residence up in his heart and mind and he could no longer imagine his life without her. A few days without seeing her made his life feel empty.

He thought about keeping his past with Aiden a secret without doing damage to his relationship with Fiona. Which would be more destructive—the truth or a lie?

∞

You're such an idiot. Fiona berated herself in the shower. She'd learned over the course of many relationships that talking about love caused more harm than good, especially early in the relationship, but the words just popped out. Connor excelled at making her feel healthy and normal. And she had needed that after holding everything in the entire day. Her mother would've been proud to witness how bottled up Fiona was. At least for the day, until she saw Connor. For some reason, seeing him made the emotion spill out.

Then she had to ruin it by admitting she was in love with him.

When she stepped fresh from the shower, smelling like Connor after using his soap and shampoo, she hesitated. She didn't know what to do because she had nowhere to go. If Connor freaked out because of her admission, she'd have to leave. Going home or to her parents' house or Aiden's didn't appeal to her, so she called Sarah.

With a towel wrapped around her, she walked into Connor's bedroom and flipped on the TV. Maybe her parents hadn't made the evening news. Something had to go her way, right? Sarah answered as the news anchors began with national headlines.

"Hey, Sarah."

"How are you holding up?"

"I'm okay. I just…" Even thinking about what she did made her feel like an idiot. "I told Connor I love him."

"You did what?"

She sank onto the bed and turned the volume down on the TV. "I don't know how it happened. When I got here, I fell apart. He didn't criticize me or tell me what to do. He just held me. And then the words slipped out."

"What did he say?"

"Nothing. I didn't give him a chance. I ran upstairs to take a shower, but I'm pretty certain he's downstairs freaking out, trying to decide how to get rid of me." She finger-combed her curls while keeping an eye on the news. "Now I'm pacing in his bedroom, starving because I brought dinner and left it in the living room."

"You need to chill out. Go down and get some food. Don't mention the whole love thing unless he brings it up. And really, what man ever brings it up? I think you're safe."

Sarah got quiet, which worried Fiona. "What's wrong?"

"I wasn't sure I wanted to tell you, but as long as your night sucks anyway...You should know that reporters showed up at the center after you left. I don't know if they were looking for you, but they did ask questions about your family's donations. I don't know how any of it fits with the accusations. I think they were grasping for anything."

"God, I'm sorry."

"You have nothing to be sorry for. Besides, the questions were pretty mundane and they got bored quickly. It's not like I could say anything bad about your family's foundation and their involvement with the center. They give me money and never check on it. I like hands-off donors."

Fiona laughed. "My parents are good at hands-off. Should I stay away for a few days?"

"It might be best. You hate the press, and I don't know if they'll be back."

Fiona's stomach sank. She loved working at the center and teaching art. She hated that her family caused a spotlight to shine on the center in the midst of bad publicity. At least Sarah's news briefly took her mind off Connor. Until her stomach growled.

She said good-bye to Sarah and turned the volume back up on the TV. A knock on the door startled her.

Connor pushed the door open.

"Why are you knocking on your own bedroom door?"

The corner of his mouth lifted. "I didn't know if you were ready for company." He took in her appearance and added, "You look good in my towel."

"I was wondering if I could borrow a shirt." At this rate, she'd end up with half his wardrobe in her possession.

He reached into his dresser and tossed her a shirt. "I heated up dinner if you're ready to eat."

No mention of love. No crazed look seeking escape. No admission on his part. Fiona didn't know exactly what she'd hoped for. She hadn't driven him away, and she should be grateful. She pulled the T-shirt on and forced a smile. A pair of socks smacked her in the face.

"I know how cold your feet get and there's no way I'm letting you warm them up on my calves." He grabbed the remote from the bed and turned off the TV. "I think a media blackout is in order. You don't need to worry about your parents' mess."

How did he know exactly the right thing to say? This was the reason she loved him, but she was afraid to point it out, so she simply said, "Thanks."

He put his arm across her shoulder and walked her downstairs and into the kitchen. Max howled at the back door to be let in.

Connor swung the door open and Max walked straight over to Fiona. "You do know you're my dog, right?"

Fiona squatted and petted Max.

"Shit. I can't compete with that. No wonder the dog chooses you over me."

"What?" she asked as she straightened.

He looked at her bare legs and the shirt riding high on her thighs. She smacked his arm. "That's just wrong. Your dog likes me. Don't turn it into something gross."

He swung her into his arms. "I like seeing you smile. I was afraid I wouldn't get to see that tonight."

Fiona felt her smile broaden. This man was good for her. She hadn't felt like smiling. Not at all, until he made silly jokes. His arms banded around her and she allowed herself to relish the strength in them as if he could restore her reserves. At the moment there was no better place on the planet.

Connor held Fiona tight and enjoyed knowing he'd made her smile. He couldn't talk about love, but what else explained the feelings he had for her? He didn't even know what love was supposed to feel like. But he knew he couldn't live with the pain he'd seen on her face. She looked defeated and it worked against every vision of her he had.

He released her and set plates on the kitchen table. He planned to do everything in his power to make this a regular night. To give Fiona every bit of normal he could.

She dumped rice on her plate and added vegetables and beef. "This looks delicious. I'm starving. I forgot to eat before I went to the outreach center." She began to shove food into her mouth and moaned in satisfaction.

Connor helped himself to food, unsure of conversation. He and Fiona never lacked things to talk about, but he didn't want to say the wrong thing. He wanted to avoid bringing up anything that might make her think of her parents. Luckily she seemed talked out. She snuck Max a few pieces of beef under the table, ensuring her status as best friend.

They finished eating and cleaned up the dishes. "Let's rent a movie or something," he offered. Anything to avoid the news.

"Sure. But I might not make it to the end. I'm pretty beat."

They walked upstairs and Connor was struck by the thought that they were going to bed with no plans to have sex. He knew he could get Fiona in the mood if he wanted; it wasn't difficult. But all he really wanted was to comfort her, give her a safe place to be. He'd never had similar feelings for another woman. To spend time with someone, sure, but to invite her to his bed for what? To cuddle? What the fuck was happening to him?

He took a quick shower before crawling into bed and handing Fiona the remote. She clicked through the channels and settled on some sappy chick movie. Twenty minutes in, Fiona nestled against his chest with an arm wrapped around his waist, and dropped sound asleep. The movie murmured in the background as he used his phone to access the news. The latest headlines about her family caused anger to bubble up.

He'd never understand how she came from the Cavanaghs. She was kind and giving, and the rest of them knew nothing but how to take and put themselves first. As much as she seemed to distance herself from them, though, she never completely cut ties. He couldn't help but think she'd be happier if she could.

They slept together all night, with Fiona half on top of him. Max whined at the foot of the bed and Fiona grunted and rolled over. Connor slid from the bed, let Max out, and started a pot of coffee. He had a couple of estimates to do and a small cabinet to finish in the basement. All he wanted to do was crawl back in bed with Fiona and pretend the rest of the world didn't exist. Halfway through his first cup of coffee, Fiona walked into the kitchen, her hair like a fiery bush. He took another drink to hide his smile.

"What are your plans for today?" she asked as she poured

coffee into the cup he had waiting for her.

"A couple of estimates and some work downstairs. You can stay here as long as you need."

She shrugged as if his invitation wasn't a huge step. He didn't trust anyone enough to leave them in his house.

"I don't have any clothes and nothing to do here. I'd go crazy. Sarah wants me to stay away from the center for a few days until things settle." She drank her coffee and stared past him out the window.

He'd never seen her so distant, so unlike herself.

"Can I use your computer? I put some new pieces on sale and I want to check if I have any bites."

"Sure. Go ahead. There's some food in the fridge if you're hungry. I'm going to grab a shower before I go."

He left his coffee on the counter and went upstairs. Navigating relationship waters wasn't something he knew how to do, but this edged toward the ridiculous. He had no idea what else to do for her.

When he got out of the shower, Fiona was sitting in front of his computer with tears streaming down her face.

He rushed to her side. "What is it? What happened?"

She pointed a shaky finger to the computer screen where she had multiple windows open to various news sites. Each window had a headline about her parents. He leaned over and scanned the top article. Sources revealed Brady Cavanagh's campaign funds were being investigated. The Inspector General commented that a ward employee filed a complaint about campaign work being done in the ward office. It looked like the rumors had opened the floodgates for legitimate accusations.

"I thought we agreed on a media blackout." He reached over and turned the screen off.

"I checked my email, but the headline just stared at me, so I had to read it."

Connor grabbed her hand and pulled her out of the chair so he could wrap his arms around her.

"It's true, isn't it?"

"I have no idea." At least he was able to answer honestly.

"But there wouldn't be an investigation unless they had reason to look. So even if my parents didn't misuse campaign funds, they must've done something else." She pushed away from him and rubbed roughly at her eyes. "I don't know what to believe about my parents anymore. And it's not like I can call them and ask for the truth."

"Maybe you need to distance yourself from them and their problems. Let them handle it." He knew it was more wishful thinking because the Cavanaghs would want the family to show a united front like they had for the election. And he wouldn't be able to be there for her. He would never be allowed in the inner circle.

Not that he'd want to be included.

She took a steadying breath. "You're right. This problem has nothing to do with me."

He pushed one of her crazy curls behind her ear. "Want to go to work with me?"

Her eyes crinkled. "Why?"

"It'll get you out of the house and away from your phone and the TV. I'm mostly driving around to do estimates, but you can keep me company." He liked the idea of spending the day with her, showing her his work.

"I don't even have clothes to wear. I don't think so."

"I'll bump my first appointment and we'll stop by your place."

She suddenly looked nervous. "With this new development,

reporters might be at my place. They were at my parents' house yesterday."

"Then I'll go and pick up stuff for you and bring it back."

"Are you sure? You've already done enough. I don't want to impose."

"I wouldn't have offered if it was an imposition."

She chewed on her lower lip and finger-combed her wild hair. "Okay. If you're sure you don't mind."

"One condition."

Her brow furrowed.

"No more news—no TV, Internet, newspaper. Grab a book to read."

She rose on tiptoe and kissed his cheek. "I think I can handle that."

Fiona watched from the window as Connor drove off. Her phone rang and she cringed. She didn't want to even look at the screen, but she couldn't help it.

It was her mother and she knew better than to answer. Nothing Sheila said would make her feel better. But maybe she was calling to tell Fiona it was all lies. The reporters had gotten it wrong and her dad was safe.

The phone stopped ringing while she ran scenarios through her head.

The idea of her dad's safety hadn't occurred to her. What if the investigation did turn something up? Would he go to prison?

In recent years, Illinois made a point of sending dirty politicians away. She couldn't picture her dad behind bars, wearing an orange jumpsuit. Maybe that was only in movies. Whenever they showed the former governors on TV, they weren't wearing orange.

She shook the silly thoughts from her mind. Her imagination ran wild. So some reporter made accusations about her dad being dirty. That didn't make it true. Over the years she'd learned that her father's enemies would say anything to take him down. There were always rumblings, but an investigation was different.

Even now, her default setting was to defend him. What was wrong with her?

Her phone rang again, startling her. She looked at the screen. Aiden. He'd be a voice of reason.

"What's going on, Aiden?"

"Hey, I wanted to check on you because you didn't answer for Mom."

"I'm avoiding her because I didn't want to get in the middle of this mess, but I saw the news. Is it true? Are our parents crooks?" She paced the length of Connor's bedroom, wanting to crawl back into bed, but knowing she wouldn't find any peace.

"I don't know."

Something in the way he said it worried her, like he believed in the possibility. "What aren't you saying?"

"Weston saying he overheard a conversation is most definitely a lie."

"How do you know?"

"Because Dad would never be stupid enough to have that kind of conversation in public."

Fiona heard all the words Aiden didn't say. Not that Dad wouldn't have such a conversation, just that he wouldn't risk being overheard.

"There are a lot of things you don't know about them, Fiona. Things they've shielded from you."

Her stomach churned. Secrets never set well with her. Keeping secrets always made things worse. "Tell me."

"It's not my place to tell you."

"How do *you* know? Why would they tell you, but not me?" She knew the answer of course, but she didn't want to acknowledge it. Her parents didn't trust her.

"I know things mostly because I figured them out. Other things, Dad consulted me on. You know he's been trying to get me more involved, wants me to run for office. It was a natural progression to include me."

"You're still not telling me anything."

"What do you want to know?"

"Are they guilty?"

Silence answered and she knew that was bad. Aiden always had an answer. It might not be the one she wanted, or the one she liked, but he always had one.

"Maybe. That's the best I can do."

Fiona sank to the edge of the bed and tried to process the noninformation. A lump formed in her throat based on the possibilities.

"Lay low for a few days while we figure things out."

His words barely registered. *We.* They were excluding her again, but this time she felt relief. She had no intention of running into the fray, so she didn't need to be told to lay low. Obvious advice was useless. Whether Connor would still want her here after a few days was another issue, but for now she was safe.

The thought was absurd. She had no reason not to feel safe. So her world was crumbling, but she'd done nothing wrong.

Using Connor's advice, she grabbed a paperback from his shelf and snuggled back in bed to wait for him, the security of his anonymity comforting her.

Chapter 13

THE FOLLOWING DAY, FIONA WAS still a mess. She hadn't slept. Connor had been thoughtful enough to grab a bunch of her supplies so she worked through the night on her jewelry, something to give her focus. As tired as she was while standing in his kitchen, she knew she couldn't continue to hide out. The media blackout Connor had imposed helped momentarily, but it wouldn't last. She couldn't let it.

She needed to face her parents. She deserved to hear the truth from them.

Her nerves churned the coffee in her stomach.

"You're up early."

Fiona turned to face Connor. "Good morning."

"You didn't sleep at all, did you?"

She kind of shrugged with half headshake, too tired to care if he fully understood.

He kissed the top of her head as he reached past her for the coffee pot. "You need to get some sleep."

"I'm going to go see my parents." She liked that her voice sounded stronger than she felt. It enabled her to straighten her shoulders and shore up her confidence.

"Why?"

"I want answers. I'm tired of them keeping everything from me like I'm some stupid little kid."

Connor leaned against the counter and drank his coffee. "What do you hope to get out of it?"

"I honestly don't know. I'm just so mad. I feel like my whole life is a lie, and I deserve better. I'm tired of the lies. I always believed that whatever my dad did, he did for a good reason, so when he'd effectively pat me on the head and send me off, I let him. I can't imagine he's a criminal though." She dumped the rest of her coffee in the sink. Connor didn't say anything, but having the chance to say it all aloud helped.

Connor pulled open a drawer and dug through the items. When he turned to her, he held a key in his hand. "Here. I'll be out all day at a job. You can let yourself back in whenever you want."

She didn't reach for the key because she didn't want to read more into the gesture than he meant. Her daydreams would always be her downfall. "You don't need to give me a key. I'll go back to my place."

"It's up to you, but this gives you options. I know you like to escape." He set his coffee on the counter and grabbed her hand. He curled her fingers around the key. "You don't have to use it, but you have it if you want to."

Connor lowered his head and kissed her. Her roiling stomach settled at his touch and she wished she could bottle the feeling to take with her to her parents' house. When he pulled away, he tucked hair behind her ear. "Let's have dinner together."

"I don't need you to babysit me. I'll be fine."

"I'm not coddling you. I want to see you for perfectly selfish reasons."

A smile broke out on her face. "What would those reasons

be?"

"After dinner, I get to have you for dessert."

She wrapped her arms around his neck and kissed the sensitive spot behind his ear that made him twitch. "Where do you want to go for dinner?" she whispered against his neck.

"Right here."

"Deal. What time?"

"Call me when you're done and we'll figure it out."

The strain in his voice had her holding back a laugh. She stepped away and smacked his hip. "Get to work before I make you late."

To keep herself from making him late, she went upstairs and changed her clothes. Connor managed to bring quite a few things from her closet, but she couldn't decide what to wear. What kind of outfit declared, "No more crap. I want the truth"?

Knowing she didn't own anything that made such a statement, she settled on jeans and a sweater. After a quick good-bye to Max, she drove to her childhood home. She circled the block twice because reporters filled the sidewalk in front. From down the block, she called her father.

"Hello."

"Hey, Dad. I'm parked down the street. What's the best way for me to get to the house?"

"Come in through the back. Fewer reporters nosing around."

"Okay. I'll be there in a few minutes." She grabbed the hat Connor had bought for camping, tucked as much of her hair into it as she could, and walked down the alley. A couple of reporters spotted her, but didn't make the connection until she entered the yard, moments too late to mob her. She let herself in the back door and went straight to her father's study near the front of the house.

His door was open and she looked around the room before saying anything. As a child, this room had always been off-limits, but sometimes she'd sneak in and sit in her dad's chair. It made her feel important to be in his spot because she recognized him as an important man. As much as things changed, they weren't all that different. She still idolized her dad.

He looked up from the papers he held, pen poised to write. "You're here."

She took off her jacket and sat across from him. "What's going on, Dad?"

"What do you mean?"

She pointed to the window behind him where the drapes were drawn tight. He usually left them open for the natural light, he wouldn't want to make it easy for the photographers outside.

"It's nothing you need to worry about."

"Don't do this. Reporters are camped out here. They're bothering Sarah at the outreach center. This is something."

"We've been through this before. People will try to take me down. It won't happen." He shuffled the papers and set them down. "Your mother will be glad you're here. You know how she likes to rally the troops."

"I'm not here to rally. I'm here for the truth." The tension knotted her shoulders and her throat tightened.

"What are you talking about?"

She stood and started pacing. She didn't how to word this, what she really meant. "I want to know if the accusations are true."

"Absolutely not. How can you even think that of me? Of us?"

"I don't…or at least I haven't, but now… This information can't be completely fabricated. It must come from somewhere.

Are you telling me there is no truth to any of it?"

His cheeks flared, but she wasn't sure if anger or embarrassment or guilt caused it. Her dad was flustered, though, and that *never* happened.

"I've worked to make this city better. Every choice I've made has been to improve the lives of my constituents."

God, all she wanted was for him to say that it was all a lie. That he was still the man she'd always believed in. But he didn't. He covered with campaign promises and political rhetoric. And in that moment, she knew her father was guilty. Of how much was the only remaining question.

She stared at her father with new eyes. How had she never seen it before? The shift in his eyes, the twitch in his cheek. "I deserve better than the crap you spew at strangers. Tell me the truth."

"How dare you come in here and accuse me, young lady?"

"I'm not a little girl any more, Dad. I'm an adult and the things you do have an impact on me, no matter how much I've tried to keep it all separate. It's always been there, creeping at the edges of my life, but now it's in my face."

"I am innocent."

"I wish I could believe you. Just tell me one thing. Is the outreach center okay, or is this going to spill over to more than a few random questions about you?" She crossed her arms and stared at the legs of his ornate desk. She didn't want to face her father, afraid he'd tell another lie.

"Every penny we gave to the outreach center we gave because we care about you and your interests."

Always a lawyer. He hadn't said he'd done nothing wrong, nothing illegal. How close to the line had he traveled?

"Fiona, darling, you're finally here," her mother called from the hallway.

Fiona turned toward the door as her mother came rushing into the room. She reached up and cradled Fiona's face with both of her hands. "You haven't been sleeping. What's happened?"

She pushed away from her mother. "What's happened? How can you even ask? Our family is all over the news. People are accusing Dad of being corrupt."

Her mother waved off Fiona's concerns as if swatting a fly. "That's nothing. Our people are working on it now. We'll be fine. I'm worried about you. Aiden said something about you bringing this Connor character to our family dinner for Thanksgiving. What's that about?"

Fiona couldn't believe her mother focused more on a stupid dinner than the accusations. "I care about Connor. He's a good man and he's part of my life now. If you have a problem with him being here, than you can expect me not to come."

Her mom blinked rapidly as she tried to process Fiona's words. "Well, of course he's welcome to join us," she stammered.

From the corner of her eye, she saw her dad flinch. They obviously hadn't discussed this. "I appreciate it, Mom, but with all of this attention on us right now, I don't know if we'll be here. He doesn't want to be part of this circus."

Her mother had moved on to straightening items around the room: fluffing pillows, shifting statues, and rearranging a handful of coffee table books. "Our life is difficult, but not a circus. Your father and I have spent years cultivating the appropriate image for this life."

"I'm not part of your image, Mom. You point it out all the time. Nor do I want to be part of the image. I want to know who my parents are. I never thought the rumors were true. I always believed you when you said it was nothing to worry about. But this feels different."

"It's not," her father finally said. "In the past few elections, you haven't noticed because I ran uncontested. There remains a certain contingency that would like me removed from office. They're playing dirty. I've been down this road before and I'll make it through to the finish line as I always have."

Why did she feel like she was on a Tilt-a-Whirl, spinning and spinning and going nowhere? She came for answers so she'd feel better, but her parents continued to talk around her instead of to her.

"I'm going home. What should I tell reporters when they inevitably stop me?"

"Tell them no comment. Do not engage them," Dad ordered.

As if she wanted to *engage* them. "Fine."

"Fiona, stay," Mom said. "I haven't seen you for so long and you've been ignoring my calls.

"I've been ignoring you because you try to run my life."

"Really, Fiona, sometimes I think you should've been an actress instead of an artist. You do enjoy the drama."

Fiona let out a frustrated scream. "You need to hear me this time, Mom. Do not try to dictate what I do with my life. Not my career, not who I date. Nothing. You have enough to worry about with Dad's mess. Stay out of my life, or I'll ignore you so much you'll wonder if you really have a daughter."

"Fiona." Her dad's voice was sharp.

She felt like a teenager again, trying to win approval and independence. Fiona stared at her parents and she knew. They would never change. They would always treat her like a child.

Grabbing her coat from the chair, she simply said, "Good-bye, Dad," and brushed past her mother without a word.

She darted out the back door and practically ran to her car.

Not that it stopped the reporters from following, yelling questions at her back. She only hoped they wouldn't follow her. She needed peace.

∞

Connor worked all day, but he worried about Fiona. He'd tried calling and left her a text. She responded with a quick, **I'M FINE. I'LL PICK UP DINNER.** He had no idea what happened with her parents or where she was.

Normally, it wouldn't bother him; he liked being alone and not having to worry about other people. It had been one of the reasons why he'd given his mother money and sent her away. But Fiona crawled under his skin and tangled in his instincts. He wanted her to talk, to be herself.

Maybe she needed some time and space. By dinner, she'd be ready to let him in.

When he got home, he knew Fiona was there because he saw her car parked in front. She was curled up asleep on his new couch with Max guarding over her. She needed to sleep to make up for what she hadn't gotten the night before, so he walked quietly past her and into the kitchen. He expected Max to follow, but the traitor didn't.

It was sad how his best friend chose a woman over him. Not that he could totally blame the dog. Fiona had many fine attributes. He checked the oven and the fridge and found no food. It didn't look like Fiona had gotten dinner, so he ordered a pizza and went up to shower. She slept through all his moving around.

The pizza arrived and the doorbell finally woke her. She sat up, startled, and looked around like she had no idea where she was. Connor paid the delivery guy and brought the pizza to the couch. "Hey," he said.

"Hey." Her voice was scratchy and he wondered if she'd been crying. "Sorry. I meant to go out and pick up dinner, but I sat down and the couch totally sucked me in. It's a great couch."

"You were exhausted. Feeling okay?"

She nodded and he wanted to pry, but didn't. Fiona curled her legs under her and sniffed at the pizza. "I'm starving. Let's eat."

Connor flipped the box open and went to the kitchen for a couple of beers and napkins. When he came back, Fiona was already chomping on a slice. Although she smiled at him, it didn't brighten her face. The simple muscle movement meant nothing. They ate in silence and once again, Connor wished he had a TV or radio or something in his living room. Quiet and solitude never bothered him as much as it did while Fiona sat beside him.

She looked him over. "You don't work like that, do you?"

He glanced down at the unbuttoned jeans he'd pulled on so he could pay the delivery guy. He flexed the muscles on his bare chest. "Why? Do you think it'll bring in more customers?"

"I'm sure it would, but I don't want other women to see what I get to see. It'll make them horribly jealous."

As much as he enjoyed her teasing, he didn't want her dodging the issue at hand. "How did it go with your parents?"

Her teeth sank into another slice of pizza and cheese stretched out as she pulled it away from her mouth. She chewed and rolled her eyes as if she had to develop an answer. He didn't like this practiced version of Fiona. He liked the woman who blurted and rambled.

"It was fine, I guess. Looking back, it's what I should've expected."

Which told him exactly nothing.

"While I listened to my parents, I had this amazing realization. Just because I'm their daughter doesn't mean I need to be part of what they have going on. I don't need to try to make it better and I certainly don't have to suffer for it." She returned to her pizza.

He'd been trying to get her to understand exactly that. "Sounds like a plan. How do you feel, though?"

"I'm still frustrated. And a little sad because they never let me in. They treat me like a kid, sheltering me from everything and, especially my mother, trying to run my life. I thought I was okay before, but I wasn't. I acted like I did whatever I wanted, regardless of my parents, but it was never true. I feel like my whole life is a lie."

Connor slid closer to her and put his arm behind her head. "We're not a lie, and we have nothing to do with your parents. Your art, your jewelry—that's no lie either." He sipped on his beer and tried to form the right words. "I don't think your life has been a lie as much as it was you choosing not to fight. Sometimes the fight's not worth it."

She settled next to him and picked at the label on her beer. "How do you know when the fight is worth it?"

"When it bothers you enough, you need change. That's all it is. You're ready for something to change. I only hope it's not us."

She turned and kissed him. As she deepened the kiss, she climbed onto his lap and straddled him, her cold bottle of beer pressed against his shoulder. Pulling away from the kiss, she leaned her forehead against his. "I don't want us to change either. I think you're the only thing keeping me sane right now."

He took the beer from her hand and set it alongside his on

the coffee table, then set to pulling off her clothes. Fiona was quiet as he kissed her and ran his lips across her chest and down her stomach. He loved every inch of this woman and he had no words to describe it.

Max began to whimper and Connor tried to ignore him, but then Fiona let out a yelp. "What?" he asked.

"Max rubbed his cold nose against my back. I think he needs to go out."

Connor grunted. First the dog ignored him to hang out with Fiona and now he was stopping Connor from getting laid. He shifted Fiona off his lap. "Don't move."

He stood and rubbed his hand on Max's head. "Come on, boy. Let's go." In the kitchen, he grabbed Max's bowl and filled it with water. He let Max out and hoped the dog would be satisfied until he finished.

Connor returned to the living room and although Fiona looked like she was in the same spot, he knew she'd moved because her bra and underwear were gone. Seeing her naked and splayed out on his couch made his dick throb. He dropped his pants and then knelt in front of her. He grabbed her knees and yanked her to the edge of the couch, spreading her legs.

Her breaths became shallow and he saw she was already wet. He dipped his head and swiped his tongue over her. She sighed with the movement, so he did it again, slower this time. Now, her breath hitched. He looked up at her and her blue eyes were hazy with lust. He lowered his head again and she closed her eyes.

Connor bit her inner thigh, making her jump before soothing it with his tongue. Her hips began to wiggle as he swirled his tongue over her and then sucked on her clit. Her right hand slapped down on his shoulder and her nails dug in. He waited for her to issue some demand, but she didn't. She let him do what he wanted.

He wanted her slow and writhing and ready to scream his name. He needed her to know that whatever secrets they'd had between them, this was no lie. They were more real than anything he'd ever known.

Later, Fiona stretched out next to him on his bed. Her head lay on his chest and she swirled her fingers around the hair there. They'd made love on the couch, but they'd gotten cold. Another item to add to his shopping list: a blanket for the living room. They got Max settled in for the night and came upstairs.

"What are you going to do about your parents?" he asked.

"There's nothing I can do. Like you said, I never fought anything. Now, I know I need to. I'm not ready to walk away from my parents. I mean, they're my family and I love them. But I deserve to have my own life. That much I made sure my mother understood. I don't know about the rest." She pushed up on him to look into his face. The room had darkened, but light from outside glinted against her pale eyes. "My dad's guilty of something. He dodged too many of my questions for me to believe he's innocent. I still want to believe him, but it's what he's not telling me that worries me."

Connor knew she should be worried. Brady Cavanagh didn't deserve her trust, but Connor had no way to explain it to her.

"I'm tired of the secrets and lies. When I lied to you about my last name, it gnawed at me the entire time. I can't understand how they live their lives shrouded in lies and secrets. How do they function?"

He stroked her back and toyed with her curls. "Maybe they lied to protect you. I can understand. Sometimes a lie is easier if it keeps people you love safe." He hoped his secrets protected her and what they shared.

Fiona fell silent for a minute, then she pushed all the way to a sitting position. "No, I don't buy it. One lie leads to more. The whole tangled web and all. At some point, don't you lose yourself? Become more of the lie and less of who you are?"

How could he explain that his lies, his secrets, allowed him to become more of himself? It sounded ridiculous. "As much as you didn't like lying to me about your name, did you ever feel less than yourself?"

She flopped back down against the pillow beside him with a groan. "How do you do that?"

"What?"

"Make it sound okay. Lying about my name allowed me to be myself because I didn't have to worry about whether you wanted something from my dad. There was no history attached to me because of who my family is. But I don't think it's the same when it comes to my parents and their lies." She inhaled deeply and released the breath slowly.

Connor watched the rise and fall of her chest and the shadows playing across her skin. He couldn't help her come to terms with her parents. He could only offer shelter for the fallout, whatever and whenever that might happen.

Chapter 14

THE NEWS ABOUT THE CAVANAGHS faded over the next couple of days, but Connor had a feeling the other shoe hadn't yet dropped. He also knew he had to address his history with Aiden. He wasn't sure how to approach it, but it needed to be done. To Fiona, he said, "I need to talk to Aiden."

She looked up from his computer where she'd been checking her online sales. "Why do you need to talk to my brother?"

"We have to talk about our past. I don't want you caught in the middle of the crap we carry between us." Although he didn't want to keep any more secrets from her, or lie to her, he didn't want to explain everything either. She'd spent a lot of time with Aiden over the last few days and she always looked better after being with him. He somehow steadied her, like a big brother should.

A crooked smile spread over her face. "You're going to not only start a conversation, but actually open up about your past? Can I get a video crew in for this?"

Her quip didn't amuse him. This was hard enough.

She rolled her eyes, but said, "I can invite him to dinner."

"No, this is something between us. I don't how ugly it will be, so I don't want you there. Can you give me his number?"

She scribbled it on a scrap of paper and handed it to him. She reached up and smoothed her hand across his jaw. "I appreciate you putting in the effort with Aiden. It means a lot to me."

Her lips pressed against his gently, reminding him once again how amazing this woman was. He would do whatever necessary to make things work because he wouldn't lose her.

He offered her one more kiss good-bye and left the room to go to work. In his truck, he called Aiden. Not surprisingly, he didn't answer, so Connor left a message.

Hours later, while in the midst of installing a seat in front of a bay window, Connor received a text from Aiden. He wanted Connor to come to his office at six.

Connor shook his head. Just like a Cavanagh to demand a time and place. But for Fiona, he'd suck it up and go to Aiden. He'd prefer neutral ground, but at least in Aiden's office no one would misconstrue it as a social visit.

At six on the nose, Connor stood in front of a Northside office building signing in with a security guard. It looked like reporters had gotten bored with Aiden, which hopefully meant they were done with Fiona as well. If so, she could go home, but he wasn't in a rush for that to happen. He'd become accustomed to having her in his home and he enjoyed it. He rode up to the eighth floor and practiced his approach.

The elevator doors slid open. Aiden stood in front of him and all calm, practiced thought fled. Anger and resentment bubbled up, so he swallowed hard. "Aiden."

Neither extended a hand. Aiden barely offered a nod of acknowledgement.

"My office is this way. I assume you don't want to have a

discussion in the hall."

"Whatever." He followed Aiden.

Aiden glanced over his shoulder and said, "Thanks for coming here. I had a late meeting, and I have a conference call coming in at seven, so leaving would be difficult. It was too much to explain in a text, so I didn't."

Connor didn't respond, but he understood Aiden's reasoning. Aiden's office was big and decorated to express success. Connor couldn't see the Aiden he knew comfortable in this space. Brady Cavanagh would be at ease here, but Aiden?

Aiden gestured to a chair, but Connor couldn't sit.

"I'm glad you called. I've been wanting to reach out to you, but I wasn't sure how you'd react." Aiden leaned against the edge of his mahogany desk.

"Worried I'd kick your ass?"

"Maybe a little." Then a slight smile turned the corners of his mouth and Connor saw a glimpse of his friend.

"I'm here because of Fiona. She told me she laid out an ultimatum to your family. I had nothing to do with that. I have no desire to be with your family for Thanksgiving or any other holiday, but it's important to her." He jammed his hands into his pockets. Standing there, he knew he and Aiden appeared as opposites. Aiden with his classy suit and styled hair and Connor with his dusty jeans and sweaty T-shirt.

"You haven't told her."

It wasn't a question, so Connor didn't know how to respond or what Aiden expected.

"Why not?"

Why hadn't he? The simple answer was because he loved Fiona. "Telling her wouldn't accomplish anything. Like your father said, we had an agreement and we both upheld our end. If I told Fiona, I doubt it would've affected on my relationship with her, but it would cause a rift between you and her. Regardless of my feelings about you, she cares for you. When all the shit with your family hit last week, I knew she couldn't handle the extra lies and secrets."

"I appreciate it more than I could ever say. Is that the reason for your visit? To tell me our secret is safe?" Aiden stood with his arms crossed as if readying for negotiations. His father must love seeing this side of him.

Connor paced. He still wasn't completely sure of his reasons for coming here, but he knew it had to happen. Part of him needed to know he wouldn't feel the urge to attack Aiden, and he didn't. More than anything, he felt a deep sadness over lost friendship. "I love your sister."

The words came out strong and clear. Aiden probably shouldn't have been the first person he declared his love to, but what the hell. "I need to know that you and your family won't try to sabotage it more than you already have."

"I have no plans to do anything, and you should know by now I can't speak for my parents. They'll do whatever the hell they want."

Connor stepped closer to Aiden and studied his old friend. "Make sure they know that if they try to ruin this, Fiona and anyone else who'll listen will know the truth."

"Are you threatening me?"

Was he? Connor hadn't necessarily meant to, but yeah. What were his other choices? Beg? He knew better. "Take it any way you want. If I lose Fiona, I'll have nothing left, so it won't matter."

Connor turned away and headed for the door.

"I'm sorry, you know." Aiden's words were quiet, but stopped Connor. "I was young and fucked-up."

Connor turned back to Aiden. "So was I."

The comfort and confidence Connor had seen in Aiden disappeared.

"I never meant for you to go to prison. I just didn't want to go. My dad gave me a way out and I took it. I didn't even know what he'd done until it was over."

"That's bullshit and we both know it. You could've ended it at any time. All you had to do was come forward."

"I was scared. And you never seemed to be. Nothing ever got to you."

Connor huffed out a breath that almost sounded like a laugh. "I wasn't brave. I was stupid. I thought I'd make a quick buck off your dad and go on my way. It never occurred to me that I'd lose my entire life."

"I lost those three years too. Everything I did for three years was self-destructive. More than usual even for me."

"I lost a fuckload more than three years. A felony never goes away. People look at me like I can't be trusted, like I'm still a criminal. Most never even ask what I went to prison for. My entire life has been limited by one stupid choice." The anger he felt fizzled. He saw the sorrow etched on Aiden's face.

Connor's feet were rooted in place. "If you were so bothered by everything your father designed, why did you disappear? Not one visit in three years."

Aiden rubbed a hand across his mouth. "I couldn't face you. I couldn't face everything I'd done, so I pretended none of it existed. Abandoning you was the shittiest thing I did. You deserved better."

It should've made Connor feel better, but it didn't. "Yeah, well, none of it matters now. Life goes on."

"Does it?"

Connor's eyes narrowed.

"You say you love my sister, but part of me thinks you're

looking for revenge."

Connor looked at the floor. Like everyone else, Aiden couldn't believe he'd changed. Guilt tugged in his chest remembering how he'd planned to use Fiona to do that. "The thought crossed my mind. But then I got to know her and I realized she's nothing like the rest of you."

Aiden shifted against his desk. "So you really love her?"

Connor nodded.

"Where do you see this going?"

"I have no fucking clue. But it's up to me and her."

"I can respect that, but my father won't. He never liked you, never saw what I saw, what Fiona obviously sees. Watch your back."

"Threatening me?" Connor's gaze locked on Aiden's face offering a cold hard stare.

Aiden shook his head. "No. It's a friendly warning. I have no idea what my dad is capable of. Not anymore."

The phone on his desk rang and Connor backed up a step. "I'll let you get back to work."

Connor left unsure if the meeting actually accomplished anything. It didn't feel like much, but it had been a long time coming.

Connor stood in his living room and stared at the couch and then at the bare walls, trying to decide how to arrange his meager furniture and where to hang the new flat screen TV. After he'd left Aiden, he'd gone shopping. He wanted his house to start feeling more like a home. Having Fiona there made a difference.

He shoved the couch to spin it again as she walked in. He looked at her from over his shoulder. Her broad smile made something turn over in his chest. As she unwound a scarf from her neck, she asked, "What are you doing?"

"I finally got a TV for in here and I'm deciding where it should go. Any ideas?" He straightened and leaned against the back of the couch.

She tossed her coat on the newel post and came to him. Something felt so right about her coming home to him that all he could do was gather her in his arms and kiss her. She melted against him the way she always did. With his hands on her ass, he said, "I think I like your ideas."

"I wasn't suggesting anything. I simply wanted to say hello."

"Well, hello then."

She pushed away from him and turned in a circle looking at the space as if she hadn't seen it before. She pointed to the wall he'd been considering for the TV. "If you put the TV there, the glare from the sun will hit it depending on the time of day." She moved to stand near the windows, and pointed to the wall adjacent. "But if you put it there, you can have the couch here. The room would still be open and airy."

But the position put his back to the door, which made him uncomfortable. "What if I put the couch directly in front of the TV?"

"It could work, but having the couch in the middle of the room might make it feel smaller."

He spun the couch again and slid it back a little. The space behind the couch made a walkway to get to the kitchen and the room might've felt a little smaller, but he lived alone. How much space did he need?

Fiona flopped on the couch and picked up an imaginary remote. She pointed at the wall and pretended to click. She tilted her head as if she watched TV.

She was so damn cute.

"You're right. This is a good spot."

He joined her on the couch and decided the TV could wait. "What are your plans for tonight?" he asked while shifting closer to her.

She twisted on the couch, creating more space between them. "I drove by my condo today. The coast is clear. Although the investigation is ongoing, no one seems interested in me."

"That's good." He laid his hand on her thigh and began massaging.

She covered his hand with hers to stop the movement. "It's safe for me to go home. I came here to grab my stuff."

She was leaving? Connor blinked a few times. She wasn't leaving him. She was just going back to her own house, where she belonged.

But it felt like she belonged here. "You don't have to go. I like having you here."

"I appreciate you letting me stay and hide out from the craziness, but—"

"But nothing. My house has plenty of space. I have a whole bedroom upstairs that isn't used."

"What are you saying?"

What was he saying? He had no idea because he hadn't planned this. He just knew he didn't want Fiona to go. "I guess I'm asking you to move in with me."

"You guess?"

He nodded. Probably not the most romantic offer, but it was real. "I like having you here. I don't see why we wouldn't make it permanent." He searched her face. "Unless you don't want to?"

Connor studied her face and waited for an answer. As usual she was open and he saw the argument in her eyes. She wanted to be here with him, but she was unsure if they were ready.

"It's kind of fast, don't you think? I mean, we only met each other a little over a month ago and for more than half that time, I lied about who I am." She played with his fingers still on her leg.

"Not about who you are—only your last name. Everything else was true. I could see that, which is why I wasn't too upset."

She sighed. "But then there was all my family drama. It's like we haven't had the opportunity to be a normal couple."

He had a feeling they would never be normal, but he didn't feel the need to say it. "At least think about it. There's no hurry. I'm not going anywhere."

"That's good to know." She interlocked her fingers with his.

∞

The rest of the night, Fiona's head was filled with questions. Connor's invitation seemed to come out of nowhere. Sure, they'd been practically living together for days, but it had been out of desperation on her part and kindness on his. Living together was a huge step. As often as she thought she'd fallen in love with a guy, she'd never taken that step. Things always fell apart before she could get there.

Then there was her family and the fallout she'd have when she announced she was living with Connor. She waited for panic to hit her at the thought of the inevitable confrontation, but it didn't happen. Maybe she really did no longer care what her parents thought.

She'd helped Connor hang the TV in the living room. Well, she'd mostly stood there and handed him tools, but she offered suggestions for art for the walls and a rug for the floor. He told her to go pick out whatever she liked. What guy told a woman to decorate his house if he wasn't serious about living with her?

She rolled over in Connor's arms and watched him sleep. The biggest question pounded down on her. Did he love her?

He cared for her and desired her, but he didn't talk about his feelings. Maybe he never would. He'd been up front about not being a sharer. What she couldn't decide was how important the actual words were. Did she need to hear them?

Being in Connor's arms, in his bed, in his house, felt natural and right. She felt more at home in his space than she did in her parents' house and she'd grown up there. The enormity of the decision and this next step in their relationship stayed with her, though. What if a few weeks from now, he decided she was too clingy or he couldn't handle her family?

"What are you doing awake?" he whispered without opening his eyes.

"Nothing."

"I can hear you thinking. It's loud. Some of us have to work in the morning." Although his eyes remained closed, the corner of his mouth quirked up.

"Sorry. I'll try to turn it down."

He kissed the top of her head. "You don't have to decide now. Forget I asked if it helps. It's okay."

She tucked her head under his chin and burrowed into his warmth. She'd never been cautious about much in her life, why was she doing it with Connor? "You might regret asking."

"Nope."

"A few weeks of looking at my jewelry mess might drive you over the edge."

"Does that mean you're moving in?"

A smile took over her face because she had been stressing over the way things should be instead of listening to her heart. "If you'll have me."

He shot up and slipped her over. So much for him being

asleep. The man moved like a ninja. His body pressed hers into the mattress. "You know I'll have you."

Instead of following with a smirk, he kissed her gently and reminded her why she loved him.

Connor's morning routine woke her, but she was more alert than usual. Maybe because she'd been getting more sleep. Connor was an early-to-bed, early-to-rise guy, the complete opposite of how she lived. It was another reminder of the adjustments they'd have to make.

He sat on the edge of the bed and tied his boots. "Coffee's made. I already let Max out, but since you're here, he'll get you to let him out again."

When he stood, he got quiet, like he was preparing for something. "You haven't changed your mind about moving in, have you?"

"In the last few hours while I was asleep? Nope."

He leaned over and planted a quick kiss on her lips. "When do you want to bring your stuff over?"

She shrugged.

"How about this? You go grab a couple of bags today and then this weekend I'll go with you and we'll pack up."

Because he'd distracted her with excellent kisses last night, she hadn't considered the logistics of moving in with him. What was she supposed to do with her stuff? And her condo?

"Uh-oh. I know that look. What's wrong now?"

"I didn't think about what to do with my stuff and if I should sell my condo. I can't pay two mortgages."

"If it'll make you feel better, keep the condo for now. Maybe sublet it. Take your time deciding what to do with it, as long as you're here while you're thinking. I don't need your help with my mortgage. I didn't ask you to move in because I want your money."

Nothing like having a pushy man. "Okay. I'll bring my clothes today. Where should I put them?"

He straightened away from her. "Wherever you want. The closet's empty. All my clothes are in the dresser. Move whatever."

No way could he be this laid back. Maybe she'd leave her stuff in suitcases until they brought her furniture. She didn't want her moving in to displace him.

While her mind headed into planning mode, Connor had headed toward the door. "I should be home by six unless I run into problems. Are you going to be around all day?"

"I might stop by the outreach center. I miss the kids."

"See you when I get home."

Fiona loved hearing those words more than she thought.

Sarah looked up from whatever boring forms she was filling out and smiled at Fiona. "You look happy."

"I am. I was relieved to see no reporters lurking around here. Has it been quiet?"

Sarah laid the papers down in front of her. "They came back when the second story broke about the investigation into your dad, but nothing since. I was going to call you and tell you the coast was clear, but I figured you'd need time to deal with your family stuff."

Fiona plopped into the chair in front of Sarah. "I tried, but failed, so I've been with Connor this whole time."

Sarah's eyes narrowed. "This *whole* time. Like in his house without him?"

Fiona could barely contain her excitement. Ever since Connor left this morning and she began planning what to bring from her apartment, everything felt so real. "He asked me to move in with him."

"What?" Sarah jumped out of her chair and came to the other side of the desk to sit beside Fiona. "When? What did you say?"

"He asked yesterday when I pointed out the reporters were gone from my house and I could go home. I told him yes last night. Or I guess it was technically morning."

Sarah's lips pulled down. "Please tell me you didn't make a decision like this while in an orgasm-induced haze."

"No. Although the celebratory orgasm was so worth it. I was going back and forth in my head about whether it was the right time, or if we were moving too fast. But then I listened to my heart. It feels right with him. I love him."

Sarah settled back in her chair and folded her hands on her crossed legs. "You've been in love before and I'm not aware of you ever considering moving in with a guy."

"No one ever asked before, or let's face it, I would've. At first I wasn't sure if he was sure, but Connor doesn't make a move unless he's sure."

"Does he love you?"

"I think so?"

"So he hasn't said it."

"No. He doesn't talk about feelings. He's an excellent listener though and he didn't freak out when I told him I love him. That's gotta count for something, right?"

"I'm not going to be able to say anything to change your mind, so I won't try. Are you happy?"

"Yes. Extremely."

"A simple 'yes' would've been fine. You don't need to rub it in. I assume you haven't told your family yet." Now Sarah leaned forward in her chair.

"They know I'm with Connor. I told them if they couldn't accept it, I wouldn't be around."

Sarah let out a low whistle. "Ballsy."

Hearing Sarah's compliment bolstered her ego. Sarah had been after her for years to fight her parents over their crazy expectations even though it might cost the outreach center funding. Now, she wished she'd done it earlier. It was freeing.

But she didn't think she would've done it if she didn't have Connor at her back. She knew he'd support whatever decision she made because he didn't want anything from her parents. He was exactly what she'd been looking for in a man.

"When I did it, it wasn't so much a ballsy move as a need for them to understand. Plus, I delivered the first blow via Aiden. I told him so he could carry the message to Mom. It might've been a little cowardly, but I choose to see it as a strategic move. You know how my mother gets when she's blindsided." She'd watched her mother lash out at everyone in her path when Aiden had gotten into trouble as a teenager. The woman could get downright vicious.

"Since your parents didn't flip out and lock you in a tower, congratulations are in order. Drinks on me tonight." Sarah stood and reclaimed her position behind her desk.

Fiona stood, itching to get back to teaching art to a group of eager kids. "Sounds great. Do you want to go right after we leave here, or do you want to go home and change first?"

"Are you asking because you need to go check in with your new roomie?"

"No, I'll text him and let him know." At the door, she turned back to Sarah. "Thanks for being such a great friend. I know you picked Connor because he looked temporary, and you easily could've tried to dissuade this relationship, but you've been great."

"I know I'm wonderful. Now if only the rest of the world would see that."

Fiona let out a laugh. Sarah was one of the most hardworking women she knew, but often overlooked. It was one of the many reasons why Fiona had gone to the Cavanagh Foundation for money for the center. Sarah had been trying to do it all with nearly nothing. She should be recognized for how wonderful she was.

On her way to the classroom, Fiona shot off a text to Connor to let him know she was teaching this afternoon and then going out with Sarah.

Immediately her phone buzzed with a response: **SHOULD I BE JEALOUS?**

Fiona snickered and answered, **NO, BECAUSE I'LL BE COMING HOME TO YOU.**

She imagined the smirk on his face and knew she'd made the right decision. She wanted to go home to Connor. She opened the classroom door and was greeted by questions and yells and friendly smiles.

This was exactly the life she wanted.

∞

Connor ate leftover pizza for dinner and scrolled through channels on the TV in the living room, which still felt weird given that he'd lived in the house for a couple of years and had never used the living room for anything other than a passageway. Max sat at his feet and chomped on the crust Connor tossed to him.

In the two years he'd lived in the house, it had never felt empty, but without Fiona and her chatter, he was lonely. Her upbeat attitude balanced him out and he found himself looking forward to it.

He should go to bed, but he wanted to be awake to say good night to her, even if she didn't join him in bed right away. He'd cleared out the few boxes he'd had stored in the extra bedroom so she'd have a place to work. Her worktable should be the first thing they moved in. As he tried to imagine all of Fiona's clutter in his house, he started to doze off.

Connor had no idea how long he'd been out, but Max's scampering across the floor woke him. Fiona struggled to drag a suitcase through the door. He jumped up to help her.

When he easily picked it up with one hand and pulled her close with the other, she smiled. "I knew having a big, strong guy around would come in handy."

"I'm handy for a whole lot of things."

"Don't I know it." She leaned up and kissed him.

He tasted alcohol on her tongue, but she wasn't drunk. Her eyes were clear and she was happy. "Were you celebrating something tonight?"

"Hmm-mmm." Her eyes fluttered closed and she came closer for another kiss.

"Are you going to tell me what?"

"You."

"Me?"

"We were celebrating me moving in with you. And me telling my parents they had no choice but to accept you. And me getting back to the center to work because the kids missed me."

"A lot of celebrating. Anything else?"

A goofy grin crossed her face. "Nope."

"Ready for bed?"

"Not really. But I'll tuck you in if you want."

He turned and pulled her with him as he headed up the stairs. "Will you be naked when you tuck me in?"

"Maybe."

"Asking you to move in was definitely an excellent decision."

Chapter 15

FIONA HAD NO IDEA WHAT was going on with her body when she found herself wide awake again at six in the morning. The only time she voluntarily saw six was by staying up all night. Now she feared it would become habit. Connor tried to be quiet when he woke and got ready, but as soon as he left her side, her eyes opened. Even on Thanksgiving, he rose as if he needed to go to work.

She tossed off the covers and got up. She'd do some work and then take a nap. After pulling on some sweatpants and a T-shirt, she settled in at Connor's computer. She really needed to bring hers and set it up. His was like a dinosaur. She heard him downstairs and she figured he was finishing his first cup of coffee.

While the computer booted up, she wrangled her hair into a knot on the top of her head. She opened the Internet and Connor's email program stared at her. She never considered herself a truly nosy person, but when something's right there... Most of the subject lines read from customers, but something near the bottom of the page caught her eye and she froze.

Her nerves tingled and her stomach turned. She blinked her eyes. She must've imagined it. She scrolled down and read the subject line RE: THE CAVANAGH CONSPIRACY – OFFER. She wanted to unsee it, but couldn't. Her finger hovered over the mouse button.

Connor had a right to privacy, but she also had a right to honesty. She clicked. She only read as far as the first line before nausea hit her. She stared at the single line through the blur of tears. Not Connor. He couldn't be like the others.

Dear Mr. Duffy,

After careful consideration, and in light of recent events, we would like to acquire your book, THE CAVANAGH CONSPIRACY.

A book. He'd written a book about her family.

She heard his footsteps on the stairs, but she didn't move.

"Hey, sweetheart," he said as he set a cup of coffee at her elbow and kissed the top of her head. "I'm surprised you're awake."

She swiped at the tears rolling down her cheek.

"What's wrong? What happened?"

She shot out of the chair, knocking the coffee over. She glanced at it running off the edge of the desk. "You happened, you lying piece of shit. How long did you plan to carry this out?"

He grabbed a discarded towel from the floor and mopped at the coffee. "What are you talking about?"

His eyes were wide with concern. At least that's what it looked like. But now she couldn't trust appearances.

She jabbed her finger at the computer screen. "Your book. Someone wants to *acquire* it."

He froze and face fell. "It's not what you think."

She shoved away from the desk. It felt like a hand reached

into her chest and twisted her heart. "You didn't write a book about my family in order to publish it?"

"I... It—" He ran a hand over his mouth and looked at the floor.

"That's what I thought." The tears were making a virtual river on her face, but she couldn't stop them. They dripped onto her T-shirt leaving little wet splotches. "How could you? I trusted you. You made me feel like my last name didn't matter."

"It doesn't." The words were barely a whisper. When his eyes met hers, they had regained their strength. "It mattered when we first met, but then I got to know you and it didn't matter anymore."

"You'll have to excuse me for not believing a single word coming from your mouth." Her gaze darted around the room to identify how many articles of clothing she had lying around. She went into high speed and scooped them up and shoved them back into her suitcase.

"What are you doing?"

"What does it look like I'm doing? I'm leaving you." She closed the suitcase and zipped it. When she grabbed the handle to heft it, his hand closed over hers.

"Don't. Let me explain."

She hated that the warmth of his skin reached all the way into her soul and she yanked free of his grasp. "There is no explaining this. You're just like everyone else in my life. Always looking for a way to use the Cavanagh name. Use me."

His face, so full of emotion, turned to stone. "Use you? You've used me for weeks. Just like the rest of the Cavanaghs."

Even shrouded in anger, she couldn't resist asking. "What do you mean 'just like the rest of the Cavanaghs'?"

Connor's eyes narrowed. "Writing a book isn't my only secret. The real secret, the one behind the book is that I used to be friends with Aiden. The night of the hit-and-run? Not only was he with me, but he was also the one driving. Your father paid me to confess to the crime. So don't you dare talk to me about using people. I only tried to give you whatever you needed."

She needed lies? Her mouth went dry and she almost gagged on the dryness of her throat. It couldn't be true. He was making this up to hurt her. She clamped her lips shut to stop the trembling. An all-over shiver shook her body.

He stepped closer, a mere breath away, and the heat radiating from his skin warmed her.

His voice barely rose above a whisper as he said, "Please. I love you, Fiona. Don't leave."

She released the suitcase as if it had shocked her. Her breath hitched. She stared at him. How she'd longed to hear those words from him. How she wanted to know how he felt. And now he soiled every emotion she'd had for him. Before she could think, her hand flew up and struck him across the face. "Fuck you. I'm done with liars."

Leaving the suitcase on the floor, she fled from the room, pausing only to grab her coat and purse by the front door. She rushed outside, the cold wind whipping at her wet cheeks causing them to sting as if she'd been slapped. Her palm held an identical burn.

She sat in her car, but didn't start it because her hands were trembling. Her crying had slowed to the annoying hiccups and she couldn't catch her breath. She laid her forehead against the steering wheel and focused on nothing but breathing. Simple task. Suck in air slowly, then release. But her chest hurt and the air couldn't force its way past the fist lodged in her throat.

Fiona had no idea how long she sat in her car, praying Connor wouldn't follow her out. She couldn't handle another confrontation. Finally, she slid her arms into her coat and tugged at it until it was no longer bunched behind her back. She started the engine and turned the heat on high in an attempt to warm herself.

The cold was so deep, she never thought she'd thaw again.

Connor stared at the empty doorway, unable to move. His heart raced and he couldn't suck in adequate air.

Fiona left him.

His brain couldn't quite process what that meant. Her suitcase sat at his feet. She would come back and he'd explain. He hadn't told her about the book because then he would've had to tell her about him and Aiden. He'd already walked away from the book. It didn't mean anything.

How could she not know that?

He turned to the computer sitting on the desk, the glowing light mocking him. He picked up the monitor and threw it against the wall. It shattered with a pop. Max whimpered and scurried in the opposite direction.

His past was still fucking up his life. Max edged forward and nudged his hand. Connor sank to the floor and held his dog. He didn't know how to fix this. He'd managed to do the one thing he swore he wouldn't. He hurt Fiona the same way her family had.

He stayed on the floor until his backside was numb. He finally pushed up and took Max to let him out. Then he grabbed a bottle of whiskey and sat on his couch to drink. The alcohol would do its job and numb everything.

Fiona drove with tears blinding her. She'd never felt so alone in her life. She needed answers, so she drove to her parents' house in search of the truth. When she got there, she realized her family expected her for Thanksgiving dinner hours from now. She was dressed in the sweat pants and T-shirt she'd put on at Connor's. Pushing through the front door, she called out, "Hello?"

Her voice was rusty from crying and she swallowed hard to try to clear it.

"Fiona, what are you doing here so early?" her mother asked and peered around. "I thought you were bringing a date." Then she glanced down at Fiona's attire. "What's wrong?"

Only after she took in the ratty clothes did her mother notice Fiona had been crying. Mother of the year she was not.

"Where's Dad?"

"In his study. Dinner's not for hours. You have plenty of time to change and get ready."

Not even a question about why she'd been crying. Fiona shook her head and walked to her father's study. He looked up from the file he held. "Fiona, what's happened? Why are you crying?"

She inhaled a slow, deep breath, determined to keep her voice steady. "I left Connor. I think you were right about him. I found out this morning that he wrote a book about us, well, probably more about you."

Her father rose from behind his desk and approached her. "I'm sorry, Fiona, but I warned you."

She jerked back. Even as she stood there, clearly upset, he still felt the need to say *I told you so*. "But you never explained exactly why you needed to warn me. Did you, Dad? You neglected to tell me about your past with Connor."

The shiftiness in her father's eyes appeared again. She could probably sell that small piece of information to the highest bidder. *Brady Cavanagh's eyes shift and his cheek twitches when he's getting ready to lie.*

"I want the truth, Dad. Did you pay Connor to confess to a crime Aiden committed?"

"Yes." He said it without flinching, without remorse.

"What kind of people are you?"

Her father tucked his hands into the pockets of his very expensive suit pants. "We're the kind of people who protect our children. I always taught you I would take care of you no matter what."

She wondered if he ever left the politician behind anymore. Everything coming from his mouth was a sound bite. "This wasn't getting Aiden out of a ticket, Dad. He hit someone while driving drunk and took off. Isn't part of your job as a parent to teach responsibility?"

So much about her brother made sense now. He'd changed after his encounter with Connor. He strove for perfection in his life to make up for all the earlier mistakes.

Dad went to the cabinet and poured himself a drink. "What would going to prison have done for Aiden? It would've ruined his life and any chance of a good career."

She flung her hands up at him. "What about Connor Duffy's life and career? Who thought about him?"

"He was well paid for what he did. It took care of his family in a way he couldn't." Her father stood there, swirling his drink like he was talking about the next move for his stock portfolio.

He was so sure in his convictions that she knew nothing she said would change his mind. He didn't believe he'd done anything wrong. For the first time, she saw her family in a clear light. Aiden suffered for the things their father had done on his behalf, and he never thought he'd get out from under it.

Their father loved them; she believed that. But he was a master manipulator, always needing control. And dear old Mom, worried most about appearances and how their name was reflected in the public eye.

They belonged on a nighttime soap.

She loved them, but she couldn't do this anymore. She needed to live an honest life and they couldn't live without their lies.

Any lingering doubt she'd held about her father's culpability in the conspiracy and bribery charges faded. Her entire being felt empty. Everything she'd believed about her life was based on a foundation of quicksand.

She didn't even have words for them. She simply turned and walked out the door. By the time she got to the curb, her mother called from the house. "Fiona, where are you going? Will you be back?"

Fiona didn't respond. She wasn't sure how to respond. Right now she didn't want to have anything to do with her family and sharing a holiday meal was the furthest thing from her mind.

Driving through the city, Fiona tried to ignore all the holiday traffic. Families traveling to see loved ones. Her body had finally settled into a strange kind of peace. It wasn't relaxation as much as emptiness. She couldn't deal with the frenzy of emotions, so she shut them down.

After driving for over an hour, Fiona pointed her car in the direction of Sarah's house. Her brain scrambled to remember what Sarah had said her plans were for Thanksgiving. She hadn't planned to travel home for the holiday. Fiona knew that much.

When she knocked on Sarah's door, she prayed her friend was home. Sarah opened the door and the tears started again. How many tears could one human being produce?

"Oh, my God. What happened?" Sarah reached for her and ushered her into the townhouse.

Fiona sucked in a hitching breath and swiped her sleeves on her cheeks. "Everyone in my life is a liar except you."

"Wow. Uh... Let's sit down and you can explain."

Fiona sat on the couch, curling her legs up and hugging them. "Connor wrote a book about my family. A publisher wants to buy it."

She looked at Sarah who took the seat on the opposite end of the couch. She saw the anger in her friend's eyes.

"That's not even the worst of the lies. He'd known who I was from the very beginning. After my cousin's wedding he told me about his past and why he thought our relationship couldn't work. He was in a hit-and-run accident while driving drunk. Went to prison for it. He made me believe he thought we couldn't be together because of his felony."

She took a slow calming breath before continuing. "He neglected to mention he and Aiden had been friends. More importantly, Aiden had not only been with him that night, but it had been Aiden who'd been driving. My father paid Connor to confess and go to prison for my brother."

"Oh, my...shit. I don't even know what to say."

Fiona rested her cheek on her knee. "There's not much to say. I don't even know who I want to be most mad at. Connor lied about who he was and he had these ulterior motives the whole time we were together. The entire time I was falling in love with him because he allowed me to be myself and wanted nothing from me, he planned to ruin my dad.

"But my father. Christ. He's not the man I thought he was. I always, *always* believed in him. He's a good man working hard for the city. I stood by him and defended him. I can't believe he did that to Connor. And then kept it from me and lied to me about it. It makes me wonder what else he's guilty of or capable of if he could do that to Aiden's friend."

Sarah scooted closer and put an arm around her. Fiona would not cry anymore. These people didn't deserve her tears.

"What are you going to do?"

"I'm not sure. I need some distance from everyone. That's why I came here."

Sarah rubbed a hand down Fiona's back. "Hon, you can stay as long as you need."

"Thanks. I knew I could count on you." Fiona straightened her legs and stretched. All the crying had exhausted her, emotionally and physically. "I hope I didn't ruin your plans for today. If you need to go, I'll be fine."

Sarah shrugged. "I'm meeting some friends for dinner later. You're welcome to join us. They won't mind. We're a ragtag group who meets up for every holiday because we don't have any local family."

Fiona shook her head. "I won't be very good company. I think I'll take a nap and develop a plan. My parents will look for me sooner or later. I need to have a response ready."

"Go take my bed. I have some work to do."

Fiona stood and Sarah followed. Fiona hugged her. "Thanks again."

Once settled under the covers, Fiona wasn't sure she'd actually be able to sleep. She closed her eyes and focused on each individual emotion roaring through her. For now, she shoved aside the rage. Betrayal was a strong one, probably next in line behind the rage. Connor betrayed her trust, but having all of the pieces to the story created mitigating circumstances. Her family had wronged him in ways she couldn't wrap her head around.

It didn't justify him lying to her and making her feel like they had a future together. God, how could he have gone so far as to invite her to move in with him? He knew she loved him. It was no secret.

Lying there, warm beneath the covers, she heard his whisper. *I love you, Fiona.*

And another tear fell.

∞

The pounding in his head became louder, so Connor took another swig from the bottle, but it didn't help. Then a far-away voice called, "Open up."

Connor pushed himself to sit up and realized the pounding was at the front door, not in his head. He shoved off the couch and stumbled to the door. It took a second to register that Aiden stood staring at him. All he had was a second before Aiden rushed at him swinging.

Aiden's fist connected with Connor's jaw and the bottle of whiskey flew against the wall and shattered.

"You son of a bitch," Aiden growled.

Connor felt himself weave, but put up his fists in defense. Aiden came at him again and instead of swinging a punch, Connor lowered himself and rammed into Aiden's midsection, carrying them both into the wall. He felt the air whoosh from Aiden's lungs and grim satisfaction filled Connor when he heard Aiden suck in a wheezing breath.

He released Aiden and stumbled back. Aiden leaned over with his hands on his knees.

"Come on," Connor taunted, his voice slurring. "You wanted a fight. Come beat the fuck out of me."

Aiden swore and came at him again. The physical pain felt good. Better than the emotional onslaught he'd been hiding from all day. Connor let Aiden pummel him until Connor lost his balance and his knees hit the floor. His lip split, and he tasted blood. His cheekbone throbbed an incessant beat. "Just finish it."

"You look like shit," Aiden said.

"Feel like it." He sank back until he sat on the floor.

Aiden slid against the wall until he sat across from him. "What the hell were you thinking? Why would you do that to her?"

"Do what?"

"I heard about the book. I get that you want revenge or retribution. But why involve Fiona? You told me you loved her."

Connor felt tears burn his eyes and his throat tightened. "I do. That's why I didn't tell her anything. The book was before. Before her. Didn't matter anymore."

"You fucked up good this time, Duffy."

Max howled at the back door. Connor flopped on his back and hit the floor hard. The room spun and he inhaled deeply to stave off nausea.

"Is your dog gonna attack me if I let him in?"

"Uh-uh." Using his voice hurt. Footsteps vibrated the hardwood and a moment later Max's nails click-clicked through the house as he rushed for Connor. The dog licked his face, but Connor swatted him away. Suddenly his dog's tongue was replaced by a bag of ice. He squinted one eye open to see Aiden hovering over him.

"Hitting you felt pretty damn good, but beating you isn't going to fix anything. When's the book going to come out?"

Connor tried to shrug. He hadn't even contacted the editor. He didn't give a fuck about anything anymore except Fiona, and he'd lost her.

"You should've just forgotten about the Cavanaghs."

"I fucking tried. Then she walked into a bar and ruined me."

"We have to figure out how to make this right for her."

Connor waved his arm. He had no way to make this right. Not for Fiona, not for him.

Chapter 16

FIONA CLIMBED OUT OF SARAH'S bed determined to improve the situation. She was done with the lies and she planned to let everyone know. The only way she could think to accomplish this mission, however, was to ask for Aiden's help. She had no idea if he would agree, but she had to try. She scribbled a quick note to Sarah letting her know she'd be back later and she went to her brother's house.

Aiden answered the door and the strong stench of whiskey assaulted her nose. He'd been drinking? Then she looked up at his face where a nasty bruise covered his jaw. Worry bubbled up in her chest. "Oh, my God. Are you okay?"

He pulled his face away from her searching fingers. "I'm fine. I didn't expect to see you."

She narrowed her eyes and studied his face. He didn't sound drunk.

"Why are you looking at me like that?"

"You smell like a distillery, but you don't sound drunk."

"Shit. I didn't drink. I went to see Connor. We got into a fight and I ended up wearing the whiskey he was drinking. I just got home and haven't showered yet." He turned and walked into his living room peeling off his shirt as he went. A splotchy pattern of bruises marked his torso.

"Must've been a heck of a fight."

He turned to face her again. "I'm sorry I didn't tell you the truth. I didn't know what to say. That entire portion of my life is an embarrassment. I did nothing right."

"Embarrassment?" Somehow the word didn't seem nearly harsh enough.

"I don't need a lecture to make me feel guilty. I've lived with tremendous guilt for years."

"And your way of getting over the guilt was to get into a fight with Connor?"

"No. I'm okay with whatever he does to me. The fight was because he hurt you."

She tried not to let the simple statement break the barrier around her that she clung to. She couldn't trust her family, but she needed Aiden's help. "I think I have a way to fix things. Maybe assuage your guilt and correct our father's mistakes."

Aiden crossed his arms. "I'm listening."

"I want to find evidence against Dad. I know it must exist."

"You want to have Dad arrested?"

"No. I want to find the information and give it to Connor. He can use it to detail everything that's wrong with Brady Cavanagh and reclaim part of his life. Whatever happens after Connor exposes him isn't my problem. I need to start a clean slate, to disentangle myself from all of it." Nervous flutters bounced in her stomach. She'd never been totally alone before. "I need your help. I'm not sure where to look for the right information."

He nodded. "I do."

That's what she'd figured. "So you'll help then?"

"Let me grab a shower so I don't smell like a drunk and we'll go to the house."

Her heartbeat raced. "Home? What are you going to do, ask Dad to give you something?"

"It's Thanksgiving. Dinner is over and they'll be making their annual appearance at the homeless shelter. You know they'll never miss an opportunity to look good. We should have a couple of hours to grab what you want." He turned and walked away.

Fiona breathed a sigh of relief. Aiden had changed from the rotten teenager he'd been. He'd turned out to be a decent brother. She didn't know what would become of him once Connor's book came out. Would he be arrested or was it too late? Would he lose his career?

The same questions had probably raced through Aiden's mind, but he didn't seem concerned. His entire life might be turned upside down, but he was going to help her do what she needed to do to feel better. Even if it made his situation worse.

More worry tugged at her. She didn't want Aiden's life to be destroyed any more than she'd want that for Connor.

Connor rolled over and his entire stomach wanted to leave his body. Max licked his face, which didn't help the nausea. Every muscle ached and even breathing hurt. He swallowed back the bile, not wanting to taste anything a second time. His liquid diet from the previous day caused his head to pound an angry beat. He pushed up onto his knees. Christ, even they hurt.

He stumbled to the kitchen and let Max out into the yard. He started a pot of coffee and tried convince himself that once he finished a shower, his stomach would be able to handle it.

He sipped at a glass of water and wished he'd drunk more of that yesterday. At least then he might not be so dehydrated.

Using the wall, and then the rail for guidance, he managed to make his way up the stairs and into the bathroom. Most of the previous day had been a blur. He'd only left the house once to walk to the liquor store for another bottle of booze.

But he remembered Aiden showing up and hitting him. Had he seriously lost a fight to Aiden Cavanagh? He must've been really fucked-up. The hot spray of the shower beat down on his face and helped clear his head.

Aiden had come to fight because of Fiona. He knew about the book, about Connor telling Fiona everything and hurting her. As the steam and water relaxed his muscles, more of the stilted conversation with Aiden returned. Aiden had told him they had to make it right. He couldn't remember much else Aiden had said, but those were his parting words, at least as he recalled.

How the fuck could he fix it?

He stood under the water until it started to go cold. With a towel wrapped around his waist, he searched for his phone to call Fiona. She might not answer, but he could leave a message. When he got to the living room, the awful stench of stale whiskey burned his nostrils and made him feel weak again. Taking shallow breaths through his mouth, he searched the couch cushions for the phone with no luck.

Then he caught sight of it sticking out from under the table. He picked it up only to find the battery dead. Before leaving the room to charge his phone, he opened the front door and the windows to air out the space. In front of the door, he stepped in a puddle that he hoped to God wasn't piss. Then he saw the shattered glass and remembered the bottle smashing.

The sunlight burned his eyes and he shuffled back to the

kitchen for coffee. He should probably eat, but the thought of food made his stomach jump. He plugged the phone in and waited. What would he say to Fiona?

He'd lied to her, even when he knew she couldn't handle any more secrets. As soon as the phone had enough juice to turn on, he called Fiona.

She pushed it to voicemail. He listened to her message and enjoyed the friendliness of her voice. After the beep, he croaked, "Hey, Fiona, it's me. I know you don't want to talk, but I'd like a chance to explain. You'll get total honesty from me this time, and then you can decide what you want to do."

Then he quickly checked his emails. If nothing else, he needed to respond to the editor and let her know the book was no longer available. He opened the message and read:

Dear Mr. Duffy,
After careful consideration, we would like to acquire your book, THE CAVANAGH CONSPIRACY. The writing itself needs some work, so I want to talk to you about working with a ghostwriter. Please call me at your earliest convenience.

So his writing wasn't up to standard, as he'd suspected. When the first rejections had come in, he thought it was his writing, but Dermott had convinced him otherwise. He shot off a quick response letting her know thanks, but no thanks.

He disconnected and went upstairs to bed. A nap would give him the fuel he'd need for the day. He knew Fiona wouldn't call back, so he had time to formulate a plan.

An hour and a much-too-brief nap later, Max scrambled for the front door. Connor's feet clomped down the stairs as he still fought off the raging hangover headache. When he opened the door, his heart stopped. Fiona stood on his porch, hair blowing wildly in the wind, skin sickly pale except for the red splotches left from crying.

His lungs seized knowing he did this to her. "Fiona," he croaked.

Her eyes widened in concern when she looked at his face. Aiden had definitely left is mark last night, but it looked worse than it felt. He swung the door wider to invite her in.

She edged inside the door enough for him to close it, but didn't walk to the living room. "Here." She thrust a packed accordion folder at him.

"What's this?"

"The proof you need against my father. It should be enough for you to reclaim your life. I'm sorry for what my family did to you." She fumbled for the doorknob.

His head screamed at her to stop, but all that left his lips was a whispered, "Wait."

"I can't." She faced the door, but it was as if she'd forgotten how it worked.

"I'm sorry, Fiona. I never meant to hurt you. I wanted to hurt your father. I can't deny that. But you were a game changer. You made me want a different life."

She hiccupped and then yanked the door open. The blast of cold air smacked him, and he had to watch her walk away from him again. It wasn't any easier the second time. He closed the door quietly and studied the folder in his hand. What had she been thinking?

Was this some kind of test? He sat on the stairs, tugged the elastic and flipped the top open. Inside, he found photocopies of a ledger and email correspondence between what looked like her father and various construction companies.

The information he held in his hand proved the allegations

of Cavanagh using ward employees for campaign work would be the least of his worries. Someone else knew about this. The question was what was *he* going to do with it? Fiona obviously wanted to offer some kind of restitution as if she'd been the guilty party.

Never in a million years did he think she would go against her father, her family. This information could bring down the entire Cavanagh name. He read through the file and the enormity of her decision hit him. She was cutting herself loose.

But he wasn't ready to let her go.

Connor spent the entire day studying the file Fiona had given him. He wondered how she managed to get her hands on it. She had known little of her father's dealings. She must've had help. If he used this information, what would it do to Fiona and Aiden?

Everything he read pointed to Brady being corrupt almost from the beginning. If this fell into the right hands, Brady would probably go to prison. Is that what Fiona wanted? He couldn't imagine her wanting that no matter how angry or hurt she was. She couldn't have been thinking clearly.

At this point, he couldn't think straight either. He tucked the files into his desk and walked down the block to talk to Dermott. At the bar, he settled on a stool, and when Dermott went to pour him a beer, Connor waved it off. He was done with alcohol for a while.

"What the hell happened to you?" Dermott asked.

"Fiona knows everything."

Dermott laughed. "She did this?"

"No. That was Aiden, after he found out I told Fiona." Connor shook his head. "Doesn't matter. She left me."

"I told you the truth would come out."

"I was afraid of hurting her. But she came back and gave me everything I could ever want on her father. An entire file of incriminating information."

Dermott leaned on the bar. "What are you going to do?"

"You told me that if it's right, it's worth the trouble. Do you still believe that?"

"Yeah."

"Then why didn't you convince my mom to stay here?"

Dermott stiffened. They never talked about Connor's mother. Not while Connor was in prison and not since. The hurt sank too deep for both of them. Connor watched Dermott swallow hard.

"You wanted her to go. Gave her the money and the opportunity."

"I was a fucked-up kid who couldn't take care of her. I had no idea how you felt. You never said."

"It wasn't my place."

"It was if you loved her. Have you ever talked to her?"

Dermott's eyes saddened and guilt smacked Connor.

"I have. I spoke to her pretty regular when she first left. The calls became fewer over the years, but we still talk on the holidays."

Connor wasn't sure how to feel about this new knowledge. Dermott had never mentioned talking to his mother. Once, while Connor was in prison and once when he got out. Connor remembered being angry and not wanting to talk to his mother, needing to avoid the disappointment she would have.

"Sorry I never told you. You didn't want to talk about her. I didn't want to risk having you disappear because I pushed."

Connor chuckled. Dermott had pushed plenty when it came to other things. "How is she? And Danny?"

Dermott smiled, relief replacing the sadness. "You should ask them yourself." He reached for a napkin and scribbled a number. "Call them."

Connor stared at the numbers. He hadn't spoken to his mother or Danny in years. He had no idea what to say.

"It's about time, don't you think? They've missed you. I hope you don't mind, but I've told them about you. They've always been eager for anything I could say."

"Really? I thought they'd be happy to be rid of me. I fucked everything up so bad. I didn't want to bring them down with me."

Dermott patted his arm. "You wouldn't have. But it's time to move forward and stop worrying about the past. Time to let it go."

Connor got off the stool and shoved the napkin in his pocket. He'd been trying so hard to let go of the past. He'd made contact with Aiden, but that had gone south. Brady Cavanagh tried to pay him off. Fiona wanted him to expose her father. There was no letting go of his past.

He'd be lucky if he could trudge forward.

Back in his house, Max greeted him and the silence bore down on him. He didn't want this to be the rest of his life. Not when he'd experienced what he could have.

The Cavanaghs weren't the only people who needed to make amends for the past. Connor picked up his phone and fished the napkin from his pocket. Hopefully the time difference wouldn't make it too late.

"Hello?"

The sound of the best thing from his childhood constricted his chest. Even after all these years, she sounded the same. "Hi, Mom, it's Connor."

"Oh, my boy, it's so good to hear your voice. I was beginning to think I'd never hear it again."

The lilt of her brogue warmed him. The accent had strengthened with her being back in her home country.

"Are you better now?"

Such an odd question for her to ask. As if he'd been sick for a few days. Was he? He thought of Fiona and knew he was better. Better than he'd been in more years than he'd care to think. "Yeah, Mom. I am better. I've missed you."

Fiona drove back to Sarah's place. Her friend had been kind enough to let her stay while she searched for a new place to live. Walking into the living room, she dialed Aiden. "It's done. I have one more favor to ask."

"What did he say?"

"He apologized." She pushed images of Connor's battered face from her mind. She couldn't handle thinking about him anymore. "I need you to get rid of my condo."

"What?"

"Mom and Dad gave me the down payment for it and they co-signed the loan. I have no idea what money they used. I don't want to have anything to do with their corruption."

"Where are you going to go?" "Right now, I'm at Sarah's, but I'll do what any other normal twenty-six year old does: I'll get an apartment and pay rent. Maybe find a roommate." She settled on the couch and the weight of all of her emotions dragged her down. All she wanted was more sleep. Real sleep that wasn't plagued with dreams of a man she couldn't have. "How soon can you get me out of there?"

"Move whenever you want and I'll take care of the rest."

He was being so supportive. He didn't question what she wanted and whether it was the best choice. Aiden actually respected her decisions. "You're a good brother."

"I haven't been, but I'm trying."

Fiona hung up, knowing she would be okay with Aiden. She still hadn't spoken to her parents, nor did she want to. She had nothing more to say to them. They believed what they'd done was right, but she would never agree. That impasse couldn't be rectified.

All she could do now was move on and out. Time to start fresh. She spent the day looking at the classifieds for an apartment.

When Sarah came home from her crazed Black Friday shopping, she tossed bags in the middle of the room and plopped on the couch. "You're looking better."

She didn't tell Sarah about the evidence on her father. She thought it best to have as few people know as possible. "I'm feeling better. I'm looking for a new place to live. I'm going to spend the weekend packing up my condo and if I have to, I'll put it all in storage and stay with Aiden until I find an apartment."

"You can stay here. I know my place isn't nearly as big and nice as your condo, but you're welcome to stay."

"Thanks for the offer, but I would drive you crazy. I will, however, ask you to give up your weekend to help me pack."

"Sure. That's what friends are for, right?"

Fiona went back to her apartment hunt feeling lighter than she had in days. For once in her life, she had a plan.

After speaking to his mother and promising to call again to talk to Danny, Connor spent the night at his kitchen table with the folder of information Fiona had given him.

This information was exactly what the editor had been looking for. But he wouldn't use it. Taking this and exploiting his relationship with Fiona wouldn't fix anything and it certainly wouldn't make her feel better. Not in the way she believed it would.

The following morning, he repacked the files and rubbed Max's head. "Wish me luck."

Unfortunately, he'd need a whole lot more than luck. He drove to Fiona's condo and hoped she'd be home. He had no idea where else she might go. For weeks, every time she wanted to escape her family, she'd come to him. Who else would she turn to? Maybe her friend Sarah. Connor hoped not because he had no idea how to reach Sarah except through the outreach center.

He rang Fiona's bell, but it wasn't her who answered. "Hello?"

"Hi. It's Connor. Is Fiona home?"

A moment of silence greeted him before the intercom clicked in and out as if they couldn't decide if they wanted to talk. Then the door buzzed.

He felt like a kid unsure of his every step. When he got up to her condo, the door swung open and Sarah stood there, staring at him.

She jabbed a finger in his direction. "I told you to be nice to my friend. Not a difficult task."

"You're right. I fucked up and I don't know if I can fix it, but I sure as hell need to try."

She fisted her hands on her hips.

"Just let him in, Sarah."

Sarah grumbled but stepped aside. Fiona looked at her friend. "Could you maybe go down to the coffee shop and get us some drinks?"

"I don't think that's a great idea."

"It's fine, Sarah." Fiona hugged her friend. "Thanks."

Sarah snatched up her purse and shot Connor a dirty look.

Shit. If her friend was that bad, he had little hope. He watched Sarah leave and then turned back to Fiona. Her living room was a mess. Boxes were stacked everywhere and piles of clothes littered every piece of furniture.

"Going somewhere?"

"I'm moving."

"Where?"

She crossed her arms and raised an eyebrow. So small talk was off the table.

"I brought this back." He set the file on the counter.

"They're copies, so you can keep them."

"No. I don't need them because I have no intention of using them."

Her eyebrows furrowed. "You have to."

"No, I don't. I don't want to." He rubbed a hand over his face. "Before we met, the one thing I wanted more than anything was to make your father pay for what he did. I'll never like your father, but going after him means hurting you, and I'm not willing to do that. I haven't for weeks."

He walked closer, half expecting her to step away, but she didn't. "I know you find this hard to believe because I kept it all from you, but I haven't thought about the book since before the election. When I met you, I had hopes for this exact thing." He hitched his chin toward the file. "But it changed once I fell for you. If you want to take your father down, you'll have to use someone else to do it."

He stared into her blue eyes, willing the tears to stay away. "I wrote the book to let go of the anger I had for years. I was out of control and writing it helped me regain part of me. I wanted the world to know what your father had done.

I planned to use you to do that. But I got to know you and things changed.

"I know I should've come clean a long time ago. When I told you about my record, your forgiveness and understanding meant more to me than anything. That's why I couldn't tell you the whole sordid story. I knew it would drive a wedge between you and your family and I didn't want to be the one to cause you pain. I know what it is to lose everything. I didn't want you to feel it as well." He shook his head. "It's a whole lot of bullshit to say I lied for you. I lied for me too. I was afraid of what you would think about what I would do for money. But I was more afraid of losing you."

Tears welled in her eyes and panic struck again. He swore he wouldn't make her cry. Each tear felt like a tiny sword scraping away at the parts of him that were still good.

"You should've had more faith in me. Trusted me to understand."

"Yeah, I should have. But I've never known anyone like you." He stepped closer, needing to touch her, but afraid to. She met him halfway and pressed her face against his chest. The moment her arms wrapped around him, every fear seeped away.

"Please don't lie to me. Don't tell me things you think I want to hear. Too many people have done that my whole life. I'd rather have the ugly truth."

"The ugly truth is, I love you, and I'll do anything for you."

"Including letting go of the past?"

"I've been working on it." He thought of Aiden and nodded. They might never be friends again, but they could learn to be civil for her sake. They'd all been victims of Brady Cavanagh, too young to stand up to him.

Connor grabbed her shoulders and pulled her from his

chest. He tilted her chin up and looked into her eyes. "I've never told a woman I love her, but there's a lot going on in your life right now. If you need time to figure things out, I'll wait."

She placed her hand on top of his. "There are a lot of things I need to figure out, but you're not one of them. I've been in love with you for a while, waiting for you to catch up." She pointed at the file. "I thought that would be the end of us. I want you to be happy."

"You make me happy. Happier than any amount of revenge."

She laughed. "I don't know how this is supposed to go."

He smiled. "Don't look at me. I just told you I have no clue what I'm doing."

"A little bit of normal is all I'm asking for." She leaned up and kissed him.

The kiss revealed they would have anything but a normal life and that was more than okay with him. A lifetime with Fiona's kind of crazy might be enough.

Epilogue

6 months later

"YOU SURE ABOUT THIS?" AIDEN asked as he hefted a box into the back of the truck.

"Yes." She and Connor had spent months rebuilding their relationship, during which time she had moved into her own apartment. She was moving again, this time into Connor's house. She slid her box beside Aiden's.

"I told you I'd hire movers for you."

"And I told you, I could handle this on my own."

It had been hard going at it alone, but she'd done it. She continued to build her online jewelry store, and she'd been working with Sarah to expand the art program at the outreach center. Being truly independent from her parents was exhilarating.

"On your own is fine, but shouldn't your boyfriend be here to help?"

Fiona laughed. "He's on his way."

While Connor and Aiden weren't exactly friends, Fiona believed they might get back there one day. What started out as civility toward each other in deference to her had begun to morph into reminiscing about good times as teenagers. Fiona hoped they could repair the damage caused by her father. Connor could use a friend.

And so could Aiden.

On the occasions they were all together, Fiona saw the down-deep connection they shared. They were two men who understood each other because they knew who the other had been as a messed-up boy, long before they became the men they were today.

"How are Mom and Dad holding up?" she asked. She hadn't had any contact with them since she'd stormed out of their house on Thanksgiving. Her dad was still blissfully unaware of the file of information she had on him.

She'd ultimately decided that if Connor didn't want it, she would just hold it. Brady Cavanagh had plenty to deal with. The investigation into his campaign dragged on for months, but earlier this week, her father had been indicted.

"Mom is stoic as ever, but behind closed doors, I don't think she's handling it well. She puts on her brave face and reassures me that Dad is innocent."

"How can she believe that? They've been married for almost forty years. She helped build his career. Has he lied to her this whole time, too?" Fiona led the way back into her small apartment.

"I'm not sure what Mom knows versus what she might suspect versus what she chooses to ignore. Mostly I'm her shoulder to lean on." Aiden sighed as he looked over the living room full of boxes. "She would probably feel a whole lot better if you stopped by."

Her heart tugged. Aiden always knew how to do that. "I don't know if I'm ready for that. I still feel betrayed. All those years of her telling me how to live, who to date, what to look like so that I could fit her image of the perfect family. But we were never that. Dad was so far from perfect. It was all smoke and mirrors."

Aiden leaned against the wall. "She did what she thought was best. Her life is falling apart. She doesn't know how to handle that."

Fiona laughed. "Like she'll listen to me?"

Aiden's shoulder lifted. "She might. You managed to walk away from everything you've known and continue on successfully. She's proud of you, Fi."

"She said that?"

"Plenty of times. She asks about you all the time, but she's afraid that if she calls, it'll make things worse."

Connor came through the door. "I'm a little late, so no progress is made? That's sad, Cavanagh."

"Hey," Fiona said as she wrapped her arms around his waist. "We got a few boxes in the truck."

Connor looked pointedly at the stacks in the living room. "Yeah, I can tell."

"Why were you late again? Slacking off?" Aiden asked.

"I was gathering help."

"Huh?" As she asked the question, Sarah came through the door with a crowd of people. Other teachers and volunteers from the outreach center filled the small space with cheerful hellos as they grabbed boxes and filed back out the door.

Sarah bumped her hip. "I told you, you're not alone."

"How?" The single word was all Fiona could squeak out because she was a little choked up.

"I can't believe you didn't tell me you were moving today," Sarah continued.

"I knew you'd volunteer to help, but you helped me move last time."

Sarah shook her head. "While Aiden and Connor are very

able-bodied men, there's no reason for you to be working at this all night, when we can have you done in a trip or two. That's what friends are for."

Fiona smiled. Growing up, most of her friendships had been superficial, everyone out to network because of who their parents were. Today, Fiona realized that she had in fact managed to collect an amazing group of friends who created a family of her own.

Connor leaned on the door of the spare bedroom and watched Fiona set up her workspace. The cabinet he'd made her took a prominent place in front of the windows and she arranged trays and containers on the shelves below. He was exhausted. He had no idea where she got her energy. Not only had she hefted her share of boxes today, she managed to do it all with a smile and carry on conversations with every freaking person Sarah had dragged along.

When she caught him staring, she smiled and sauntered over. She wrapped her arms around his waist. "Thank you for today."

"No thanks necessary. Moving a few boxes to get you in my house was nothing."

"No. I mean bringing Sarah and everyone else to help. I know that was hard for you."

He almost brushed her thanks aside again. Asking someone for help had always been hard for him, but not when it came to her. He knew she'd been lonely since separating herself from her parents. Every now and then he caught the sad look in her eyes. "I want you to be happy."

"You make me happy." She rose up and nipped his ear, followed by running her tongue on the sensitive spot just behind it.

"Not nearly as happy as you make me." Having her here in his house, in his arms was much more than he'd expected.

She suddenly shifted in his arms. Something on the small TV in the corner of the room snagged her attention. Without letting her go, he turned as well. The screen was filled with an image of Brady and Sheila Cavanagh. Fiona didn't stiffen like she used to.

"Are you okay?"

She nodded and pulled away to grab the remote. She turned up the volume and wrapped her arms around herself.

A voiceover said, "Alderman Brady Cavanagh was in court today in an attempt to get the charges against him dismissed. His lawyers argued that the evidence against him was gotten illegally."

Fiona snorted. Connor pulled her against his chest. "He has to put up a fight. He wouldn't be Brady Cavanagh if he didn't."

"I know." She waved a hand at the screen. "Look at the smug expression on his face. He really thinks he's going to get away with this."

Of course, Brady stopped in front of the cameras. The man never missed an opportunity. He straightened his jacket and took Sheila's hand. "I have every confidence that the court will rule in my favor. These charges are fabricated. I've done nothing but serve this city for my entire career."

Reporters lobbed questions, but Brady shook his head and waved. Something on Cavanagh's face caught Connor's attention. Fear. The man was afraid. Good.

Even better was the fact that Connor didn't really care anymore. The usual rage that surged whenever he saw a Cavanagh no longer existed. He'd finally been able to put that chapter of his life behind him thanks to the woman in his arms.

"I think I need to call my mom."

"Okay." Her declaration wasn't much of a surprise to him. Fiona turned. "Are you?"

"What?"

"Okay with that."

He ran his hands down her arms. "They're your family, Fiona. It's completely up to you to decide what your relationship is with them."

"I know, but I don't want them to come between us."

"I'll never be friends with your parents, especially your father. But I would never keep you from them. I don't expect you to walk away from a relationship with them in order to have one with me." He smiled. "I've been putting up with Aiden just fine, haven't I?"

Her lips curved, but it wasn't quite a smile. She laid her head on his chest, her wild curls springing up and tickling his chin.

"It'll probably get uglier long before this is over, you know that, right? If the case moves forward, the reporters will be back, looking for me and Aiden to comment. I'll have to hide out like I did last fall."

"So we'll go away."

"What?" she asked as she pulled away again.

"We'll pack our shit and move." He'd made the offer months ago, when she'd first distanced herself from her family.

"Like I said before, our lives are here." Her eyes hardened. "And I'm not about to run away."

He'd come to expect no less from her, but she'd forgiven him for so much, he'd do anything for her.

She tugged on the waistband of his jeans. "But it makes me all hot to know that you'd leave everything for me."

He threaded his fingers through her wild curls and brought

her lips to his. He didn't care if she remained loyal to her family as long as he continued to get all of her love. "I think the best part about you moving in here is having you whenever I want."

About the Author

SHANNYN SCHROEDER is the author of the O'Leary series and the For Your Love Series - contemporary romances centered around large Irish-American families in Chicago. She also authors the Hot & Nerdy series about nerdy friends finding love. When she's not wrangling her three kids or writing, she watches a ton of TV and loves to bake cookies.

Also by Shannyn Schroeder

For Your Love
In Your Arms (For Your Love #2)
Under Your Skin (For Your Love #1)

O'Learys
Hold Me Close (O'Learys #6)
Just a Taste (O'Learys #5)
Catch Your Breath (O'Learys #4)
Something to Prove (O'Learys #3)
A Good Time (O'Learys #2)
More Than This (O'Learys #1)

Hot & Nerdy
Hot @nd Nerdy
Hot and Nerdy 2

Keep reading for an excerpt from *In Your Arms*

In Your Arms

(For Your Love #2)

A KNIGHT IN SHINING LEATHER...

Sean O'Malley has never tried to hide who he is. He shows it in the motorcycle thrumming between the legs of his tight jeans...the shaggy hair that falls in his gorgeous eyes...the wicked gleam in his smile when he asks Emma out for a drink. Sean is a rebel, a bad boy, and a ton of fun: exactly the kind of guy she's sworn off forever.

Emma isn't just the prim kindergarten teacher she appears to be. And somehow Sean can tell. As soon as he pulls up to her overheated car he knows that a fast bike and a cold beer will fix her rotten day better than compliments or a bubble bath. Her straitlaced exterior and her wild heart light him up. But Emma wants to escape her past and settle down—and if her desk jockey dates don't understand where she comes from, at least she doesn't worry about them bringing her back.

One weekend of intense connection can't change the paths Sean and Emma have chosen. But with a little space to be themselves together, maybe the rest of the world can wait...

Excerpt

In Your Arms

SEAN TOOK THE QUICKEST SHOWER possible and ran his hands through his hair. Back in his bedroom, Emma sat in the same spot on his bed, scrolling through her phone.

"Telling all your Facebook friends about the great guy you met?"

She looked up and around the room. "Who would that be?"

He grabbed his chest. "You wound me." He keeled over on the mattress.

She poked him with her foot. "Seriously, as great as you are—and compared to some guys I've known, you're ranked near the top—but I don't do Facebook."

Sean let her words sink in. She hadn't talked much about herself last night; neither of them had. Hearing how he compared to her past boyfriends or hookups, or whatever, helped. "Near the top, huh? I'll have to see what I can do about that."

She smiled.

"You're really not on Facebook? I've never met a girl who wasn't." Hell, most girls couldn't wait to log on and change their status. They went straight from meeting to "in a relationship" within a night.

She shrugged. "I used to be. Then a couple of years ago, my college adviser pointed out that principals and eventually parents would be looking up my social media."

"So?"

"My mom has a habit of posting some inappropriate stuff.

Stuff I wouldn't want my boss to see. Or the parents of my kids."

"If you're not on Facebook, what are you doing? Sending out messages for a rescue?" He sincerely hoped not. He didn't think he'd done anything to warrant a rescue call.

"I was on Pinterest."

"Huh?"

She turned her phone to face him. "It's a virtual bulletin board. I collect recipes of stuff I want to try. Sometimes books."

He took the phone and scrolled. "Yeah, shirtless dudes are really recipes. Aren't you worried about your boss seeing that?"

She reached for her phone, but he pulled it away.

Emma slumped back, not engaging in his game. "I guess you didn't notice the words 'secret board' above that one. No one can see that board or what I have pinned to it except me."

He handed her the phone. When she took it, he whipped off his shirt.

"Want a picture for your secret board?" He flexed and posed, and Emma doubled over laughing. "What are you saying? That even though I'm better than the losers you know, I can't compete with your eye candy?"

She laughed harder, and Sean felt like he'd accomplished something. If he got nothing else done for the day, this would be enough. He'd seen her smile, which was pretty great, and she'd snarked at him jokingly, but her laugh was fantastic.

With a hand on her chest, she inhaled deeply. Then she raised her phone. "Hold still." And she snapped a picture of him.

"Wait. I can do better than a sneak shot." He crawled closer, straddling her outstretched legs as he did. He lifted an eyebrow. "How about a smolder?"

Another peal of laughter had him joining in and almost falling on top of her. He couldn't remember the last time he'd laughed so hard with a girl, especially in bed. It was a good feeling. Sean rolled next to her and they caught their breath, sides touching, and even though they were both fully clothed, something sparked between them. God, he loved it when the chemistry was hot.

He bumped her thigh with the back of his hand. "Ready to go?"

"Yeah." She sat up and put her phone in her bag. "Any idea when I can get my car?"

He swung his legs over the side of the bed and sat next to her. "I haven't called yet. I'm sure it'll be ready by the end of the day. Let's just take my bike around and I'll get you to the garage before it closes."

She bit her lip. "Are you sure it'll be ready? I need my car. I have to go home at some point."

"But for now, you're good. Let's go have some fun." He pointed at her bag. "You got room in there for a few bottles of water for us?"

"Sure." They stood and went upstairs for the water. As he came through the kitchen, Sean saw Norah at the sink.

She spun to face him. "You know, it's bad enough you ate all of the breakfast so I couldn't bring any to Kai, but you could've done your dishes."

"I was gonna get to the dishes, but thanks for taking care of it, squirt." He felt Emma at his back, but even if he hadn't, the look on Norah's face would've told him she was there.

Norah quickly dried her hands on a towel and stuck one out to Emma. "Hi, I'm Norah."

They shook. "Emma."

Sean had no idea what that was about. Norah never introduced herself to any of the girls he'd brought home. Of course, part of that was because they usually came and went through the basement door.

Norah pointed at Sean. "It would've been nice for you to save some crêpes for Kai."

"Why? He doesn't live here. In fact, when are you moving out? You've been dating that big lug for a year. Shouldn't you be living together or something by now?"

"What's the rush?"

"If you move out, I get the sweet apartment upstairs Jimmy made. I still don't think it's fair he gave you his place."

"Of course he gave me his place when he moved out. First, I'm the only girl. There's no way I'm sharing space with either you or Tommy. Second, I'm the baby. It's his job to protect me from the debauchery in the basement." She peered around Sean and looked at Emma. "No offense." Coming back to Sean, she said, "And third, he loves me best."

Emma chuckled behind him.

"Whatever. So what's your timeline here?"

"I'm not moving in with Kai until after I graduate. Next summer. Is that soon enough?"

Sean opened his mouth to respond, but Emma cut in. "I know it's none of my business, but good for you. Finish your education and you can always take care of yourself. You'll never need to rely on a man. It's a smart move."

Norah practically beamed. "Thank you."

Chicks. He'd never suggested she not finish school. Or that she should rely on Kai, although he was a good guy who clearly loved his baby sister. He moved past Norah and opened the fridge. Emma wasn't much of a talker, but when she opened her mouth, her words meant something. She was independent. He liked that. A woman who could take care of herself. She might be the perfect woman. Someone who wouldn't expect anything from him but fun.

He handed her a few bottles of water. "See you later, squirt. Coming to practice tonight?"

Norah had the water running in the sink again. "Probably," she said over her shoulder.

He led Emma through the living room to leave. As usual, his dad was in the same spot on the couch. Sean was sure there were permanent ass imprints from his dad. The man had done nothing since retirement, other than drive them all a little crazy. "Hey, Dad."

Dad grunted back. Sean paused and considered introducing Emma but decided not to. Seamus O'Malley wasn't exactly a pleasant guy. Sean had managed to keep Emma's interest this long. He didn't need his dad to screw anything up.

Sean paused at the front hall closet and grabbed his spare helmet. He handed it to Emma and headed out the front door. It was near noon and the sun blazed. Humidity weighed heavily in the air. It would be a great day for a long ride.

www.ingramcontent.com/pod-product-compliance
Lightning Source LLC
Chambersburg PA
CBHW062136170626
46813CB00002B/724